UNDERCOVER
GENTLEMAN

Marlborough Books
presents

The Undercover Gentleman

About the Author

"There are tons of novels available, but the ability to write a singularly perfect story is rare. That's why I especially enjoyed Anthony Pour's work because in just a few pages he takes you into the lives of the characters he creates, gives you a sense of where they are, and then, at the end, never fails to surprise you. Pour is equally at home writing about ordinary folk or the rich and famous. It is their human weaknesses that interest him and there are plenty to satisfy his wicked sense of humor that will thoroughly entertain you."

Alan Caruba, Bookviews

THE UNDERCOVER GENTLEMAN

Marlborough Books
Paperback edition July 2009

This book is a work of fiction. Characters, names, places and events are the products of the author's imagination. Any resemblance to actual persons, events or locales is entirely coincidental.

All rights reserved
Copyright © 2009 by Anthony Pour
Library of Congress Control Number 2004104193

ISBN 978-0-615-27595-6

Edited by Dawne Brooks
Printed in the United States of America

Anthony Pour

THE UNDERCOVER GENTLEMAN

A Novel

Knowledge comes,
But wisdom lingers.

Alfred Lord Tennyson (1809 - 1892)

California
Winter 1969

The rains came early that year. Creek beds that had been dry all summer filled with a muddy runoff from the mountains, grazing ranges turned from parched yellow to lush green streaked with ripples of red poppies and blue bells, and by Christmas, Southern California ranchers were grumbling about a darn soggy winter comin' up.

The storm clouds kept on rolling in from the Pacific, dumping their payload on contact with land, and a hundred miles north of Los Angeles, in the Santa Ynez Valley, the river ran way above normal. The sandbar in the bend above the Teeple Ranch had been washed away, wiping out the only ford in miles, and on the last Sunday before Christmas, Hank Teeple woke up with a knot in his stomach. It had been raining all night and crossing the river on horseback was going to be a toss-up.

Other than that, things did not look half bad. The storm had moved on shortly before daybreak, and there was not a cloud in the sky as he got out of bed to turn on the transistor radio perched for the occasion on a sunlit window sill. The signal was good on a day like this. The local station that sometimes barely reached out here was doing the Sunday morning hit parade, and in a window facing the hills with the broken antenna pointing in the direction of town, Dean Martin's latest number one was coming in loud and clear. It was a lone cowboy tune about trotting on to nowhere with just *my rifle, my pony and me*, and Hank could not but feel sorry for the guy as he brushed his teeth and put Vitalis in his hair. Not all cowboys were loners like in the song, with just a rifle and a pony for company when *the cattle began to go down to the stream* . . .

In Hank Teeple's case out here, the stream was the currently raging Santa Ynez River, and waiting for him on the other side was a runner-up for Miss California 1969. Her picture had made the *Los Angeles Times*, the *Santa Barbara News Press*, and most of the smaller papers up the coast all the way to San Francisco, and people who knew her were scratching their heads. The consensus was that she'd missed the crown by a hair just because the judges couldn't see her on horseback.

She sure was the best horse woman he knew, Hank thought as he put on a freshly ironed flannel shirt with mother-of-pearl buttons and a belt with the buckle he had won in the Fiesta rodeo this summer. It looked pretty special on Sunday jeans on this pretty special Sunday and, pretty pleased with himself, he pulled a little jewelry box out of the back of a drawer in his nightstand. His heart skipped a beat as he slipped it in a pocket and turned sideways in front of a mirror to check the bulge it made in the tight jeans. Not bad. Not even mother might notice. But since there was no need to try her, he did not put on his boots yet.

He just turned off the radio, grabbed his hat from a peg on the door, and carrying the boots by the straps, tiptoed around the creaky spots in the hallway floor. Mother was in the kitchen, kneading bread dough with her back to the open door, but she heard him anyway.

"Going out, Hank?"

"Yeah." He stopped to put the boots on.

"The river's running high."

"I know."

"Is she worth it?" Mother went on working her dough, and Hank groaned.

"Mom, come on."

"Just want you to be sure, that's all."

"Sure like what?" He had his boots on by then and felt taller.

"You're so different, you two."

"Because her family has money?"

"That's what they want everybody to believe."

"Right." Hank did not want to go into that. It had been a bad year for everybody around here. Beef prices were rock bottom and quarter horses would fetch next to nothing at local auctions. Mother's legs were swollen from the ankles up, but she would not see a doctor because they had already defaulted on health insurance payments. Instead, she would put on an extra bright smile to pretend all was well on the ranch — the mere thought of which made Hank drop a hand over his pocket to camouflage the bulge of the little jewelry box.

The engagement ring in it was just a sort of sterling silver, ten dollars at the Chumash Indian shop in Los Olivos, but without Dean Martin on the radio backing up the notion of a cowboy with a girl of his own, Hank's guilt kept creeping up. His father and younger brother had taken a couple of horses to town before dawn, and the money they would bring back, if any, would not pay half the bills piling up under the pans in the kitchen cupboard. Because Father was what he was, straight as an arrow even in horse trading; he just wouldn't shut up before shaking on a deal.

"Just so you know before you lay out good money," Father would tell prospective buyers, "the stallion has a tendency to weak knees. The mare's all right, though. Maybe a bit tender around the mouth . . ."

It ran in the family. The Teeples would go out of their way to do right by their neighbors, which in Hank's case might have been the reason his knees buckled whenever Roni Pitt, the runner-up beauty queen and a neighbor from across the river, looked his way. He would do anything to do right by her . . .

"You're not twenty yet, Hank," mother said, startling him out of his reveries. "Don't rush it."

"I'm rushing nothing."

"Promise?" She dipped her hands into flour to peel the dough off her fingers and turned around. She was a strong, red-cheeked woman with graying hair and clear blue eyes that were doing their best to smile. The family would be going to church in the afternoon, and she wanted the mood in the car to be just right on the way to town. "Be home for lunch, all right?"

Outside, the yard was still wet from the night storm, and Hank made deliberately casual detours around rain puddles to cover up for the jitters in his legs. He was sure mother was looking after him from the kitchen window.

Inside the stables and out of sight, though, he took his hands out of the pockets and skipped a step to sprint for Primo's stall. Primo was a seven-year-old quarter horse whose gait was a match for the thousand-dollar Andalusian mare Roni would ride to their Sunday dates, and he hoped they wouldn't have to sell him, too. The way things were, they would be lucky to get a hundred for him these days.

"Good boy." He stroked Primo's velvety nose and felt goose bumps pricking up on his arm. Saddling up on Sundays would by now stir all kinds of tremors in his gut in anticipation of Roni's soft lips and firm breasts, and he almost dropped the saddle as he pulled it off the rack.

"Damn." He better watched what he's doing.

It was Primo's old trick to breathe in while the cinch was being tightened. That way, anytime he chose later on, he could exhale all the way, let the saddle slide sideways and turn his head in fake surprise as the rider hit the ground with a thump and the bumbling clank of loose tackle—a cowboy's worst nightmare.

"Wouldn't do that to me today, would you?" Hank smiled at the horse, his mind drifting back to Roni's breasts as he waited for Primo to breathe out before he tightened the cinch another notch.

He eased the bit into Primo's mouth and threw the reins over his ears to lead him out by the bridle. The sagging barn door was in need of new hinges, but he did not want to think about that now. He led the horse to the rim of the water well from where he could jump into the saddle without stirrups — his right hand on Primo's rump, his right knee swinging over the saddle pommel high enough for the heel to clear the mane. The trick was in the timing of the high kick. Roni had asked him several times to teach her, but somehow they never got round to it. He always seemed to have time for just one thing when they were together.

Maybe after they jumped the broomstick, they'd have the mind to work on jumping into the saddle, he thought, feeling the engagement-ring case in his pocket rub against his thigh as he prodded the horse into trotting out of the yard.

The range was still wet, and Primo's hoofs were kicking up spurts of sparkling water drops from the lush new grass. But the long-stemmed poppies had already turned their brittle petals into the sun to dry, flooding the range with bright red all the way to the river, and it seemed that another storm was on its way. The sun felt prickly on the skin. A hawk up in the sky rode the rising hot air undisturbed by the slightest breath of wind, the snow on the distant mountain tops sparkled, and in the bend above the ranch, the river ran even higher than Hank had thought. So, before he could think again, he slipped his feet out of the stirrups to hold them up to Primo's neck and clicked his tongue to prod the horse into the muddy torrent, making a couple of cows on the bank turn their heads in disbelief. There were holes under the swirling surface.

Yet Primo made it across with just a few drops of water on Hank's upstream boot, and the cows went back to grazing. They looked disappointed, and Primo seemed to get a kick out of that. He needed no prodding to break into a gallop up the hill on the other side.

"Ayeeee." The pent-up anticipation in Hank's voice spilled into the horse's muscle, and the air filled with the smell of crushed grass and wet earth kicked up by pounding hoofs.

They stormed the hill at full gallop, and on the sunlit top

Primo all but reared to a screeching halt so as not to fly off the other side that was sloping in a bold, green sweep all the way down to the blue of the Pacific. The thunder of hoofs mellowed into a gentle trot as the horse, his flanks heaving and needing no directions, turned towards a small lake at the edge of the brush where Hank and his girl would sit on the trunk of a fallen mesquite tree on Sundays.

Today, though, she was not there yet, and Primo strolled all the way to the edge of the water. Flies flew up from a muddy shoal and to fight them off the horse shook his head, scaring a bunch of newts basking in the mud into propelling themselves with their paddle-like tails into deeper water—lacing the placid surface with jittery trails that stirred up jitters in the pit of Hank's stomach. He was late today on account of his mother and the flooded river, so it was not out of the question that Roni had been up here already and got tired of waiting. Because, no matter how much he tried not to think of it, he could not but remember her acting funny on more than one occasion lately.

"Come on." He steered Primo away from the lake and to the edge of the crest from where he could see the Pitt ranch on the other side of the hill. Its red roofs and white porticos were gleaming in the middle of sunlit pastures sloping all the way down to the beaches and rolling surf, and Hank tipped his hat to shade his eyes. It had always been a treat to watch Roni Pitt take that hill at a gallop, leaning low over her mare's mane, her Miss-California-runner-up legs so easily taming the jolts of raw horse power, the taut denim of her jeans barely touching the saddle.

Right now, though, nothing stirred on the hillside above the Pitt ranch. Over the ocean, a new storm was already brewing, with soggy gray clouds beginning to heave and swirl in preparation for a landing, but the wind was not up here yet. Even the curtain in the open window of Roni's room was still—as if she were daring him to play a game that was meant to get him worried at first, but would make them both laugh in each other's arms in the end.

Because, after all, there had to be a pretty laughable explanation to all the stupid rumors about Roni and an older guy that had been on the beauty-pageant jury. That guy was way over thirty, for Pete's sake, and married to boot—a smart-ass lawyer who was a lot on TV—a Fitch from the Fitch family.

Over the years, the Fitches had developed a lot of prime land in Southern California, and rumor had it they were after the Pitt property to build a fancy-pansy hotel. And as always, the local ranchers were quick with their two bits to the fray. They claimed to have inside knowledge of old Joe Fitch pulling strings to get his son, Richard, on the beauty pageant jury for the sole purpose of having him get into Roni Pitt's pants. The ranchers were sick of the Fitches. Whenever Richard's pampered, charismatic face appeared on TV, whining and ranting about inner-city poverty, the whole Santa Ynez Valley was up in arms. No one doubted that he had been worming his way into politics to manipulate zoning laws, not to give his shirt away—for sure not to the inner-city poor.

Many of the Santa Ynez ranchers were poorer than the poor in Los Angeles, only they would not rant and rave about it. They just kept their mouths shut and worked their butts off to make ends meet. And nothing would upset hard-working country boys more than the big-city media praise for the throngs of women pushing and shoving to get themselves interviewed for volunteer jobs in Richard Fitch's phony philanthropic agenda. The interviews were said to take place in his Beverly Hills law office, on an oversized couch riddled with hi-fi speakers oozing elevator music, and the nickname Slick Dick was born.

Hank had never met him, but every time he saw his face on TV or in the papers, slick was what came to mind. He wouldn't stop to think that Roni might not see it his way. She wasn't stupid, for God's sake. He could not imagine her lining up with hundreds of women who could not hold a candle to her to beg Slick Dick for a job in some off-the-wall social program to mobilize the city vote. No way. Not her. Not Roni, he was sure.

Yet there was nothing he could do about the lump in his

throat as the storm clouds over the ocean darkened the white caps of the surf and began to move inland. Shadows hit the beach, paused briefly to gather strength to scale the cliffs, and began creeping up the hillside towards the white porticos of the Pitt ranch—where a sudden gust of wind billowed the curtain in Roni's window, like an impish magician shaking his sleeve to show there was nothing in it. From Roni's empty room, the wind blew an empty path in the grass all the way to the hilltop to ruffle Primo's mane and flap the brim of Hank's hat to finally blow away the wool he so stubbornly had been pulling over his eyes.

All right . . . so be it. Fine with him. But . . . what now?

To start with, he wasn't going to tell a soul—not his mother, for sure. He wouldn't dream of crying on her shoulder. The trouble was, she'd just know, like she most likely knew about the engagement ring in his pocket, too. And the guy at the Indian store he had bought the ring from was not going to keep his mouth shut either.

So if stupid rumors not be stupid, he could forget standing tall around here. As he could forget riding down this hill ever again.

Swear to God, should those rumors about Roni and Slick Dick be true, he'd never ever come nowhere near here. He'd go as far away as . . . who the hell cared. If he had to leave the ranch, the range, the lake, and Primo, he wouldn't give a tinker's damn where he went and for how long.

Singapore

Thirty years later

1

"Won't see a rat tail stir in lunchtime, Mister Hank," the Chinese man said, and Teeple put his binoculars down to wipe sweat out of his eyes.

"That's what they want us to believe," he said, checking his watch. It was noon and the Chinese man was hungry. "Didn't you bring a bag of chips or something, Golden?"

Actually, the name was Gordon, but since everyone in Singapore made it sound like Golden, Teeple went right along with it. The two of them were sitting in a small fishing boat, rocking on the tidal swell of the Johor Straits with the outboard motor turned off to lend credibility to the pretense of fishing where there were hardly any fish left. The sluggish tidal current carried oil slicks, floating debris and clusters of foam from untreated detergents, but high above all that, the crisp little white clouds in a pristine blue sky seemed to have nothing to do with either pollution or the omnipresent stifling heat. Steamy moisture was invisible in the steamy hot air, and the sun was all but obvious. It did not shine into one's eyes or roast the back of the neck. The equator was within a stone's throw, and at midday the sun stood in the dead center of the sky, casting no shadows, zeroing in on the top of people's heads with a relentless cosmic precision. The feel was that of a sultry furnace, and Teeple tried not to speculate how many more equatorial fishing adventures were in store for him this close to his 50th birthday.

"They'd have to use womens to get anything done in the middle of the day," Golden went on, giving the notion of lunch one more try even though Teeple already had his binoculars back up, trained on the flat, hazy Malay shore before them.

The haze, the omnipresent smoke from cooking fires burning cow dung, was getting thicker now as the fires had been left to smolder during siesta, yet Teeple would not give up. He expected to see at least something stir in the row of rundown waterfront warehouses he had been watching since dawn, and Golden knew better than to insist.

He was a body builder who thrived on regular meals, but his impressive physique made him also worry about coming across too strong. So, for right now he refrained from carrying on about lunch and made do with just a wistful glance homewards, to the coastal dunes and marshes on the Singapore side from behind which rose the shiny steel-and-glass skyline of a modern city—where the traditional siesta had been replaced with a quick lunch break on the fly.

Air conditioning had turned the leisurely old midday nap into a distant memory of a not-so-distant past in Singapore, when the dazzling, high-tech metropolis used to be just a muddy fishing village run by all kinds of bad guys: pirates, headhunters, beads-and-mirrors salesmen and hard-drinking rubber planters. By now, their descendants had either taken jobs in the air conditioned steel-and-glass palaces, or, like the *orang asli*, the shallow-water pirates, pulled up stakes and moved to the less glitzy and less regulated Malay side of the Straits—where self-respecting men were still in the habit of taking a nap at noon.

The old, run-down warehouses along the Malay waterfront had been built by the British prior to the Japanese invasion in

1942, and the one Teeple had been particularly interested in must have had its name GOLDSTAR painted on the brown-brick facade well before it began to crumble. The one-story high letters were full of holes where brick had cracked and crumbled, and the whole place bore the unquestionably genuine signs of deferred maintenance under tropical conditions—except for the adjacent pier that had recently been upgraded to accommodate mid to large trawlers.

"Bet you the gofers over there are snoring right now," Golden said, tackling the subject of lunch from a different perspective. "It's all Muslims out there, Mr. Hank."

"No kidding."

"Betcha a hundred U.S., no Singapore dollars."

"Even money, Golden?" Teeple smiled, referring to the current hotly contested controversy down here.

The neighborly relations between the tiny, bustling Republic of Singapore and the big, lethargic Constitutional Monarchy of Malaysia were at a standoff at best. Unresolved issues were snowballing even in the tropics, and the polluted Johor Straits, where Teeple and Golden were at the moment pretending to fish, was just one of many. The Singaporeans had categorically denied the pollution was their doing, and the Malays threatened with the UN and all kinds of punitive actions for negligence resulting in an environmental calamity.

Consequently, when a U.S. company specializing in the tracing of illegal waste dumping called the Singapore Department of Environmental Protection, they had the contract wrapped up literally before the second ring. The fact that the polluted Johor Straits connected to the pirate-infested Malacca Straits seemed totally irrelevant in view of a high-profile dispute about sewage, and the Singaporeans were eager to shine in front of a third-party referee. Their sewer system was impeccable, complete with state-of-the-art clearing stations, while on the other side, sewage ran in shallow channels under crumbling sidewalks. Singapore welcomed an international scrutiny of its sewers, the closer the better, and no one in either the local press or the government gave second thoughts to the possibility that the American offer could have had something to do with the local pirates.

It was accepted on the fly and at face value. The environmental commissioner, an ambitious young spark with no brains, made an abrasive call to the prime minister, who in turn obediently leaned on the immigration service to cut the red tape, and an unrestricted visa for an American waste-dumping expert, Hank Teeple, was issued on the spot.

The one and only string attached, they told him when he arrived with a suitcase full of meters and gages, was for his own good. He was required to hook up with a local sidekick, a paralegal, in case some minor authorities or the media gave him trouble. The man's name was Hang Hing Hua—Gordon Hang to Westerners—a charismatic muscleman with clever eyes who looked like anything but a legal whiz. His impressive physique and cheerful grin were incompatible with law books and legal forms, which, as it turned out, did not matter one way or another. The local authorities were happy to lend a hand to an environmental expert any way they could, and Golden's legal assistance boiled down to telling Teeple where to eat, shop, or see a movie.

Not even the media, hard pressed for a controversy in the orderly little republic, professed doubt about Teeple's professional standing, not to mention the slightest suspicion that he was no waste-dumping expert and that his salary in Singapore dollars had been converted from U.S. dollars drawn in a roundabout way from the CIA payroll. When it came to sewage, the local politicians and journalists chose to unite and keep their mouths shut about American expansionist ambitions. Even the few and far between leftists closed both eyes to the capitalist decadence demonstrated by the bulge Teeple's omnipresent travel flask made in the back pocket of his trousers.

So, no eyebrows were raised when a couple of days after his arrival, Teeple, his breath smelling of peach brandy, launched an investigation into alleged waste dumping from an obscure waterfront warehouse on the Malay side of the Johor Straits.

"Wanna double the bet that they won't be dumping during siesta, Mr. Hank?" Golden said presently, allowing a touch of rueful intensity to creep into his voice as his gaze rested on the boat landing on the Singapore side. Their cars, a fire-engine red hotrod and a beige compact, had been parked there since sunrise. "How about it, ey? A quick dim-sum and we'll have our noses back to the grinding stone before the gofers on the other side wake up."

"I came prepared." Teeple put the binoculars down to pat his back pocket, and Golden rolled his eyes.

"Sweet liqueur only makes you dry."

"Does it?" Teeple made sure to keep a straight face. So far, he had never offered Golden a drink, nor had he told him what he carried in the flask.

"Trust me, Mr Hank." Golden shook his head at the sweat stains on Teeple's shirt. "In this heat, the only thing to keep you cool is hot tea."

"Which also happens to be served with dim-sum?"

"I'm serious."

"I know you are. So go. You go rehydrate, I stay."

"You mean it?"

"I won't tell your boss, don't worry." Teeple started the boat engine and put the binoculars into an empty bait box to secure them from tossing about. He was not a boating man and tended to take jerky overcorrections of unsteady turns. "A couple of hours OK with you?"

"All work, no play makes a Jack dull boy," Golden grinned back. He loved flaunting dated American proverbs, some better than others, and the implications were obvious. Most of the southeast Asian intelligence bureaus (IBs), had been founded by the British a long time ago, but many of their younger agents had trained in the U.S. Golden might have picked up his dated American idiom at some boot camp in the backcountry of Georgia or West Virginia — making it quite likely that he worked for the Singapore IB. But so what? Teeple was quite sure that Singapore Intelligence knew nothing about the real job at hand.

At the moment, the charismatic muscleman seemed merely puzzled by anyone's resistance to lunch, which made sense up to a point. Golden wasn't stupid, and Teeple knew he would have to tell him something as close to the truth as possible. The Goldstar warehouse on the other side of the Straits went on looking as abandoned as ever, most likely not air-conditioned, and he decided to take the plunge sooner rather than later. Midday heat inside an old building with a tar roof would sap up a man's strength faster than swamp fever.

"I have a man in there," he said.

"Inside Goldstar?" Golden stopped smiling. "You're kidding me?"

"Nope."

"You sent a man in there just like that?"

"I need someone to pinpoint the waste conduit." Teeple had used the technical term on the spur of the moment and, probing for signs of suspicion in Golden's face, forgot to concentrate on landing the boat. He approached the pier too fast, and Golden's reaction was lightning swift. He choked off the motor by kicking the speed lever into reverse and jumped on the landing to grab the boat by the bow railing before it crashed into the siding.

"Mister Hank! Careful." The muscles on Golden's arms bulged to hold the boat off. He had been quick to grab the bull by the horns—the most uncharacteristic behavior for a legal whiz of any nationality—and, as if he had realized his mistake, he let his muscles deflate the moment he steadied the boat and dutifully put on a would-be legal face. "The laws down here are pretty straightforward about break-ins."

"My man got no stamp in his passport before crossing over, if it's legal headaches that worry you."

"Headaches will be the last thing for your guy to worry about if he gets caught. I told you, it's all Muslims out there."

"He won't get caught."

"An old pro?"

Pretending not to notice the sarcasm, Teeple said nothing,

and Golden pushed the boat away from the landing. He was already browsing a dim-sum menu in his head and could not help grinning.

"Don't do anything I wouldn't while I'm gone, Mr. Hank."

In the parking lot, Golden jumped into the red hot rod to take off with an elegantly aggressive acceleration, and Teeple waited until he was out of sight. As soon as the throaty throb of the powerful engine died down among the sand dunes, he started the boat motor to return to the pier. He landed more carefully this time around and took care to step onto the landing only when all was at a reasonable standstill.

He tied a semblance of boating knots on the cleats and all but heard his back creak as he straightened up. Even the pretense of fishing had made his joints stiff, and he pulled the flask out of his back pocket. It felt light and hollow, and he sucked out whatever there was left inside. The warmth that flooded his stomach had an eerily cooling effect in contrast to the heat blowing in his face when he opened the trunk of the one and only remaining car in the parking lot — the beige, energy-efficient compact that an environmental expert would drive.

He carried a case of full-size brandy bottles in the trunk and took one out. It was hot to the touch and he held it with two fingers by the neck to refill the empty flask. Then he put the flask in his pocket, secured the bottle back in its place in the trunk, and got behind the wheel to drive to the main road where road signs for Kuala Lumpur would lead him onto the bridge to the other side of the Straits.

To get to the main road, though, the deserted narrow path winding through the dunes was slow going. It gave him plenty of time to think of Golden's quip about headaches being the last thing for Danny to worry about if he got caught. And, one thing leading to another, the sheer thought of the stifling heat under the Goldstar tar roof made him feel directly responsible for Danny's misery out there — even though he did not believe in global warming and had had nothing to do with the Provisional Operational Approval (POA) for this operation.

It had been a botched job from the start, its objective lost in a tangle of conflicting legal guidelines, its purpose blurred by the random morality of the day. The agency's legal eagles, anxious to keep the moralists pacified, must have warned all kinds of human-rights organizations prior to giving Danny the green light to infiltrate Goldstar. They had learned the hard way how to anesthetize loud mouths beforehand to avoid class-action lawsuits afterwards. Casualties on one's own side played a second fiddle to considerations for the well-being of the enemy. The agency lawyers knew better than anyone else that the word "bizarre" had not been banned from American legal terminology for nothing. Defense against defamation lawsuits no longer had a leg to stand on, even in the spy trade.

In the 30 years since he left California, Teeple had neither managed to get out of lawyers' ways nor to keep them out of his. Washington crawled with the likes of Slick Dick, the TV shyster who had — 30 years ago back at the ranch — turned Hank the cowboy's life upside down.

As for Slick Dick himself, he was Senator Richard Fitch now, jockeying for a spot in the next presidential elections. In that kind of scramble, a compassionate face was a must to fool the largest possible number of voters and Slick Dick — sorry, Senator Richard Fitch — was deep into human rights. He had been instrumental in passing a new law that forbade US government agencies to seek information on unsavory characters from other unsavory characters who knew them best, thus forcing men like Hank Teeple to rely on CNN as the sole source of legally admissible information. And, just as it seemed that legal guidelines in the spy business could not get more absurd, lawyers' associations, scrambling to drum up more business for an overcrowded profession, played a crucial role in getting the Clintons into the White House.

Good men, many of whom Teeple had known for a long time, began to leave the CIA in droves, while the cocky ones like Danny Craig chose to stay on to kill two birds with one stone — America's enemies abroad and political correctness gone mad at home. A task that was getting more confusing with every passing day, Teeple thought as he turned onto the main road and saw the first road sign for Kuala Lumpur.

Outside Washington, things were much simpler. Right here and now, for instance, on his way to a lurking enemy's lair, the best Teeple could do about political insanity was not to dwell on it while trying to stay alive. Slick Dick and his like-minded cohorts had already seen to it that the old spy business maxim of grabbing the enemy by the balls to make his heart and mind follow was officially placed on par with genocide, and that retributions for offenders were swift, harsh and painful. Logic was dead as a doornail back in Washington. But then, what was new? Out here and right now, Teeple's best bet was getting his flask out.

He knocked back a couple of quick ones, and the whole thing was back in his pocket before the border guards on the Johor Straits bridge could see him drink and drive. Even with a valid driver's license, he had to keep both hands on the wheel and behave — for he was about to enter the realm of a sworn enemy whose feelings he was strictly forbidden to hurt.

2

The bridge was long and narrow, one lane in either direction, and Teeple kept an eye on the railing that was rushing by just inches away from the side mirror on his weaker side, the left. He was still not used to a steering wheel on the right, but that was not what bothered him. It was the memory of the bizarre bureaucratic wrangling over Danny's Provisional Operational Approval that was making his skin crawl—as if an old nag in the passenger seat were trying to hold hands with him.

In the Goldstar case, the legal eagles at Langley had been between a rock and a hard place. Some of the tangled branches of Goldstar's overgrown ownership tree reached as far as Saudi Arabia and the United States, making it quite likely that some variety of a partial owner would suddenly pop out of the shadows, waving some kind of a receipt for a contribution to global democracy. So, eager to be on the safe side, Operations sent out a toothless wolf that could inflict no prosecutable injury.

Teeple had met Danny Craig in Sarajevo in the mid-90's during the Bosnian civil war. Danny was in his 20s back then, doing his apprenticeship in hell. His first job was to pitch a double agent in a three-way conflict, and Teeple, a senior case officer on temporary assignment (TA), would try to slow him down. Danny was eager to shine. He was tall and handsome and felt no politically correct guilt about his good looks. He was a misfit in the MTV generation, and Teeple appreciated his predicament. The two of them hit it off despite the generation gap between them.

Once a week, rain or shine, Danny would have his hair trimmed and fingernails manicured to challenge the growing belief that a grubby appearance was the proper backdrop for a heart worn on the sleeve. He would tell everybody, regardless of their politics, about the problem he had with wearing *his* heart on *his* sleeve. Not that he was heartless or mean-spirited; no way, comrades. He was just a regular guy—a guy worried like hell that his heart would jump off every time a wiggly ass passed by, hoohaha.

His real problem was that with so few shapely female rear ends wiggling about a war zone, he had had no choice but to zero in on the best one at hand. It belonged to a dumb but rather pretty Harvard graduate who had flunked the bar exam in Arkansas and came to the war-torn Balkans to dabble in human rights. There was no way he could tell her the truth. First of all, his employment contract forbade him to do that; secondly, she would drop him like a hot potato if she knew he worked for the CIA. So, he pretended to be a biologist studying the reproduction pattern of a rare strain of Bosnian bee, for which purpose, he told her, he needed manicured fingernails to perform micro-inseminations under a loupe, which was not a smart thing to do. A tongue in cheek was a no-no in a civil war. The battle lines among the Croats, Serbs and Muslims changed on a daily basis, along with their motives for killing one another, and Danny's wacky pursuit of a woman who had hung out her shingle in Sarajevo as a peace-now mediator attracted the attention of the warring parties. The Serbs, who had been told by the Russians who Danny Craig really worked for, leaked the information to the Iranians, who in turn told the militant faction of the Bosnian

Muslims because at that time the U.S. seemed to be siding with the moderate faction of the Croats.

The Muslims were only too happy to grab an American, never mind why, and chain him to a stone in a cave. They promised the world videotapes of cutting him to pieces alive, starting with his decadent manicured fingernails, and the telephone lines between a cave in Sarajevo and the executive floor at Langley got busy. The story made it as far as the National Security Advisor, who became furious. The first lady and her daughter had been planning a goodwill tour around the world, and the unofficial guideline, which came with plenty of an official pep talk, was to distance American interests in the Balkans from Danny Craig's name. To hell with the bastard when a goodwill tour was at stake.

Yet, just as Teeple received his orders, Danny surfaced in a pub in the Serbian section of Sarajevo with a cocky grin on his face and a beer in his hand, all his manicured fingers intact and his shirt collar only slightly soiled. A rookie in a civil war environment, he refused to believe he had been liberated by a roving band of Serbian gangsters in military fatigues, who had jumped at the opportunity to kill a bunch of Muslims without making the squeamish west yak about it. He told a CNN camera he had outwitted his captors all by himself because fanatics were no smarter than their ideology. In his youthful euphoria, he let the reporter trick him into putting an equal sign between fanaticism and Islam, and when the peace-now lawyeress saw it all on the evening news, she went ballistic. She kicked up a fuss about CIA arrogance on foreign soil, and the media had a field day. The networks let her get as long-winded as she wanted on the talk-show circuit, and she had no problem making the CIA's arrogance abroad sound synonymous with the glass ceiling in its Directorate of Operations at home.

Teeple was reprieved and demoted, while Danny Craig was unceremoniously tucked away to Johor Bahru on the southernmost tip of Malaysia.

Yet the banishment did not seem to dampen his spirit. On the contrary, there were all kinds of rumors of his growing conviction of invincibility that made Teeple tighten his grip on the steering wheel as he now approached the end of the bridge.

The red and white barrier in front of the Malay customs shed was open, and the armed guards in crumpled khakis did not look particularly interested in passing vehicles. With Singapore license plates and an American passport, Teeple was waved on, no questions asked.

The change from Singapore's immaculate roads and stringent traffic regulations was instant. Swarms of pedal bicycles, motor scooters and oxcarts kept to the middle of the road, where the potholes were shallower and less jagged, while pedestrians in flowing robes and rubber flip-flops were all over the place. The road led due north, along the Western shore of the Malay peninsula where the Johor Straits merged into the Straits of Malacca, and Teeple turned off onto the first passable-looking side road. To get to the row of waterfront warehouses he had been watching from the boat, he had to double back as close to the border crossing as possible.

So, under the circumstances, a dirt road leading into a chaotic cluster of wooden houses on piles near the water's edge looked like a reasonable choice. The houses had thatched roofs and floor-to-ceiling openings in the walls that served as both doors and windows into lethargic domesticity, and the air was thick with smoke from cow-dung fires. Here and there, the smoke was mixed with dust raised from the parched ground by naked children, scruffy dogs, pigs and chickens, and it took Teeple several laborious U-turns in tight spaces to worm his way through.

Past the stifling bedlam of the shanty town, the dusty, potholed road delved into a wide open countryside, and the change felt like a breath of fresh air weighed down by a sudden, abrupt, eerie silence. No more pigs, no more dogs and chickens, no naked children—as if the locals knew something they would not share with strangers.

3

The deserted dirt road cut through low brush that Teeple suspected was growing out of fly and mosquito-infested swamps. The countryside was pancake flat and the sea was very near. Here and there, a straggly cluster of tall reeds broke the monotony, and except for a few flabbergasted rodents along the roadside, he met no other living soul all the way to the dilapidated brown-brick facade of the Goldstar warehouse. The company name was painted on crumbling brick in the same bleached-out letters as on the waterfront, and he pulled up on a sort of a road shoulder. There were no warning signs here about private property or prohibited entry, and no sign of Danny Craig.

The place looked ostentatiously deserted, and Teeple restarted the engine and put the car back in gear to turn around. Chances were he might have to leave here in a hurry, and facing in the direction he had come from could do no harm. Then, with the last deep breath of air-conditioned air, he shut off the engine and got out.

The heat struck him in the face from below, reflecting from parched ground that made his shoes instantly dusty. Something flew in his mouth and he spat it out. A fly. Another fly bumped into his eye, leaving behind something that burnt his eyeball, and he was still rubbing it when he was stopped by a knee-high rusty gate in a vaulted passageway that he had almost overlooked in the twilight. It was not locked.

It opened with a squeak, and as the flies became more persistent in the musty shade, he hurried through into a sunlit, unpaved, square yard with the same hot dirt as outside.

At first, with the burning eye watering up, he thought it was a pile of clothes lying in the center of the yard. The windows in the crumbling brick facades of the surrounding buildings were boarded, and the overall sense of deterioration was in sharp contrast with the clothes on the ground. The trousers were freshly ironed, as if they had just been delivered from a dry-cleaner's—except that there were legs in them. The shoes looked as if the man had planned to hit either a dance floor or the footrest of a five-star hotel bar counter instead of lying in hot dust with ants swarming around his ankles.

The ankles were tied to wooden stakes in the ground as were the wrists of the spread-eagled arms. Four limbs, four stakes, and Teeple felt a surge of bile rising in his throat when he saw the face. Danny looked surprised—embarrassed, rather—about lying here like this.

It took Teeple a moment to realize that the surprised look was the result of the upper eyelids being taped to the forehead with packing tape. The tension of the tape had wrinkled the forehead, and the wide-open eyes stared into the blazing sun even though they could not see it. There were neither pupils nor irises in them. The eyeballs were covered with skin-color flies, and Hank went down on his knees to rip the tape off.

His hand was trembling. He could not get a fingernail under the edge of the tape and had to take a deep breath to pull himself together. He was about to try again when the hand tied to the stake by his knee moved. The fingers were clawing at dust, and Teeple was about to rip the stake out of the ground when a shadow fell over him and a firm, hard hand grabbed his wrist.

"Haste makes waste, Mister Hank." It was Golden, not smiling. "It's only muscle contractions."

"What are you doing here?"

"Working." The hand on the ground stopped moving, but Golden's grip on Teeple's wrist would not relax. "You've never seen anyone die on the stake, have you?"

"Let go." Teeple jerked his hand, but Golden was strong like an ox. He lifted Teeple by his struggling arm to put him on his feet, like a stubborn child that was not supposed to play in dirt. "I told you, the twitching fingers, it's just nerves."

The hand on the ground was dead still now, and Golden relaxed his grip on Teeple's wrist a notch to talk sense into him.

"Why the taped eyelids, you think? Because they got you figured. The first thing a Westerner would do in a situation like this is to rip the tape off, wiggle a pressure switch under the head and boom." With his free hand, Golden illustrated an explosion.

"Ow, come on."

"I'm talking about conventional explosives. Nothing radioactive. Nothing to do with the stuff you and your partner came down here to look for."

"What?"

"Ow, please. Cut to the chase, Hank." Along with the abrupt switch to contemporary Americanism, Golden also dropped the outdated Mister to test Teeple's comprehension of the more current facts of life. The jig was up. The Singapore IB had known all along who Hank Teeple was. "By the way, where's your gun?"

"I don't carry one."

"Sticking to your cover story even between a rock and a hard place, huh?" Golden gave Teeple a probing look to make sure they finally were on the same wavelength. Then he let go of his wrist. "There's nothing you can do for your partner. Come on."

"I'm not leaving him behind."

"The body will be taken care of." His eyes darting back and forth in a purposely random sequence over the boarded windows, Golden nudged Teeple into an all-out retreat. They began backing off towards the exit, where four Chinese men in office suits stepped out of the shadows of the vaulted vestibule to block their way.

They carried freshly oiled machine guns, holding them well away from their jackets, and looked relieved to take their fingers off the triggers when Golden gave them the nod. He exchanged a few staccato words in Chinese with the leader, then turned back to Teeple and his diction simmered down to English.

"Just in case you are right and the dust is radioactive around here," he smiled a little, "my guys will make sure to be done before the sundowner wind kicks up."

With the armed suits covering their retreat, Golden led the way through the fly-infested passageway and past the squeaky gate.

"Your embassy in Kuala Lumpur will have the body in a couple of days. The family name's Craig, isn't it?" He was not really asking. He knew. "A CIA case officer, right?"

Outside, on the parched roadside, he ushered Teeple into the hot driver seat of the energy-efficient beige car and stood by as if to prevent him from dashing back to the dead body. It was only when he was absolutely sure Teeple was going to do nothing of the kind that he squeezed into the back seat, extricated a gun from under his belt, and made himself small in a corner to keep an eye on the rear.

"Fast as she goes, Hank."

Even with the engine squealing in high pitch, the insipid air conditioning kept on blowing hot air for another half mile or so, but Golden did not seem to mind. He was relieved. The cards were on the table. They were brothers in arms, and he approved of Teeple driving in second gear to keep extra acceleration in reserve in case they began taking fire.

But nothing happened. No shots were fired, and they both smiled a little when the nearby village came in sight and the dusty road burrowed into the chaotic cluster of shacks on piles.

Teeple shifted into third and eased up on the gas to reduce the squeal of the engine and the dust trail. Still, the little car's narrow tires and anemic shock absorbers kept on bouncing wildly on potholes, broken driftwood and flattened Coca-Cola cans, scattering pigs and children and annoying the adults. Stoic, dark faces were staring at them from the floor-to-ceiling openings in thatch walls, and Teeple could feel the hostility in the nape of his neck.

It was only after they turned into the chaotic bicycle and ox-cart traffic on the main road that Golden expanded back to his full size in the backseat, and the bad feeling in the nape of Teeple's neck went away—to make room for scolding guilt.

"Sorry about your partner," Golden said, guessing right at the reason for Teeple's clenched jaws. "A buddy of yours?"

"I thought you knew everything . . . damn it," Teeple slammed on the brakes to avoid a lumbering oxcart that had popped out of nowhere—or, rather, out of the blind spot of his painfully divided attention.

"Do you want me to drive?" Golden said, softly.

"No."

"The thing is," Golden went on, watching the ox in front of them straining to drag the cart out of the way, "I'd hate to do you injustice, you know that."

"Then don't."

"Orders. We're switching to Plan B."

"What's that?"

"Plan B . . . like 'B' in Bye Bye Blackbird?"

The ox cart finally made it to the side of the road, and Teeple moved on. "What the hell are you talking about?"

"'B' like a Beeline to the airport."

"I have a valid Singapore visa."

"That's why our people are packing your stuff at the hotel with extra care and will bring the suitcase straight to the gate; hopefully before the press finds out you are not here to clean up our sewage. Get my drift?"

"What the hell . . ." With his side mirror, Teeple had bumped a bicycle handle bar and knocked down an old man in white garb. Fortunately, Teeple had been driving at a snail's pace and could stop without screeching tires to attract attention.

"I'm sorry, sir," he told the guy on the ground, quietly.

But the old man was not expecting an apology. He got up from the dust and picked up his skullcap with a cheerful toothless grin as if to say, "No problem, my friend, nothing to worry about."

"You see?" Golden leaned forward to tap Teeple's shoulder. "Do these people look to you like they are stockpiling weapons of mass destruction? You and your partner have been barking up the wrong tree down here."

The traffic became lighter the closer they got to the bridge, and in the end they were the only car in the Singapore-bound lane. The air conditioning was working by then, and Golden moved his hand off the gun in his lap to mop up his forehead. Then he wiped the hand on his trousers and gave Teeple's shoulder a shyly affectionate squeeze.

"No hard feelings, OK?" He was anxious to part on good terms. He liked America and Americans and wanted Teeple to see his dilemma. "My boss says it's politics, not your fault. Told me to buy you a bottle of peach brandy at the duty-free in the airport. At his private expense."

"Does he know something I don't?"

"About the toes you stepped on back in America with this job? I don't think so."

Golden's hand was still on Teeple's shoulder, but there was no use trying to pat it and insist on calling a spade a spade. Look here pal, let's be honest with each other . . .

"I know it's a bummer," Golden went on, making up his mind to drop a more explicit hint on his own authority. "They've got your number, Hank. But don't worry. No one's gonna get you on my turf. Call it taking pride in my work."

They were approaching the checkpoint on the Singapore end of the bridge, and Golden made sure to move the gun off his lap before they stopped in front of the red-and-white barrier. He slipped it under his buttocks to sit on it just as a bespectacled officer in immaculately pressed shorts and colonial-British knee socks reached inside the car.

"Papers."

There were no cars behind them, and the officer took his time to give Teeple's passport a thorough check. He found the Singapore visa, read it line by line—column by column, rather—looked up, shook his head, and pointed an accusing finger at Teeple's chest.

"No good."

"Huh?"

"Are you coming to Singapore to die, sir?"

Teeple's first thought was that Danny's body had been radioactive after all. Had the radiation already begun to distort his own face? He glanced over his shoulder, but Golden just grinned and pointed to a billboard by the roadside. It featured an oversized seat-belt buckle and a pretty Chinese girl raising a concerned eyebrow. "Buckle up if you want to meet me sometime," the caption read, and Teeple obediently put on his seat belt.

"Thank you, sir." The spruce officer returned Teeple's passport with a smart salute and waved them on.

Up ahead, against the backdrop of the gleaming Singapore skyline, a sluggish commercial jet was descending into the sand dunes and marshes where the airport was, and in the shimmering hot air, the red and blue United Airlines logo on the plane's tail looked like writing in the sky.

Teeple was going to be home in time for the witch hunt.

Washington, D.C.

4

After the scorching razzle-dazzle of the tropics, a rainy dawn in Virginia sent a shiver down Teeple's spine as the plane broke through the sagging bottom of gray clouds on its approach to Dulles. The soggy fields and wet roads along the Potomac looked drab and dull in the gray morning light, and the implications of gazing into doom and gloom through a rain-splattered window in the back of a plane were obvious.

Teeple's job seniority made him eligible for business class, thus allowing no room for illusions that an arrival in a cramped economy seat was a prelude to a hero's parade. In a government job, seniority was the ticket to a bag of perks. So, when perk after perk was being taken away from an aging government employee, seniority became merely a sort of mature ability to read the writing on the wall. He was in for more than just a slap on the wrist and the consequences were obvious.

Old friends, worried about their own pension benefits, were going to pretend not to know him, while the younger set was bound to dance in the aisles, feeling validated by the demise of a grouch of the old school. A grouch who would not see the rise of a new, gentler generation of spies without an eye surgery, Teeple thought as he watched the teenager in the next seat out of the corner of his eye. The back of the plane was full of such creatures—carbon copies of one another's individualism.

The boy had spiky green hair, a nose ring and body odor. He wore a sleeveless undershirt to show off tattooed arms that ended in stubby fingers constantly fiddling with a miniature electronic gadget—forcing Teeple to count and recount the years since he had seen America last. Had it really been that long?

Back in the old days, men used Vitalis to keep their hair tidy, while body piercings and tattoos were strictly for weirdos from the wrong side of the tracks. Regular guys wore long-sleeved shirts ironed by their mothers to look crisp and neat while dating girls who would go on ironing their shirts 'til death do us part—a prospect that Roni Pitt had turned down with a yawn.

She had been interested in neither ironing nor him—a thought that made Teeple sit up and shift his weight from one buttock to the other in the hard, cheap seat. He realized he must have looked to the green-haired punk next to him like an old man with a pickle up his rear end that became outright painful as the plane touched down.

The landing, a homecoming kiss of a rain-swept runway, brought forth all the gossip he had heard over the years about the new America where disciplinary actions and demotions were relics of the past. People were no longer being yelled at for messing up. A failure, no matter how big or small, was treated with a massive overdose of loving re-education, and Teeple could not help shuddering when he saw George Twombly, a reeducated old timer, waiting for him at the arrival gate.

"What's up?" Twombly was struggling to keep his voice down as they shook hands. A few years back, he had been accused of an unfeeling attitude towards the enemy and duly reeducated to focus his energies on politically correct gossip around the office water cooler. So, a chance of hearing news, any news, from the horse's mouth, so to speak, made him all but tremble. "Talk to me, Hank."

"What do you want to hear?"

"What the hell's going on?"

"I've been out of the loop for sixteen hours at thirty thousand feet."

"In coach, huh?"

Teeple forced a smile. "News travels fast around the water cooler."

"A lot of buzz, buddy. It's a pissing contest back at the office." Twombly used a plastic card to open a no-admittance door to skip Immigration, and in the dimly lit, bunker-like bypass, he felt safe enough to say more. "They're like dogs marking over each other's piss on a street corner. Only if you ask why that particular corner, no one knows. Danny must've hit a goddamned nerve somewhere."

Teeple said nothing, and Twombly clammed up when they entered the bustling arrival hall. At the luggage carousel, Teeple picked up his suitcase packed by the Singapore IB almost 24 hours before, and followed Twombly to a gray, no-extras Ford parked at a restricted red curb outside. There was an airport security man standing guard by it, and Twombly gave him a pat on the back and a conspiratorial wink to confirm that Teeple was that big wig he had told him about, just between the two of them.

"Thanks, Charlie. You made my day." He seemed to have worked out a routine of picking up people at the airport and would not talk until they were out of the chaotic traffic around the terminal. It was still raining, and in the swirling spray from speeding cars on the parkway, the wipers began to smudge the windshield.

"What a mess," Twombly said, fiddling with something in the dashboard. "How bad was it?"

"We don't know yet, do we?"

"I mean . . . the way Danny died."

Teeple leaned back on the headrest, but would not close his eyes. He did not want to see Danny's eyeballs swarming with flies again. Nor did he want to talk about it, and Twombly could understand that. He used to be out in the field himself; but he had to get at least something firsthand.

"They say you were still on STU-III down there," he whispered hoarsely.

"That's all we had."

"The techs swear they started sending out the next generation hardware last fall."

"Not to Malaysia."

"Couldn't you have waited?"

"Waited for what? For the Washington Post to have a copy of Danny's POA pinned up on the editors' message board?"

"You said it, man . . ." Twombly lapsed into a moody silence. Then, as if on second thought, he took a deep breath and opened the safety valves of frustration a notch. It made him sound like the hiss of water coming under pressure from a crack in the wall. "Don't you feel like shit sometimes?"

"Why me?"

"Because shit happens." Twombly decided he had said too much already and changed the subject. "By the way, how's your bladder?"

"Fine."

"You'll have time for a quick a leak, but that's about it. They're waiting for you up in the attic, tapping their feet."

The proverbial attic was the executive 11th floor, and Teeple pinched his lips and bit his tongue. He had hoped they'd leave him alone for at least the rest of the day, which was obviously not going to happen.

By the time they got off the beltway at the Langley exit, it stopped raining, and the sun began pushing through the clouds over the CIA areal, reflecting in the card Twombly used to open the parking lot gate. It had several metallic strips and a hologram of something.

"Eyewash," Twombly shrugged when he saw Teeple looking at the glitter. "Can sign for it under any name at personnel."

He pulled into a reserved parking and brightened up when Teeple asked him to open the trunk to get into his suitcase.

"Looking for your six-shooter?" Twombly slapped Teeple on the back. He obviously loved to fantasize about shooting up the place himself, and Teeple hated to disappoint him.

"Just a necktie, George."

"Are you kidding me?"

"No."

"The dinosaur look?" Twombly himself wore a white business shirt open at the neck. It was the same kind of shirt he used to wear with a tie, making him look like a stockbroker commandeered by his wife to take out the garbage after he had made himself comfortable at home after work, and Teeple shook his head.

"Can't teach an old dog new tricks." He got a necktie out of his suitcase and tied it while crossing the parking lot.

In the lobby, the sprawling Central Intelligence Agency seal in the floor was obscured by metal detectors. An X-ray gate stood on the American Eagle's head, and Teeple and Twombly queued up on the eagle's talons to wait their turn to empty their pockets.

Teeple put his key chain, loose change and the travel flask on the conveyor belt of the scanner.

"Are you on the hard stuff now?" Twombly grinned at the flask as they put their things back in the pockets on the other side of the X-ray gate. "Your tummy's got to have a steel lining."

"It didn't set off the alarm, did it?"

"Don't cancel your health insurance on account of that."

"Meaning what?"

"Nothing." Twombly waited until they were in the elevator. No one joined them, and after the door closed, he threw caution to the wind. He had to tell somebody.

"Just so you know." He showed Teeple his shoulder holster and the gun the metal detectors had failed to detect.

"Is it plastic?"

"'course not. And it's not the first time."

"Have you reported it?"

"Reported to whom?" He grabbed Teeple's sleeve. "They're in, Hank. The body snatchers are in, anywhere they want to be, from the basement to wherever."

The floor indicator showed three floors to go, and Twombly cut the story short. "Like the Vietnamese used to say back in Saigon, remember? The best way to knock out our high-tech weaponry was to grab us by the belt buckle. Somebody's doing it right now, man; only it ain't the slopes."

There was another security check on the 11th floor, the attic, and Twombly's name was not on the guard's clipboard. He was sent back downstairs, while Teeple was directed to corridor C, all the way down to the office of the deputy director of operations, where a spaced-out receptionist with black lipstick and dilated pupils shot him a shifty look. She could not have been quite 20.

"What's up, guy?"

Teeple told her his last name, using the outdated Mr. prefix, like in the old days when a necktie was a must on the 11th floor, but she ignored that.

"What is it your mother called you? John? Eduardo? Ahmed? What?"

She was even too young to be his daughter, but Teeple wanted no fuss, not the moment he got in. He obediently stated his first name and watched the girl make a tick mark in an appointment calendar. He better get used to the new America fast.

"Take a . . ." she wiped her nose with the back of her hand, "take a seat, Hank."

She went on pushing papers without looking at them, unable to sit still, and Teeple could not help wondering why she had not been given a drug test yet. She was most likely on some civil-rights committee, he thought to keep himself from getting into doomsday conjectures about both the upcoming interview and his homeland's future. He did his best not to tap his foot and forced himself not to stare when a big, broad-shouldered blonde in a red dress and rubber flip-flops on bare feet barged in with a thick document binder under an arm.

She nodded gravely to the spaced-out receptionist and was immediately waved on to the deputy director's inner sanctum, fitting the door frame like a square peg in a square hole.

A minute later, a swarthy young man in a football jersey and sneakers followed the same route, carrying nothing and passing through the inner-sanctum door with a lot more wiggle room than the woman in red before him. There was the number seven on the back of his jersey, and to prove he was a sportsman, he shut the soundproof door behind him with a hop and a kick. It closed with an airtight thud, and in the ensuing silence, the receptionist's sniffing went on marking time until the intercom on her desk buzzed a good half hour later.

Teeple was to go in.

5

The deputy director looked tired and uncomfortable behind his executive-grade desk. His hair was thinner than Teeple remembered, his hands were fidgety, and there was a shaving nick on his chin. He wore a gray business suit, but as a concession to the current individualist dress code, he also wore an old-fashioned white business shirt open at the neck, looking meek and humble before his underlings.

The big blonde in red and the number seven sportsman were hanging out in front of his desk in comfy armchairs and acknowledged Teeple with stony smiles. The sportsman added a barely perceptible nod, while the woman, her heavy legs crossed at the knees, moved the toes of her upper foot to make the flip-flop slap her heel by way of a hello.

"I guess you haven't met." The deputy director smiled, a smile as worn out as the rest of him, and waved Teeple onto a chair without elbow rests.

He introduced the blonde in red as doctor of something; Teeple did not catch of what. The sportsman was Hasan El or Al something, about 30, grim and unshaved, with a pockmarked face and thick, black hair that grew low over his forehead and temples. His jersey had the Washington Renegades RFC logo, and Teeple did not bother to remember his last name either. Should he ever want to know it, he was sure Twombly would be only too happy to oblige.

"Hank," the deputy director said, a touch too loud to show he was not embarrassed by being on a first-name basis with a man in disgrace. "One of ours is dead."

"Yes."

"What's your take on it?"

"A textbook leak," Teeple shrugged, aware that no one was interested in his take on anything.

"An outdated phone security, maybe?"

"I thought of that. But all Danny told me on the phone was that he had reliable information that no one was supposed to be inside that warehouse on that particular day. I'm pretty sure neither of us mentioned what warehouse and what day."

Teeple could tell that no one in the room really wanted to go into that either. They all looked smug about having made a decision before he came in. For some reason, though, they felt obligated to keep on making conversation for a while, and the blond doctor of something barely managed to suppress a yawn when she spoke up.

"I pulled your old field reports from way back when the agency files got computerized." Her watery eyes made brief contact with Teeple's, and her parched, pasty face all but crackled when she smiled. "Way back when I was still in grade school."

Having shown a flicker of humor, she turned serious and undid the clasp on the document binder in her lap. She had notes scribbled on the inside of the cover, and Teeple wondered if one was supposed to do that with a top-secret, numbered file. But then, things were different now. Secrecy had no place in the better world of the future.

"A fascinating read," the doctor said, tapping the binder.

"Thank you," Teeple nodded. The dislike was mutual.

"Tell me, Hank. The name of that place where officer Craig got killed, Goldstar, is sort of typically Chinese, right? Meaning good luck and fortune and all that down there in . . ." she consulted her notes, ". . . in Malaysia?"

"The registered lessees are not Chinese."

"Oh?"

"They are Malay."

"Meaning Malay Muslims?"

"Yes."

"You're on thin ice, Hank." The doctor heaved a sigh. She had done her bit to warn Teeple about the pitfalls of discrimination and turned to the sportsman. "Your witness, Hasan."

"Thanks." Hasan gave her a clipped, strictly collegial smile, pretending not to notice the affectionate glow in her paltry face. She was in love, but Hasan was all business. "All right, Hank, my friend. Go on."

"That's it."

"No it's not." Hasan forced a razor thin smile. "Convince us you played by the rules raiding Goldstar."

"It was not a raid."

"Answer my question, please." Hasan hated stubborn old guys. "Have you resorted to profiling? Yes or no."

"What the hell are you talking about?"

"You heard me."

"The *bajak laut* have been the subjects of sultans for the last thousand years and proud of it. It's just common sense to assume that . . ."

"You do know what assume means, huh?"

"What?"

"Making an *ass* of *u* and *me*." Hasan shook his head with a wink to the doctor. This was going to be fun. This guy was setting himself up and didn't know it. "Because Hank, my friend, reading between the lines of your report, it's clear to me you're convinced that the Malacca Straits pirates, the *bajak laut* as you call them, are Islamic extremists."

"I am?"

"Aren't you?"

"I thought that between the lines, I particularly pointed out that the weaponry they use is far from extreme: standard handguns and commercial duct tape. They work in pairs, two fast boats per hit, like in the old days. They just no longer fire lead cannon balls over wooden bows. Steel hulls call for magnetic climbing irons and night vision gear; and sometimes not even that. Some hits happen in broad daylight. Every ship radar has a blind spot in the wake of the vessel, and the crew often find out that something's wrong only when they have a gun muzzle shoved between their eyes. Then the pirates get duct tape out of their brand-name khakis and head for the GPS on the bridge."

"Just like that, huh?" Hasan was not trying to be on his legal best yet. "No swashbuckling, is that what you mean?"

"Big freighters are operated by computer nerds who don't fight back. If the pirates kill a few here and there, then it's just for fun. In a couple of cases, they sliced an uncooperative skipper in two with a saber, but generally, they don't need Captain Hook to help them get the boatswain on duty taped up so that they can have both hands free to pop the chip."

"Pop the chip? No kidding," Hasan grinned. This old guy was something else. "We're lawyers, man, not engineers. We need the record to show something in proper language. What?"

"What I said."

Hasan rolled his eyes. "Let me tell you what. We don't have all day."

"All right."

"Why don't you try to speak to us like we're dumb, huh?"

"No problem." Teeple dropped his eyes to his shoes, and Hasan was pacified, for the moment.

"Just give us the basics, Hank—one, two, three."

"OK."

"Go."

"One, the pirates extract the encoded ID microchip out of the freighter's global positioning system; two, they transfer the chip into a portable transponder working on the same frequency and tracking pattern; three, they throw that transponder into one of the waiting fast boats and sit back to enjoy the ride. Make sense to a lawyer?"

"More or less."

"A man with good fingers can execute items one and two in less than a second. It causes no more than a blip on the PSA monitors—PSA being a big tracking outfit out of Singapore. A blip on one out of their two hundred monitors is just another atmospheric disturbance, especially since the speed boat with the freighter's chip continues along the regular shipping route at the right speed to keep the signal on track. The other speed boat then escorts the no longer traceable freighter into one of the uncharted tidal estuaries in Sumatra."

"Uncharted? Christopher Columbus sailed in uncharted waters. What happened to satellite photography?"

"Satellites can't keep up with the bore."

"The bore? You mean like an FBI guy?" Hasan grinned, and the blond doctor gave him a loving smile. She was so proud of this handsome, clever guy, and Teeple looked away to seek refuge from syrupy emotions in technicalities.

"In southeastern Sumatra, the incoming tide gets held up by a mangrove-root mess that stretches for hundreds of miles along the coast. Water backs up till it packs enough inertia to push through into the tidal estuaries, like a sort of tsunami wave that moves at 30 to 50 miles an hour. That's the kind of "bore" I'm talking about. It changes the look of the coast in minutes, and by the time an annotated satellite picture gets to the right hands, the data about the shape and depth of any coastal estuary might do more harm than good. The Indonesian Navy would be in violation of their own safety regulations if they attempted to send cruisers in hot pursuit into places like that. The pirates don't have to rush it. With a tide calendar and a local fisherman who knows the layout of the submerged mangrove mess, they can maneuver a hijacked freighter to a place where they can take all the time they need to pick just specific items from the cargo manifest."

"How specific?"

"As specific as they want to make it. A freighter can carry up to nine thousand containers, starting at ten tons each."

"Not all of them loaded with enriched plutonium, I take it?" Hasan frowned at his wristwatch. It was time to get serious, and the doctor got the message.

"Well, Hank." She sat up to do her bit. "Tell us, how much enriched plutonium did you actually find down there?"

She and Hasan were a team at semantic games, and Teeple was not going to be sucked in. He turned to the deputy director.

"All this has been spelled out in the POA application."

"Do we have a copy?" The deputy turned a meekly authoritative glance to the doctor, who in turn tore her loving eyes from Hasan to fuss with the papers in her lap, pouncing on one and making a show of holding it up for Teeple to see.

"Is this what you're talking about?"

Teeple nodded, and she handed the document to the deputy director with the appropriate running commentary. "A Provisional Operational Approval for a single, local-agent-conducted investigation — a single investigation into a single act of piracy in the Malacca Straits. I see nothing in it that would authorize a case officer to do a follow-up footwork himself."

The deputy director hardly looked at the document, and Teeple, thinking of the flies on Danny's eyeballs, felt bile rising in his throat as he spoke up. It was tough to keep from gagging.

"To start with, all that officer Craig had to go on was an iffy container identification purposely muddled in the accompanying letter of credit. There was no chance to get an authorization for a break-in on that kind of evidence, and he had to get creative. He bribed a local roof contractor in Johor Bahru to make sure the Goldstar roof peeled off in the next typhoon so that he could take a peek inside from the air."

"That so?" the doctor smiled, confident that Teeple would shoot himself in the foot any moment now. "Are you telling us that a U.S. government official condoned a bribe?"

"Danny used the local agent as a go-between. He had nothing to do with the actual handover except making sure the right sum of money changed the right hands."

"In other words, a bribe, no matter how you slice it."

"Baksheesh is king down there."

"Which in your opinion is a valid reason for an American government agency to proliferate corruption abroad?" The doctor sat up, shaking her head. This was her turf where she was in command of a stock of clichés sufficient to convict Mother Theresa of an uncaring attitude towards the poor. But when she saw that both the deputy director and Hasan wanted her to get on, she archly nodded to Teeple to proceed with his, in her opinion, dubious story.

"After the last typhoon down there, Danny used a local asset who owned a small plane to take him up before the takeoff ban was lifted. He took pictures of the Goldstar storage space, passed them on to the Directorate of Intelligence, who passed them to OTS, who took a month to digitally enhance a partially readable container number. It jived with the first five digits of the number of a container that had been previously reported stolen off a Vietnamese ship in the Malacca Straits."

"Bingo." Facetiously, the doctor singled a page out of her binder and handed it over to the deputy director. "What Hank is talking about is a Vietnamese ship belonging to a Singapore-based firm with ties to a Swiss holding company in Zurich that happens to be a subsidiary of a movie studio in Hollywood owned by an American citizen."

"Thus proving that officer Craig was in violation of a federal law about separation of criminal investigation and intelligence gathering. On top of which . . . " Hasan sat up and raised his voice to come up with the kicker, ". . . officer Craig was in violation of Executive Order 12333 from 1981 about spying on American citizens?"

"Unless there is viable evidence that an American citizen conspired with the enemy," the deputy director put in. "Which, I'm afraid, Hank, you failed to come up with."

"I am working on that." Using first person singular, Teeple

conceded that he was alone on the case now, but would not go as far as reverting to past tense. "The Goldstar warehouse is the logical starting point. That's why Danny went in himself. He did not want someone to screw up in his name. He was scared stiff of being called home."

"What's so scary about that?"

"A desk job." Teeple could not help smiling as both the doctor and Hasan stiffened, and the deputy director held up a hand.

"You're being abrasive, Hank."

"Am I?" Teeple took a deep breath. They had done it to him again. He had been sidetracked into a crusade against stupidity and had lost sight of his objective: to speak for Danny who could no longer speak for himself. "Danny had circumstantial evidence that the goods stolen off commercial vessels in the Malacca Straits are being hauled in broad daylight by fishing trawlers from Sumatra to Malaysia for repackaging and relabeling, so that they can be smuggled back to Singapore and stolen again under a different insurance coverage. The one and only official land crossing between Singapore and Malaysia is there to enforce seat belts and put exotic stamps in tourist passports. The control of the waterways falls to Port Authority, a privately owned outfit that handles twenty millions containers a year. A pound of anything, enriched plutonium if you want, can be traced in one out of millions of containers at five hundred tons each only by its money trail—a trail starting with letters of credit issued by a Saudi bank which, as it happens, also controls manufacturer export licenses and undersells Lloyd's of London as an insurance underwriter."

"Aaah," Hasan butted in with a flippantly exaggerated awe. "A Saudi bank, a Saudi insurance, Saudi this, Saudi that. A nasty, red-hot trail going cold where the terrorists are supposed to live. Is that it, my friend?"

"All I said was that the letters of credit on the Goldstar goods we're talking about had been issued by the Emirates Bank of Riyadh. The Muslim pirates you're so concerned about don't figure into the big money equation. Whether they work on commission or straight salary, we don't care. We are not after them."

"Ow, come on, Hank." The blond doctor had heard enough. The technicalities of letters of credit, manufacturer export licenses, bogus insurance claims, magnetic climbing irons, and popping microchips sounded to her like vintage macho humor out of James Bond, whom she despised. She had always thought it so grossly demeaning to women to name one of Bond's supporting characters Pussy Galore. So, to be on the safe side in a real cloak-and-dagger case, she chose to bring in human rights, a subject no one in his right mind would dare to challenge her on.

"Perhaps Hank has never heard about presumed innocent before proven guilty?" She looked for approval from the deputy director. But the man was looking at his hands on the desk, and she went back to rifling through the file in her lap for something to attract his attention. She dropped a few pages on the floor, picked them up, found something she thought might do, and cracked a smug smile. She had an accusing finger ready, but would not point it yet.

"Danny Craig was twenty-nine when he died, right?" She was laying a course to a direct accusation in a roundabout way. "Is it totally out of the question that at his age, he might have still been playing games? Like cowboys and Indians, for instance?"

"I'm not sure I follow you," Teeple said, keeping his eyes on the inventory tag at the side of the deputy director's desk.

"What I mean is," the doctor smiled condescendingly, giving the deputy director a nod—now watch this, "weren't you by any chance raised on a farm out west, Hank?"

"A ranch," Teeple nodded.

"In which case, we can reasonably presume that you used to play at cowboys and Indians as a kid?" The doctor's smile turned motherly now that she brought in childish games. "And when you got older, I take it, you rode in rodeos?"

Teeple said nothing, trying to see where she was going with this. There was a speck of foam forming in a corner of her mouth.

"Bucking bulls, bucking horses, animals made crazy by tight belts around the loins — wild, wasn't it?" The doctor was talking to Hank while looking at the deputy director, who kept staring at his hands. It seemed he had missed her point again, and she took it once more from the top, this time with names and dates. "Danny Craig did his apprenticeship under you in Sarajevo in 1994 — am I right Hank?"

"Yes."

"In other words, in rodeo-cowboy lingo, you were breaking in a green horse." The doctor was on a roll, but Hasan knew her passion for overkill and stopped her in time.

"Now," he butted in with a painfully false conciliatory smile, "aren't we supposed to work together?"

No one said anything, and Hasan assumed it was time to turn the legal screw, which was his job.

"Regrettable as it may be, in our business, we are too often forced to operate closer to the legal borderline than we want to," he said, his voice thickening with sympathy. "The trick is not to cross it."

Again, no one said anything, and for a moment Hasan looked worried he had not turned the screw right and they were going to take the screwdriver away from him. It made him come down harder on Teeple.

"By your own admission, my friend, you disregarded the unwritten rules about bending the written ones," he said gravely, bringing his eyes down from somewhere above the top of Teeple's head. He loved to see people's faces when he pushed them over the edge. "In which case, there is precious little we can do for you."

"You tripped over your own feet, Hank. Profiling is a no-no when it fails to produce viable evidence," the deputy director nodded and, having no gavel in hand, tapped his desk with a finger. "What you came up with so far does not in our opinion justify an investigation into an alleged link between Muslim pirates in the Malacca Straits and a money-laundering operation allegedly sponsored by a Saudi bank with ties to a holding company owned by an American citizen."

"I told you, I am . . ."

"Yes, you are, Hank. You are out of line."

"I am working on this thing. So far, we have barely scratched the surface."

"Scratched it with extreme prejudice, as you 007s out in the field like to brag over your dry Martinis," the doctor butted in, the speck of foam still showing in the corner of her mouth. "Shoot first, leave questions for later."

"I don't carry a gun."

"A man is dead, Hank."

Teeple turned his eyes back to the inventory tag at the side of the deputy director's desk and bit his tongue. There was no use arguing with a cliché that had been repeated often enough by all and sundry to be taken for a fact. Guns killed people, and the mere mention of a gun in connection with a person's name was as good as an accessory-before-the-fact conviction. The blond doctor had it pat. Hasan seemed to know that, too, and decided to save his breath. It was the deputy director's turn to draw blood.

"As the lady said, Hank, a man is dead. One of ours. Which, as you know, means an inquiry." The deputy director smiled, a difficult smile. "An FBI inquiry. And you know those guys."

"Does that mean you want me out before they get here?"

"We cannot afford an accusation of illegal practices resulting in a fatality."

"You are a hot potato, Hank. But," Hasan nodded, thoughtfully smoothing the Washington Renegades logo on his jersey, "we are not dropping you like one. We don't throw people under the bus just because they made a mistake."

"The fact is, Hank," the deputy director heaved a sigh, "there are people in this building who want to see you hanged high and dry."

"Had a hell of a lot of explaining to do," Hasan nodded with impeccable timing. They all sounded as if they had rehearsed this before. "Some people wouldn't hear of helping Hank Teeple straighten out and fly right. They want your head, man."

Teeple tried hard not to think of Danny Craig. He was afraid he would jump up to wipe the snicker off Hasan's face, and the deputy director seemed to be reading his thoughts.

"A good psychoanalyst will have you back on track in no time, Hank." The deputy director leaned over his desk to flip through a Rolodex. "Besides, the personnel people will need your psychological evaluation before they decide what to do next. If that's OK with you, of course."

He scribbled a telephone number on a scrap of paper, and they all looked at Teeple as if they knew it was OK with him.

"You need help to get your act together, that's all," the deputy director said as he handed Teeple the paper. "Any questions?"

Teeple thought he had seen a twinkle in the man's eyes. But under the circumstances, it might have been just wishful thinking on his part, for there was no trace of a twinkle in either Hasan's or the doctor's eyes. They both looked smug and proper, proud of the human face they had managed to put on discrediting a senior employee—letting him down so gently that he still was not quite sure what hit him. They had made yet another step in the right direction to make the office a safer place to work on making the world a safer place to live in, and in their minds, they were already working on the wording of their report about that.

In Washington, reports would make or break careers, depending on how much heart one managed to squeeze into the opening paragraph. Heartless first paragraphs were as sure as not to earn the author a burn mark. A mark that in the mean old days used to be reserved for treason, Hank thought, almost sure by now that the twinkle in the deputy director's eyes had not been just a misconceived illusion of his own wishful thinking.

The man seemed to be reading his thoughts.

6

With the shrink's phone number in his pocket, Teeple took the downtown shuttle that departed every hour on the hour from the main gate of the CIA complex. It went straight to the FBI headquarters in the Edgar Hoover Building on Pennsylvania Avenue, a cost-be-damned manifestation of an exemplary cooperation between government agencies, and as such it was empty. It merely provided a comfortable transportation to occasional lost souls—at the taxpayers' expense of course—and when Teeple got off at the end stop, he could not but feel expelled from a cozy freeloaders' club.

The avenue before him—the extra wide, grand connector between the White House and the Capitol—looked perfectly indifferent to the plight of a small pawn in a big game. The thunder of eight traffic lanes left no doubt what would happen if he stepped forth in pursuit of one man's trifling chore. On the other hand, the mere thought that his punishment might have been an olive green desk with a pencil tray and a file drawer under the all-seeing eye of this or that committee made him feel glad to be out in the street, breathing carbon dioxide. It also made him less squeamish about using a public phone to call the number the deputy director had given him with that potentially conniving wink.

His cell phone still had an Asian chip that didn't work globally, so he found a phone booth at the corner of 10th Street. The receiver was sticky, smelling of someone's cigarette breath, and he held it in two fingers, well away from his face. A man answered at the other end and Teeple introduced himself.

"Yes," the man said unenthusiastically. He gave Teeple an address on O Street. "Come on in."

"Now?"

"Now."

It was Friday. All along Pennsylvania Avenue, the sprawling monuments of the Administration's administrative power were disgorging their nameless multitudes early, and even though the stream of liberated paper pushers on foot flowed faster than the traffic in the roadway, Teeple took a cab. The last thing he wanted was to arrive at a shrink's office on foot with a shirt sticking to his back. Washington humidity had already made the palms of his hands sticky, and he had no doubt that a psychoanalyst grasping at straws would zero in on perspiration in cold weather.

But the taxi smelled of overflowing ashtrays, and he got off at the next gridlock to walk after all. He could not stand ashtrays. Even as a kid back at the ranch, he could pick up cow pies with his bare hands, no problem there, but the mere sight of a cigarette butt would make him throw up. A psychoanalyst, he was sure, could read anything into that, too. So, he was relieved to find out that the address the man on the phone had given him was no psychiatric clinic. It was a cocktail bar with an elegant awning supported by two polished brass posts.

Inside, people were standing three and four deep around a brightly lit bar counter, but the back of the room was dark and almost deserted. There were small, marble-topped tables with flickering candles, and out of habit Teeple picked one away from the walls in case the dark wood paneling was bugged.

He ordered a beer and looked around.

It seemed to be an AIDS-awareness week in Washington. The men at the bar wore the appropriate ribbons on the lapels of their office suits, while the women wore theirs lower, where their cocktail dresses began. They were here to show off bare shoulders and cleavage rather than a commitment to a cause, and it did not take Teeple long to figure out the routine. Men made their pick at the bar and moved with their chosen ones, females only it seemed, to the tables in the back to settle the particulars — cash up front. Dollar bills changed hands in flickering candle light, and the couples left the bar as fearlessly as if their AIDS-awareness ribbons were charms bestowed upon them by an infallible shaman who would not let anything bad happen to them.

Instinctively, Teeple wiped the rim of his beer glass, and when he looked up again, he caught a pair of male eyes staring at him from the crowd at the bar. The stare was businesslike and unsmiling, decidedly not fawning, and Teeple returned it in kind.

The man raised a finger as if to indicate one of something, and Teeple nodded, hoping it was not just step one in the routine service around here. The man passed the nod on to one of the girls at the bar counter, who finished her drink, slid off the barstool, and crossed the room towards Teeple's table. She was not pretty, 40-plus, petite and brisk, walking with rapid little steps on kinky high heels. She quickly descended on a chair across from him and, perching on the edge as if the clock were already ticking, she touched his knees with hers and leaned forward to reveal a tattoo in her cleavage.

"They tell me you need a drink," Teeple thought she had said. She spoke in a low, husky voice, and it took him a moment to realize she had not said drink, but shrink. He nodded and she put a hot hand on his thigh. "Slip me a few bills, will you."

Teeple peeled off a few singles from his money clip, folded them twice to hide the denomination and pushed them down his thigh, not ostentatiously but clearly enough.

"Midday sex makes a man inconspicuous in this town," she smiled, slipped the money into her bra and got up to lead the way out of the bar. The doorman had a taxi waiting for them at the curb, and as she bent over to get into the backseat, she pulled up her skirt to reveal muscular thighs and black underpanties.

"Time's money," she reminded Teeple when he paused to look discretely the other way until she was seated. "Come on."

She took him to a brown-brick, four-story tenement behind the Capitol. It was a walkup, shabby but fairly clean, and she led the way to the top floor where she unlocked a door but would not go in herself. She just returned the small wad of bills he had given her at the bar and began to leave. Her services had obviously been prepaid by a third party.

"By the way," she smiled over a bare shoulder, her kinky heels already clattering down the raggedy stairs. "Should we meet again, I'm Heather."

7

Stuffing Heather's money back in his pocket with one hand, Teeple knocked on the unlocked door with the other. There was no answer, and he stepped in. It was one of the typical 1930s railroad-car apartments, long, narrow and dark, with an old man smoking a cigar in an orange armchair against the backdrop of powder blue wallpaper. The place looked as if it had been furnished in a hurry by some charity bent on making poor folks jump up and down from joy over a wacky color scheme.

"I'm Josef Verhagen," the old man said. His handshake was firm and dry, but his arthritic fingers made it feel skew. He seemed even older than his legend, for Teeple certainly knew the name.

In the old Cold War days, Verhagen had been the master of battling the Russians with smoke and mirrors that reflected their own nasty techniques. Some of his old stunts remained in the CIA training manuals to this day. And as if to retain at least some of the old glory, his hair was discretely dyed, even though he must have known he was out of the game for good. The new generation of spies was swamping the business with goodwill and benign spirituality, and Cold War spy masters with icy hearts and controlled emotions had gone out of fashion together with Fedora hats, three-piece suits and the Berlin Wall.

"Your father and I go way back," Verhagen smiled, a controlled smile. "Korea, 1951."

Teeple nodded. As far as he remembered, his father had never mentioned Verhagen by name, but he did not want to hurt the old man's feelings. Despite the ice-and-steel reputation, Verhagen looked fragile and vulnerable—too small for his suit and hopelessly out of place in an orange-and-blue dump.

There was rap music throbbing behind a wall, and it was obvious the old man did not live here. On the other hand, he might have. There were rumors that some of President Clinton's aides, who wore hammer-and-sickle pins on their T-shirts inside the Oval Office, were gung-ho on cutting pensions for old communist bashers.

"Your father carried me on his back when my toes froze off. We could hear the Chinks on our heels . . . kha-kha-kha," the old man smiled, letting the controlled warmth in his eyes flicker. "You should've heard your old man, huffing and puffing, but he wouldn't let go of me. They don't make guys like that anymore."

Teeple said nothing, and the old man nodded. "Pity he's no longer with us."

"Yes."

"The old-boys' network is dying out. The liberals are ecstatic. But . . ." Verhagen gave Teeple a slow once-over from head to foot,". . . one thing will never change. A good son will be a chip off the old block no matter what."

With a glance at a clock ticking on a crochet cover on a chest of drawers, Verhagen allowed Teeple a moment to ponder what he had just said, then pointed to another orange armchair. "Take a seat, son."

"Thank you."

"Don't."

"Huh?"

"Don't thank me, Hank. I have merely carried out your father's wish to follow your progress from a distance. He absolutely insisted that I let you earn your spurs yourself."

The old man sounded slow and spaced out, as if he were pursuing a train of thought he had honed before Teeple came in and was now trying to remember the point.

"This whole Malacca Straits mess . . ." The old man's cigar went out, and he relit it. "It makes Danny Craig's dossier a fascinating read. Sounds like your kind of man, Hank. Was he?"

"I liked him."

"Do you feel he died for naught but a conciliatory gesture to the foe?"

Teeple said nothing, not sure about the high-flown language, but Verhagen was bent on hearing an answer — a simple one, if need be. "Well?"

"Probably."

"Wouldn't you want to know for sure?"

"What difference would that make?"

"Good question." The old man paused to collect his thoughts. "The fact is, Danny Craig is the first dead case officer in the Malacca Straits mess. The others were just agents. An Indonesian man was shot in the head in his bed in Djakarta; a liaison woman in Bangkok who liked wearing short shorts had her legs cut off with a chain saw from the window of a passing car; a chain-smoking Vietnamese in Paris had his head blown off when he lit up with a lighter filled with napalm in the middle of the Champs Élysées. Now, what did these killings, including your buddy Craig's, have in common?"

"I never heard about the others before."

"Now you did."

"Right." After 14 hours on a plane followed by a bizarre debriefing in Langley, Teeple was having a hard time thinking of anything but his next meal and a hot bath. He had not slept much on the plane from Singapore; he couldn't close his eyes without seeing ants pouring into Danny's pants.

"Are you with me, Hank?"

"No." Teeple suppressed a yawn. "I mean no, I don't know what the killings had in common."

"A smell, Hank. That's what. Doubts about a dead man's integrity are like sneaky farts let loose in a crowd of reverent mourners—a stink impossible to trace back to the source." Verhagen puffed on his cigar as if to overpower some imaginary intestinal gases, while Teeple was trying to figure out what meal his jet-lagged body needed. Lunch, dinner, a snack? He just needed to eat something before he passed out, but Verhagen was stubbornly refusing to see that. The old man went on, thinking aloud.

"The first farts pursuant to doubts about Danny Craig's integrity are already in the air here in Washington, Hank. Makes you feel like quitting, doesn't it? Quitting to care, I mean."

The rap music behind the wall stopped. Then it started again, same tune, a slightly different beat to dazzle some brain-dead neighbor, and Verhagen gave Teeple a slow, sad smile.

"The blame is on my head alone, my boy. It's all been my doing. Without me, you wouldn't be in this hellhole."

Teeple could not see where Verhagen was going with this, but was too tired to speculate. He just watched the old man sit up without changing position in the armchair. He had merely moved inside the suit.

"Love me or hate me for it, Hank, just don't tell me which."

"All right."

"After your father and I returned home from Korea, he went back to ranching and I got a job here in Washington. We would write Christmas cards when we thought of it—happy holidays, how's the wife, what about the kids, that kind of thing. Then, years later, he called me on the phone; his older boy had to get away from home for a while on account of a girl next door. He asked me to get you a job, but do you no favors. 'Just watch him hack it,' he told me. You know how he was, ready to walk through fire for the next guy, but hating charity like the pest . . . you listening, Hank?"

When Hank returned home after Roni stood him up on that infa-

mous Christmas Day 30 years back, his father was already back from town. The horse trailer stood in the yard, unhitched from the truck. The flap gate had been left open to clean out manure, and after Hank let Primo into the corral to cool off, he got himself a shovel. He had to stop moping about Roni.

He had the trailer almost cleaned out by the time his father finally showed up.

"How did it go in town?" he asked the old man, knowing the answer.

"Not good." Father leaned on the corral railing. He was tall enough to keep an elbow on the top rail and have his thumb hooked behind his belt buckle at the same time. "Your mother told me you were out to see the Pitt girl."

"Oh yeah?" Hank kept on shoveling horse manure, wishing there was more.

"Well?"

"Well what?"

"Were you?"

"Yeah."

It was not hot, but father took off his hat and wiped his leathery forehead with a sleeve. "You know it ain't gonna work?"

Hank bit his tongue, and father put the hat back on and hooked his thumb back behind the belt buckle.

"There's this guy I met in Korea way back when. Ever told you about him?"

"Which one?"

"The one that had his toes freezed off."

"Oh, yeah?" Hank leaned the shovel against the trailer siding. "What about him?"

"I once carried him a couple of miles on my back. Uphill." Father paused to draw patterns in the dust with the toe of his boot, as if he were trying to remember long forgotten bends and turns of some frozen, faraway road. "Called him last night on the phone."

Fighting bad vibes, Hank stuck his thumb behind his belt buckle too and waited for father to go on.

"Anyway, he may have a job for you."

"Me?"

"It's something with the government, but don't worry. I told him to make sure it's outdoors work." Father stopped kicking dust and looked up. "The pay's good. Lots of extras when you ship out. You'll see the world and at the same time help us over the rough times."

On the other side of the railing, Primo came up and poked at father's elbow on the rail.

"It's one damned thing after another. Regular horses don't sell," father said, turning to stroke the horse's nose, and Hank knew what was coming. "Gotta take Primo to town next week."

"You do?" The frog in Hank's throat was burrowing straight into his heart as he looked up the hill on the other side of the river and thought he saw Roni up there, but it was just a storm cloud beginning to peek over the top. His eyes had been playing tricks on him — making one thing clear. If he stayed at home, it would be like in the old song about seeing you in all the familiar places. He might as well see the world instead.

"What are you thinking?" father said, going back to kicking dust.

"I don't know."

"Your kid brother's back is getting pretty strong."

"Sure is."

"We'll be all right here . . . with whatever money you can send us."

"You sure?" The lump in Hank's throat would not go away as he looked from father to Primo, then back to father. He took his thumb from behind the belt buckle and put his hand on the old man's arm . . .

But it was Verhagen's hand on his arm that brought him back to the blue-and-orange rathole in the heart of Washington, D.C., 30 years later.

"Tea, my boy?" Verhagen wanted to know.

A white-haired lady in black had brought in a silver tray with an elaborate tea service. She wore a string of pearls and black pumps and, having caught Verhagen's last words, she smiled at Teeple as if to say, "Listen to him, young man, for he knows what he is talking about."

"Thank you, darling," Verhagen said as she began laying out elegant china and cute little spoons, doing her best to ignore the rap beat next door. She looked as if she had come from some cozy neat quarters on the other side of town where she lived in style.

"My wife of fifty-one years," Verhagen said after she left the room. "Being married that long to one woman makes a man reek of conservative values, if you know what I mean. Might be better if no one knows you're here."

Verhagen paused to give Teeple's weary brain a fair chance to catch up. "Officially, Hank, you have been granted a leave of absence from your job, time off to repent until your psychological profile can be reevaluated, which in your case might take forever. You are a good man, therefore, a good riddance in their eyes. America's their country now. They won't be sorry to see you fade into oblivion."

"What kind?"

"Of oblivion?"

"Yeah."

"Does it matter if it gives you a clear shot at Danny Craig's killers?" Verhagen watched Teeple with a quizzical twinkle over the tea cups between them. "No lawyers in your line of fire, guaranteed."

The music behind the wall was making the fragile cups rattle on their saucers, and the old man picked up his. He emptied it back into the tea pot and nodded to Teeple to do the same with his. Then he leaned back, took a bottle out of a drawer, and showed Teeple the label. Peach brandy. "Your favorite brand?"

Teeple had no favorite brand, but he nodded and Verhagen nodded back.

"Let's hope the rest of my intel's at least as good." The old man broke the seal, poured two generous helpings into the tea cups, and lifted his. "Cheers."

Teeple took just a polite sip from his cup, and Verhagen nodded again.

"Should you agree with what I am going to suggest to you, you may have to keep up the tipsy image for a while longer."

"All right."

"It's all fairly complicated; but, fortunately, it's the weekend now. The architects of a better tomorrow are off. They play stick and ball with the kids or are out fishing. We have two days to figure out the next move, which I promise won't be all work." Verhagen lowered his voice confidentially. "My wife's an excellent cook."

"Great." A hot surge of adrenalin flooded Teeple's frazzled brain with images of a hot meal, and things began to look instantly better. Had the old man been building up to a tidal wave of male bonding, it worked. The two of them were not going to let Danny Craig's name be routinely added to the No Politically Correct Action Taken (NPCAT) list of casualties. "Great," Teeple said again.

"We'll just have to find you an extra pair of pajamas and a toothbrush. No shaving gear, though."

"I have no job to go to on Monday, do I?"

"Exactly." Verhagen clenched his teeth to fight rheumatic pain somewhere in his body as he leaned forward to pick up his notepad. He ticked off the top line on a densely handwritten page and moved to line two. "Remember the deputy director, the man who fired you this morning?"

"He looked sick."

"He is." Speaking of which reminded Verhagen to finally pay attention to Teeple's increasingly obvious fatigue. He packed the deputy director's role in all of this into a single sentence before he ticked off line two on his notepad. "Long story short, Hank, the man's on our side and will see to it that the report on your debriefing today falls into unauthorized hands tomorrow, at the latest."

8

A copy of the report on Teeple's debriefing in Langley, Virginia, landed the following morning on Joe Fitch's breakfast tray in Malibu, California.

At the age of 99, breakfast was old Joe's best meal of the day and his all but lipless mouth began to water when the wonted clink and clatter inside the bedroom door frame woke him up from a fitful sleep. Like every morning on the stroke of eight, Woolsey, the butler, had put a finger into the fingerprint reader outside to disengage the stainless-steel door latches guarding his master's nights and slithered in with the breakfast tray.

"A very good morning to you, sir." Woolsey opened the heavy velvet curtains a crack to let in daylight minus the proverbial Southern California sunshine. Then he straddled the breakfast tray over the fragile outline of the master's body underneath the satin blanket.

The tea was the right temperature, the toast had been no longer than a minute out of the toaster, and the egg was soft-boiled to perfection. The only unsavory thing on the tray was a folded batch of documents underneath the toast basket. It had been put there in the foyer by Mr. B, the master's right hand, and Woolsey had to live with it whether he liked it or not, which did not mean he had to mention it right away.

"Your son is holding a speech at the University of California at Berkeley this morning," Woolsey said to start the day on a more agreeable note. "Beginning just about now, sir."

Old Joe nodded, and Woolsey opened a Louis XIV armoire opposite the bed. He made sure the TV inside was set to the right channel and respectfully punched the power button.

"Also, sir . . ." Woolsey could not help smiling as he watched the master dig into the soft-boiled egg. The yolk looked perfect, dark yellow and beautifully runny. "Mr. B added some papers for your perusal and insisted on waiting outside."

The TV came on, and Woolsey bowed himself out of the bedroom with another smug smile. Master was in good appetite this morning, and he passed the good news to Mr. B in the foyer, hoping against hope that even someone whose real name was Buzz Blewitt would get the message.

He had always found it difficult to say the man's name aloud, especially in master's presence. Both Buzz and Blewitt sounded ever so common, so much like the man's unseemly squint. So it had become a matter of accepted practice that the butler would refer to his master's trusted lieutenant as Mr. B. But not even an accepted practice gave Woolsey the authority to talk back to Mr. B.

"Show me in," Blewitt said, neither of his disparate eyes amused by the butler's antics.

"At once?"

"Now."

Looking gravely pained, Woolsey led the way back into the bedroom, but once he was in, he could not help smiling again. Like the beautiful yolk of the the master's egg, the happening on the TV monitor inside the Louis XIV armoire seemed equally satisfying. The station had preempted its regular programming to give Mister Richard's speech the impression of an unbiased newscast. The lighting and camera angles made Richard's jawline handsomely authoritative, the cuts to the predictably enthusiastic crowd were well timed, and the sound was on the decibel level used for commercials. Obviously, the right technician had been put on it by the right people in charge, and Joe Fitch did not look displeased to see Blewitt enter the bedroom at the butler's heels.

"What the hell's this, Buzz?" The old man tapped the papers under the toast basket with his egg spoon. He had not looked at them yet and showed no inclination to do that anytime soon.

"A gut feeling, sir." Buzz Blewitt's lead eye swerved to Woolsey, who was still standing by, and old Joe dismissed the butler with a hardly perceptible nod.

After Woolsey was gone, Blewitt placed himself at the foot of the bed, where he knew the light from the window would be least disturbing to the old man's failing eyesight.

"I thought you ought see these documents. In view of . . ." Blewitt nodded to the TV, "your son's election campaign."

"Oh that." Joe Fitch shook his head at the TV where his son was speaking about the moral obligation of one and all to let their feelings hang out and vote for a man like himself. He would drive the crowd into a screeching frenzy over and over again. High-pitched voices had the undeniable lead in the mayhem, and old Joe nodded to Blewitt to turn the sound off. He had been watching that farce merely to make sure the network executives were taking no shortcuts on the salaries he paid them. Other than that, he could not care less about his son's drivel about a glorious rainbow bridge into the new millennium—or whatever else he might have been telling the idiots out there to make them go bonkers. Mob hysterics would make old Joe sick to his queasy stomach.

"A pack of dolts." With his fragile, crooked fingers, the old man broke off a piece of toast, and for a moment it was not quite clear what snapped. "Tell me, Buzz, were we that stupid when we were their age?"

"Makes one wonder, doesn't it?"

"Not even your generation would've bought this crap. Women weren't screaming in public yet, were they?"

"They say it's the bullhorn that makes them go crazy about men on pulpits," Blewitt shrugged, wondering how many of his son's nicknames the old man knew about. Slick Dick for sure; maybe even what the Arizona Indians called him, Walking Eagle—a bird so full of shit it could no longer fly; some people even compared Richard Fitch to Charles Manson because women would kill for him, too. But so what. Buzz would not dream of bringing irrelevant folks' wisdom to his boss's attention.

"Women love Richard," he said instead.

"Can no longer run a country without playing up to them, can we?"

"No, sir."

Blewitt was a married man himself, but would not call the few hours a week he spent at home quality time. He loved his work. He was pushing 50, short and lithe, with a good head of graying hair and heavy eyebrows that accentuated the determination in his steely gray cross-eyes. His lead eye was the left one, and it would look his master straight in the face even when the news was bad.

Buzz Blewitt was the son of old Joe's first and only business partner from the real old days, Lord Henry Blewitt, one of the oldest baronetcies in England. As a young man at Oxford back in the early 1920s, Lord Henry had become infatuated with progressive thinking and decided to prove to the bloody commoners that a member of the idle class had it in him to make a living. With his family name as collateral, he had no problem raising capital to set up a revolutionary sporting venture, a sort of predecessor to off-track betting. No problem there. Except that his proverbial knack for backing the right horse on the racetrack turned out to be an elusive fluke when performed wholesale over telephone lines. His picks began to go bad at a truly wholesale rate, and just before his staggering debts were entered in the docket of a bankruptcy court in London, he used his word of honor to hustle up more credit for a first-class passage to America. He was 26 when he landed in New York, beautifully dressed, aristocratically debonair and charmingly spiteful about the scourge of Prohibition. He quickly became a hit with silly middle-aged wives of important old men and would work magic in bringing top politicians together with top crooks. He was the rage of the town, and Joe Fitch, a struggling mid-list bootlegger back then, was quick to offer him a partnership before the competition realized the handsome Lord's full potential.

Within just a couple of years, the two of them became major players among racketeers, and the partnership was doomed. Lord Henry did understand that keeping millions of illegal dollars in a mattress was impractical, but as a gentleman, he could not see himself fiddling with bookkeeping ledgers and bank statements. Joe, on the other hand, being the son of a bricklayer, considered paperwork a step up. So, when Joe decided at his 30th birthday to get himself a seat on the Board of Directors of a major bank and stop packing a gun, Lord Henry was happy to pack two to watch his newly respectable partner's back.

He had to live dangerously or not at all. His ancestors had built an empire on which the sun never set by the sword, charging enemy cannons with no more armor than skin-tight red coats, and he could not let them down. He would be damned to have a hand in building an empire from behind an office desk. He was a free spirit and a sportsman, and the possibility of taking a bullet for a bottom-drawer commoner like Joe Fitch kept him intrigued to no end—especially since the pay was 10 times what aristocrats in the old country took in from their sacred land leases.

By the age of 40, Lord Henry had more money than he could spend alone and married a dazzling high-class hooker with a heart of steel and a mind that could wreck high-flown academic arguments with an innocently low-key mention of down-to-earth detail. She was a piece of work and, eventually, the two of them passed their genes to their son to keep him safe from the petty implications of the human tragedy. The cross-eyes were merely an accident no one was allowed to mention aloud, and in view of making a true Yank out of him, they had him christened Buzz, no middle initials. He was not expected to carry on the family title.

So, when Lord Henry Blewitt finally took the long anticipated bullet for the both hated and idolized Joe Fitch, Buzz took over his father's job and dropped the title the same day it was passed onto him. He became a pillar of the Fitch empire just like his forebears had been pillars of the British one, and Joe Fitch trusted him implicitly. He trusted him more than his favorite son, Richard, not to mention his in-laws and grandsons. He knew Buzz would die for him because of the noblesse-oblige in his blood and bone, and saw to it that if he himself died first, the loyal lieutenant would be a very rich man.

Yet Buzz Blewitt did not want his boss to die. He dreaded the boredom of being a rich man with nothing to do but hit golf balls and slaughter partridge together with other bored rich men. As for women, he liked their looks, but their chatter was something else. Except for his wife, he never saw a woman in private more than once. And the last thing he would ever dream of was attaining fame by shooting off his mouth to the press. With Richard running for president on the fair-taxation ticket, a revelation about Joe Fitch's tax evasion practices through a mammoth network of offshore accounts would give a man more that just the proverbial 15 minutes of fame—as would a revelation about old Joe's disdain for women whose vote was expected to get his son into the White House. Buzz Blewitt would never do anything of the kind. He couldn't care less about fame. A celebrity status ranked pretty low in his view of the good life. He had seen too many famous faces cringe and cower when he dropped by their mortgaged-to-the-hilt mansions with a message from his boss.

Blewitt loved to be what he was; so when his boss chose to ignore the papers on the breakfast tray, he took care not to look overly concerned. The batch was still where he had put it, sticking out from under the toast basket, and a brief explanation was called for.

"It's minutes of a meeting held yesterday at the CIA Department of Operations," he said, his left eye looking straight in his boss's face. He saw no need to go into detail about the potentially sensitive connection between the report's prime subject, Hank Teeple, and Veronica Pitt, one of Richard's ex-babes. That kind of a smoldering fire was up to him to put out. "All in all, the meeting was a low-level affair; but still . . ."

"Still what?"

"The Emirates Bank, sir. It's mentioned by name in these papers. Twice."

"You said the meeting was low level."

"That's what worries me."

"Hmm." Old Joe went on nibbling on his toast, while on the mute TV screen in front of the bed his son's handsome face seemed to be on the verge of tears, most likely telling the mob about feeling their pain. They were putty in his hands, and Joe Fitch heaved a sigh. It was so damned easy to sway the riffraff with a rhetoric that resonated in the tingle bells of their mushy little hearts. Which, by the good old rule of action and reaction, gave the opposition an equal chance to sway a compatible bunch of dolts the other way by waking the devil in their nasty little souls. So, in a world that could be so easily rocked to and fro by gullible humanity, what could have possibly been so important about a dog-eared batch of bureaucratic drivel on his breakfast tray?

With his son in a cutthroat race for the top government job — a race that could go as easily to mushy little hearts as to nasty little souls — the last thing he wanted to know about was a bunch of classified government documents.

"Tell you what, Buzz." Joe Fitch stretched his fragile limbs under the satin blanket as if he already saw himself putting his feet on his son's desk in the Oval Office — or, rather, having

Woolsey put his feet that high. It made him smile, and Blewitt was puzzled.

"Sir?"

"Tell you what. Don't rock the boat just yet."

Outside the bedroom window, a single file of pelicans sailed along the beach in majestic slow motion, yet they merely flashed across old Joe's narrowing field of vision. The world's best oncologists had been unable to predict when the inoperable retina ailment would allow the creeping black curtain to shut off the light for good, and there was no time to waste. Old Joe wanted to see, not just hear his son taking the oath of office on the steps of the Capitol, and Blewitt, having an eye problem of his own, saw the boss's point clearer than anyone else.

"Whatever it takes, sir," he said, ready to go and do his part.

"That a boy." Once more, old Joe tapped the classified documents with his egg spoon, and Blewitt leaned over to get the unsavory stuff out of the boss's sight.

"Sorry," he said.

"Had breakfast yet, Buzz?"

"No. I . . ."

"I know, you thought this was important."

"Yes."

"Go tell them in the kitchen to make you an egg. Soft boiled, eighteen seconds under two minutes. Will you remember that?"

"Eighteen seconds under two minutes."

"Good," old Joe nodded, thoughtfully. "After that, you go and keep an ear to the ground."

"Right."

"And depending on what you hear, don't be shy about kicking butt and taking names, my boy."

"Yes, sir." Blewitt tweaked a corner of his mouth, his lead eye shining. Whenever the boss called him my boy, he had been given a free hand for as long as he did not report every little misdemeanor like a good boy should.

9

In the mean streets behind Washington, D.C.'s Capitol, on the steps of which old Joe Fitch was hoping to see his son Richard take the Oath of Office sooner rather than later, Teeple and Verhagen had spent the weekend huddled over legal pads filled with notes, time charts and photographs of people and places. Then, on Monday when Washington returned to work, Verhagen, still in his pajamas, made Teeple go back to page one of pad one and mull over the "what-ifs" in the margins.

The two of them were, as the old man put it, up to their eyeballs in a reasonably realistic speculation when Mrs. Verhagen brought in a sealed manila envelope. A very nice young man had just brought it, she told her husband, brushing lint off his shoulders. Knowing him, she feared that the contents of a hand-delivered envelope would make him forget the fun part of life.

"Will you want me to wait with tea?" she smiled, doing her best not to sound disappointed, and was greatly relieved to see him chuckle when he took a closer look at the urgent missive.

"Tea as usual, dear," he grinned.

"Oh, good."

"Good?" Verhagen tapped the batch of typewritten pages he had pulled out of the envelope. "This is not good. It's great."

"Well, then." The old lady was delighted to hear that. She wanted her husband to have whatever fun there was left in life. It was so good for him. "I better go figure something sweet with tea today."

She left the room in a quest for suitable biscuits, and Verhagen gave Teeple a wink as he pushed the papers over to him.

"Your psychological evaluation. It seems you hit the bottom and already started to dig."

The title page had Teeple's name, date of birth and 3MS-7 rating: emotionally unstable on retroactively subconscious multilevel base corollary to compulsive alcohol consumption. The next couple of pages were shop talk about symptoms, tolerance levels and physiological disfunction bordering on a chronic medical condition—a dull reading except for the conclusion. By a new law recently passed by Congress, summaries in governmental reports had to be written in a language comprehensible to the academically challenged, and when Verhagen got to that, he could not resist reading the last paragraph aloud.

"The said employee's uncontrollable (impossible to control) alcoholism is the inevitable (impossible to avoid) consequence of a mean-spirited upbringing resulting in lifelong suppression of his natural craving for sweetness resulting in clandestine (secretive and crafty) consumption (guzzling) of peach brandy (alcoholic beverage)."

"Thanks."

"Don't mention it," Verhagen chuckled. "Originally, the man who wrote this wanted to bring in sexual abuse by the father. I told him you'd punch his face in if he did that."

Teeple said nothing, and Verhagen pointed out the date on the "Received" stamp on the first page. "The original of this report's been entered into your personal file this morning. The 3MS rating means mean-spirited level 3, which makes you ineligible for full pension. So, I guess, we better figure out how you make money out of all this, too."

*　*　*

The following morning, Washington was hit by a major storm. High winds and a heavy downpour made the streets look as if they were being hosed down by some higher power, and to do justice to Teeple's psychological evaluation, Verhagen decided to send him out without an umbrella. His beard was four days old by then and with a generous sprinkling of gray in it, he was bound to look like hell in driving rain. On top of it, Mrs. Verhagen knew a special tea guaranteed to cause bad breath for the rest of the day.

Teeple had two cups, then took a bus to Langley. It took three transfers in driving rain, and by the time he got to the main gate of the CIA complex, he did look like hell. He held up his old ID card in the same hand as a soggy Mc Donald's paper bag, and the guards did not look too close. There was ketchup leaking from the bag, and they cringed away from a protracted exposure to Teeple's breath.

His tousled hair, messy beard and soaking overcoat, a loaner from the much smaller Verhagen, left a drip path in the lobby, all the way into the elevator where he made a puddle. The Human Resources Department was on the 10th floor, and everybody who saw him in time, talking to himself and shuffling towards the payroll office with water sloshing in his shoes, made sure to scramble for cover. They were all gawking from behind partitions and potted plants, and the department supervisor had been warned in time. She managed to get out of her office before Teeple barged in without knocking. Her chair was still warm, but he did not make a fuss about that.

He just wrote her a rambling note about putting him on ice a month before he would get into a higher pension bracket. It was not true but fitted in with his whining tone that made it doubtful that anyone would dare to check facts. His psychological evaluation made him untouchable. He was a guy with a mental issue, and whatever he did was not to be snickered at. So, leaving the handwritten note on top of a pile of ledgers where everybody could read it, he knocked back a couple of quick ones from his flask and went to say hello to George Twombly.

"Hey, buddy," he slapped Twombly on the back and made sure to speak close to his face to let him have the full benefit of bad-breath tea and peach brandy point blank.

"The sweet smell of freedom." Twombly pretended to be amused, and they shook hands. "You stink like a wino."

"Nah."

"Getting swamped with job offers, yet?"

"You bet."

"A guy with your experience can write his own ticket. Just like that," Twombly snapped his fingers without conviction. "In the private sector, the sky is the limit. Six-figure pay before you know it."

"Flipping burgers?"

"Ow, come on."

"Selling snake oil?"

"You don't know beans about snakes, man. Your background's in banking and investigation. You'll be a top-notch private eye before you know it. I'll yet come work for you."

"Send me an application."

"You betcha."

"In triplicate, you hear me?" Teeple did his best to fake a laugh, remembering that as a boy he once briefly wanted to become an actor, but could not figure out what acting was. "I'll hire you the moment I scrape up the first and last months' rent for an office and two chairs."

He always found it damn hard to sound like people he did not like and was worried it would show, but Twombly seemed to have bought it—most likely to get him out faster.

"Hey, what's a couple of months' rent to a guy like you?" Twombly poked Teeple in the ribs. "You know the drill. Get yourself an address and a job, open a savings account and bingo, banks will be throwing money at you. Any old job to start with."

"Like what?"

"Anything. Any last outpost, man."

"Like the IRS, maybe?"

"Hey, how about that?"

"How about that." Teeple suppressed a hiccup, took his flask out, and pulled a long gulp. "Know what?"

"What?"

"I like it."

"The tax collectors won't believe their luck." Glancing at his watch, Twombly poked Teeple in the ribs again. "Who the hell knows more about monkey tricks with offshore accounts, ey?"

"You said it." In return for the poke, Teeple patted Twombly's cheek. "Watch out with your next tax return, pal."

"You take care, you hear me."

Teeple left the soggy Mc Donald's bag on Twombly's desk, feeling bad about it even though the whole stunt had been Verhagen's idea. The old man was sure Twombly would be flaunting the IRS idea at the office water cooler before Teeple was out of the building.

From Langley, Teeple took a train back to town. He could not face yet another bus ride. By the time he got off at Dupont Circle, it stopped raining and he took off the overcoat. People were well dressed here, and he saw no reason to look like the only bum around. He dropped by a supermarket, pinched a plastic shopping bag at the cashier's, stuck the soggy coat in it, and walked all the way to the unemployment office on Q and 5th.

The Social Development Services Administration office was crowded. He checked his plastic bag at the security counter, put the stub in a pocket, and joined a gloomy queue at the P to T counter. People seemed to be ignoring each other with a vengeance here, as if to make it perfectly clear to one another that striking new acquaintances was not worth the effort because they were not coming back. The silence was outright hostile.

The P to T line was a good 30 feet long, progressing about a foot per two minutes, and Teeple made peace with the prospect of a good hour wait. Over the years out in the field, he had learned the hard way that it never was the wait itself but one's fretting about it that sapped up energy.

The movement of the line slowed at lunchtime, and the air thickened with the odor of wet shoes and damp clothes—making it impossible not to think of the sea breeze on the wide-flung slopes above the old Pitt ranch back in California . . .

In the Pitt's yard, the clatter of Primo's hoofs on brick brought Roni's mother out of the house to check what was going on. She was not pleased to see Hank.

She seemed to be expecting people for lunch. Her fingernails were painted red, matching the color of her dress and shoes, her hair was done up, and there was classical music coming out of the open door behind her back—one of the reasons the Pitts were not popular in the county. Mrs. Pitt had the reputation of a darn snob, a snotty bitch according to some, and for a moment Hank could not decide between speaking up and running away. But then, he was not here to see her.

"Hello, ma'am," he said, bravely.

"I'm busy, Hank."

"'s Roni home?"

"Veronica."

"Yes, ma'am. Is Veronica at home?" He slid off the saddle, and they were talking over Primo's rump. He could not but think of it as griping over a horse's ass, but Mrs. Pitt was dead serious.

"Veronica is in Los Angeles. Mr. Richard Fitch invited her personally to attend a convention on pressing environmental issues."

"Why . . ."

"You're asking me, Hank?" Mrs. Pitt pointed an angry finger over Hank's head to the top of the hill. "Those poor newts in that lake of yours up there, that's why."

Mrs Pitt's mercilessly exacting pronunciation sounded as it was supposed to, socially distant, giving Hank the impression she was talking to him from across a river—a waterfall, rather. The sound of rushing water was so real that it took him a moment to realize it was not a waterfall but Primo. The horse was relieving himself on the brick pavement, and he could see droplets of urine bounce off the brick and land on Mrs. Pitt's red shoes.

"Gosh, I . . . I'm sorry."

"Forget it." Mrs. Pitt, busy as she was, had no time to look down at her feet and accepted his apology at face value. "I have nothing against Veronica and you remaining friends for as long as you promise to do right by her. My daughter wants more from life than baking cookies for a bunch of kids on a ranch."

"Yes, but . . ."

"You're thinking too much, Hank. It's not complicated, is it?"

"No."

"So what are you waiting for?"

"To clean your shoes."

"Huh?" Mrs. Pitt finally looked down at her urine splattered feet, took a deep breath, and held it. She was not going to lose it in front of a cowboy, and Hank saw a chance to finally get in a whole sentence.

"Can I have a hose and a rag?" He was half hoping Roni would show up while he was hosing the yard and polishing her mother's shoes, but Mrs. Pitt preferred a puddle of horse piss to having him around when her lunch guests arrived.

"Just get out of here, will you." She spun around and went back inside without wasting another word on a hopeless case. The door banged shut on her and her classical music before he had a chance to ask whether Roni — sorry, Veronica — would be home later on, which was just as well. He might not have managed to get a word out.

The sinister weight that had squashed the air out of his chest deprived not just his lungs but also his brain of oxygen, making him walk right through the urine puddle as he led Primo out of the yard. He climbed into the saddle like a weary old man, and the clumsy burden of his misery prodded Primo into beating retreat at an all-out gallop.

The pounding hoofs were tearing out chunks of wet earth, wild poppies and blue bells, wreaking havoc among the bees working in the lush blossoms — which only reassured Mrs. Pitt, who had been watching from behind a curtain, that she had done the right thing. Her daughter was well rid of a never-do-well hulk with a tight butt, a fancy belt buckle and . . .

. . . no respect for the environment, Hank thought as he now finally pressed his plain city belt buckle against the P to T counter at the Washington, D.C. unemployment office.

It was mid-afternoon by then, and the agent, a dark-eyed man with beautiful teeth, must have just returned from lunch. He was chewing on a toothpick and glanced at Teeple's application with the alacrity of a chain-gang regular.

"So, Hank Teeple," he began, not bothering to hide his distaste for new claims. Things had to be typed and papers filed. "What is it you're good at?"

"I wrote it all down."

"That so?"

"It's under previous employment."

"Sure it is. Let's hear it, buddy."

Teeple suppressed the urge to get facetious about the man's reading skills and took a deep breath instead.

"My last job was in the investigation of domestic and international banking fraud," he said.

"That's a mouthful."

"Tax evasion tricks, if you prefer."

"Geez. And you're out of a job?" The man smiled, a beautiful smile. He put Teeple's application in his in-tray, pecked something into a computer keyboard, scrolled through a list on the screen, and sent an item to the printer.

"Good luck, man." With a wiggle of the toothpick and an eye on the next customer, he handed Teeple the job ticket. "This should do it."

The ticket was for a position loosely associated with financial fraud, a telemarketer for an investment scheme, which made it difficult to object. Besides, before Teeple could say something, the next man in line already pushed him aside.

Clutching the job ticket in one hand and the plastic bag with the wet coat in the other, Teeple walked out into the street. The sun was out now, and he had a week to kill ahead of him. Verhagen had thought it wise to take at least a week between supplications. An eager beaver did not fit the image of a peach-brandy addict going to seed.

10

The next day, Teeple moved from Verhagen's tiny, dark apartment to an even tinier and darker room at a transient hotel that offered rock-bottom weekly rates and picked Thursdays to drop by the unemployment office. Rain or shine, every Thursday, the man behind the P to T counter would print a new job ticket, too busy chewing on a toothpick to ask questions about the previous one.

The second job ticket was related to banking, too: a security guard at a bank in Maryland. The third one was for a waiter at a coffee shop in the lobby of a bank in Virginia. The fourth time around, though, the toothpick chewer was not in. He had been replaced by a neat, middle-aged lady with a pleasant smile who looked like someone from the management filling in for a gofer who had either gone on strike or eaten a bad burger for lunch. She showed interest in the history of Teeple's quest.

"Telemarketing didn't work out for you?" she smiled as she went through Teeple's record on the computer screen.

"Most of the people on the list they gave me spoke no English."

"How many have you tried?"

"Enough."

"Maybe you should have tried a few more."

"The company would've back-charged me for all calls if I didn't sell anything for two days in a row."

"How about the security guard position?"

"Tough security clearance. They wouldn't take anyone who's not lived at the same address for at least a month."

"And the coffee shop?"

"I didn't go there."

"Just like that?" She sounded displeased but not vindictive as she studied the computer screen with clever, alert eyes. "How about relocating, Mr. Teeple?"

"Relocating?"

"I might have something for you in the Big Apple."

"New York?" Teeple took care to sound reluctant to severe his ties with Washington, D.C. The woman could not have possibly known that besides Verhagen, all the people he knew here were just a handful of spaced-out derelicts he met in his hotel's lobby. "I don't know. Not gladly, if you ask me."

"Would you rather throw away all those years of experience?" She tapped the computer screen with a painted fingernail. "The IRS office in New York has an opening in Surrogation. Looks like something right down your alley."

"I don't know," Teeple repeated, stupidly.

"They won't believe their luck when you show up," the woman smiled. End of story. She printed a ticket and pulled out a relocation form to fill out by hand. "Have a lot of furniture, Mr. Teeple?"

"No."

"Knick knacks, clothes, books?"

"I live at a hotel."

"Well then." Her smile became even more reassuring. "I don't think the Internal Revenue Service will make a fuss about reimbursing you for a one-way train ticket. I'll write it in, plus a cab to the station here and from the station in New York."

She made it sound as if there was no doubt in her mind that he would be doing his prospective employer a favor by just showing up.

* * *

So, the welcome Teeple received at the IRS Human Resources Department on West Broadway in Lower Manhattan was a downer. A dusty looking man with sunken cheeks and thin, white hair sounded gravely unenthusiastic about the idea of the right man for the right job.

"You know that on this salary you won't find a decent place to live in Manhattan," he told Teeple with the chronic fatigue of a lifetime commuter from the far-out suburbs. His idea of the right man for the right job seemed to depend solely on subway connections. "If you want to live in the city these days, you better look for something in highway robbery."

"I'll be all right."

"No you won't." The man had obviously never had anything good happen to him.

"Do I have the job or not?"

"If you believe you can cope, it's no skin off my nose."

The starting salary was $1,800 a month, $1,400 to take home, and Teeple found a furnished studio apartment within walking distance from the office. The rent was $800 and the building was shabby and dirty. The street was teeming with would-be artists, out-of-work actors, dope dealers and the standard second echelon of hookers and pimps of either sex who did not make the cut in the neighboring Greenwich Village. It made the shabby privacy of a tiny apartment on the third floor of a four-story brown-brick tenement feel almost cozy. The door had three massive steel latches, and the hard-to-open window in the living room somewhat dampened the din of traffic in the street below.

A rickety gas range and a solid iron bathtub in the kitchen made it the ideal home for a man bent on washing his one and only shirt every day — Verhagen's idea of a loser who was down on his luck but not ready to give up quite yet. As for cooking, the gas range was good enough for warming up cans with expired sell-by dates that he would buy at a local grocery store run by an odd couple who spoke no English. And since his salary did not warrant singles bars, he would spend his evenings at home, sprawled on a threadbare sofa in front of a small black-and-white TV, trying to ignore the smell of burning weeds seeping in under the door.

The TV, good for only the few free networks, stood on a rickety old chair in a dark corner, and he would have preferred to turn down the volume to just keep the picture tube warm in order to make the dusty cobwebs under the ceiling flutter. Watching fluttering cobwebs in total silence would have been a welcome break from most TV shows; but he had to keep the sound on to outdo the perpetual shouting match in an unintelligible language that one male and two female voices were having every night behind the thin wall next to his sofa.

Then, after a couple of beers, he would take a sleeping pill and stare at the cobwebs until he fell asleep, usually about 10:30. Police sirens, roaming drunks and knocking in the water pipes would wake him several times every night, often keeping him awake for hours—until it was time to get up. His one and only shirt that he washed before going to bed was usually dry by then, and he would take the subway to the two-by-three olive green desk at the IRS office that he gradually began to consider his.

The desk was one of 120 identical desks lined up in 12 rows and 10 columns in a common room lit by rows upon rows of fluorescent lights. There were stacks of manila folders on all the other desks, but he had been given just one thin file to start with.

The division supervisor, who spoke passable English, was a stickler to duty bent on testing new employees' reading skills first, and Teeple's inaugural file contained just a copy of a single 1040 tax return. His job was to check line 35 on Form A, where a construction worker claimed a deduction for 365 pairs of expensive socks as a medical expense on account of a foot condition. A doctor's certificate was enclosed, which Teeple had no problem identifying as a clumsy forgery, and the construction worker was charged $43.78 in back taxes. With interest and penalties, the total was almost $400, and the division supervisor was pleased.

"Good work, man," he told Teeple and dropped three new cases on his desk.

By the end of the second week, the pile of manila folders on Teeple's desk began to grow, making him feel as if he belonged, which in turn made his trips to the men's room more frequent. He chose not to be obvious, sucking at a worn flask at his work station, even though his coworkers appeared to pay very little attention to him. Despite the praise he had received from the division supervisor in the socks case, nobody seemed to care whether his frequent trips to the bathroom were the result of chronic alcoholism or a bladder condition.

He remained wretchedly anonymous at his olive green desk, or so he thought. Because under the harsh fluorescent lights, his new lifestyle was beginning to show. The fretful sleep in his hellhole of a home made his bloodshot eyes tear up in the draft from the office air conditioning, catching the eye of a girl who worked at a desk three rows ahead and two columns to the right.

She had noticed Teeple the first thing in the morning of his first day on the job as he slithered in with a Styrofoam coffee cup in one hand, the employee rule book in the other and a doughnut in his mouth.

She thought he looked rather nice and sad, and her heart went out to him. She was a lithe, flat-chested girl with untidy chestnut hair. There was no trace of lipstick on her lips, no mascara to bring out her lively green eyes, no blusher on her pale, freckled cheeks. She was used to getting overlooked and felt safe to glance in Teeple's direction several times a day.

She saw him having doughnuts number two and three during the afternoon coffee break, and found it amazing that a man with that kind of eating habits should look trim and fit. Also, she thought, he was quite handsome for his age; so, normally, she would have left it at that. Handsome men paid no attention to her. She had no illusions there, but Teeple's perpetually bloodshot, red-rimmed eyes and frequent trips to the bathroom were encouraging. He was a man with a health issue, maybe even a mental one.

He talked to no one, doing whatever he was doing with his manila folders in a monk-like silence, and whenever she saw him look up from his work, she thought he looked startled when he realized where he was, which was something she could identify with.

By the end of the week, she was beginning to suspect that she might understand him better than anyone else in the office and decided to do something about it.

She knew a girl in human resources, who also had no luck with men, and invited her for a drink after work. She asked about the new guy in Surrogation straight out.

"Hank Teeple?"

"Is that his name?"

"A has-been." The girl rolled her eyes. She handled all kinds of files in her line of work. "You get tons of those at your department. Crooks tripping up crooks."

"You think so?"

"I know so."

"Some kind of a tough luck story?"

"Hey," the human resources girl grinned, chewing on the candied cherry from her drink. "You're getting ahead of yourself, sister."

"It's not what you think."

"Whatever. You asked me a question and I answered it as best as I could. There are rules to what I can say, you know."

"Thank you."

"The guy took a whopping pay cut getting this job—you know that, I suppose?"

"Wow." Beth was impressed.

Hank Teeple wore a clean white shirt every day and his shoes were always polished. No dirty sneakers, no sloppy blue jeans, no chewed-up T-shirts—always neat like a new pin. So, considering that everyone working in the common room was more or less in the same pay bracket, she assumed he did his washing and ironing himself. It never occurred to her that he was married. He did not look like a family man, not by a long shot. She could not tell why she thought that. She just did—a gut feeling.

"He seems all right," she told the human resources girl, calling for another round of cocktails. She had the bartender put in two candied cherries each, and the girl lowered her voice.

"All right my foot."

"What do you mean?"

"You should see his file."

It was only over the fourth drink and seventh candied cherry that Beth's new best friend would go into detail.

"Your Mr. Right's sure right." She looked around to make sure no one was listening. She was not supposed to do this. "He was too right-wing even for the fucking CIA."

It was the right-wing angle that touched Beth's heart. She had to be fair. She had been too young to vote for Bill Clinton the first time around, but she had helped get him reelected, which did not mean she agreed with whatever his wife was screaming about a right-wing conspiracy in America. There was something about Hank Teeple that cried for a helping hand.

So, the next day at lunch time, Beth brushed her hair, moistened her lips with her tongue, and joined Teeple at a small corner table in the cafeteria.

"You probably think I only talk to people when I need something," she told him for openers.

Their lunch trays touched in the middle of the narrow tabletop, and he gave her a curious look.

"Doesn't everybody?"

"No."

"Oh."

"Sometimes it pays to look for the best in people."

Teeple dropped his eyes back to his cheeseburger, and she remembered what the human resources girl had told her about him—an ex-tough guy who was not into eternal love and understanding and things like that. So she just wiped her hand on a napkin and held it out.

"I'm Beth."

She liked his firm handshake and the way their eyes locked, albeit for just a split second. The last man that had asked her out a couple of months back had mushy, sweaty hands, would never look her in the eye, and made a big deal out of taking her to the cheap seats at an irrelevant baseball game.

"I hear you used to work for the government before," she said, careful not to sound accusatory. "The CIA?"

"You're overtaxing my memory."

"Would I do that in the IRS cafeteria?"

They both smiled, their eyes met over the lunch trays, and again Teeple dropped his first. But she was determined to keep the conversation going.

"Maybe you can help me. I imagine you spent a lot of time abroad . . ."

She told him about the case she was currently working on: a dentist who had padded currency exchange rates on his expense account for an orthodontic convention in Paris. "I have trouble checking the French franc on a particular day four years back."

She wrote the date in question on a paper napkin, wondering whether or not it was a good time to mention something about Teeple's coffee-and-doughnuts diet. On second thought, she decided against it, hoping to be able to do for him something more meaningful later on—something to make those real nice eyes of his look less bloodshot.

Teeple got her the exchange rates later that afternoon, and at quitting time, they stood next to each other in the down elevator.

"You take the subway home?" she asked.

"I walk."

In the lobby, he was about to go his own way when he noticed she had a limp. It made sense, the way she dressed, flat shoes and baggy brown pants to camouflage her legs. Instinctively, he slowed down, and she gave him a thankful, bright smile that showed very nice teeth. But she quickly closed her mouth when she realized he was looking at them.

Out in the street, assuming she took the subway, Teeple turned to walk her to the BMT station at the corner of Park Lane. It was quitting time. The sidewalks between the World Trade Center and Wall Street had turned into stampede trails, teeming with home-bound people who had no patience with anyone's limp, and Teeple suggested a detour through the City Hall Park.

"We must be the only ones in no rush to go home," she said.

It was a pleasant, balmy evening, and after the stampede on the sidewalks, a gravel path alongside of a straggly lawn felt almost romantic.

"You're not a family man, are you?" she said.

"Because I walk home?"

"What do you do when it rains?"

"I take a bus."

On the other side of the park, Teeple stopped at the subway entrance. In the shadow of City Hall, they ran out of conversation and he held out a hand.

"Good night," he nodded. He had learned by now that among office employees, "good night" was the salutation of choice at quitting time, as if after work there was nothing a heart could desire but a good night's sleep. Beth did not seem to fit that mold.

"Well," she smiled, holding Teeple's hand a split second longer than necessary. "See you tomorrow, I guess."

She looked after him, watching him cross Park Lane and turn towards the Supreme Court building and Little Italy further on. Then she hailed a taxi and sunk into the back seat, thinking. She was 23 and had not dated many men, certainly no one close to her father's age. Yet she could not stop thinking about Hank Teeple, a has-been, wondering where and how he lived. He was a man down on his luck, a brooding loner with a dark secret, a wounded bird whom she could not imagine living in a nice nest.

*   *   *

When Teeple entered his building, it was hard to tell what it smelled of. It just smelled. Some of the lights were out, and he almost stumbled over a young couple sitting on the stairs, shooting something into each other's arms.

On the second floor, a few apartment doors were open. He noticed more open doors on the third floor, including his, but there was no one inside the apartment. He looked into the bedroom and the bathroom, but nothing was missing. The place seemed to be OK. The old TV set was still standing on the old rickety chair under dusty cobwebs, and there was a preprinted notice taped to it. The cable service had been disconnected because the landlord had failed to collect the payments from all tenants.

"*Hey, dude,*" a xeroxed handwritten note from the landlord said, "*Say NO tonigt, give me the money you safe and we watch the fucking TV again. Get it, ashole?*"

Teeple dropped the note in the garbage can in the kitchen, took off his shirt, threw it in the bathtub, poured detergent over it, and ran hot water. While the water was running, he took a can of Spam out of the fridge, the only place clean enough to keep even canned food in, and turned on the only working burner in the gas range. He had to melt the jelled fat so that he could eat with a spoon out of the can. And while the can was heating up, he thought of Beth eating from a proper plate, using proper cutlery and a napkin—most likely alone. She seemed to be that kind of girl.

11

The following week, he met Beth several times in the elevator at quitting time, and at one point it occurred to him she had been to a hairdresser. Her hair was tidy and cute, and she looked quite good even in her usual baggy clothes. Also, she wore lipstick, and when she saw him looking at her, she smiled back. They got out of the elevator side by side and crossed the lobby together, with Teeple slowing down to accommodate her limp.

"Big plans for the weekend?" she smiled, tentatively.

"No."

"I do."

It was Friday, sunny and pleasantly cool, and it felt quite natural that they should avoid the crowded sidewalks and once again walk together across the park, where she tackled the subject of healthy diet.

"I bought myself a cookbook."

"Oh."

"I know. You prefer doughnuts," she smiled. "What's your favorite filling?"

"Custard."

"Really?"

"Yes." His tone pre-empted further discussion about bad eating habits.

They just shook hands in front of the subway entrance in the shadow of City Hall, and again she made the handshake last a split second too long, while he pretended not to notice.

"See you Monday," he said.

There was no room for women and new cookbooks in Verhagen's scheme. Or was there? Because, come to think of it, the old man had not expressly excluded either, and Teeple had a feeling she would try again.

But on Monday, it was raining. By quitting time, it was obvious the rain was not letting up, and Beth left the office 10 minutes to 5:00. By the time Teeple came out of the building to head for the bus stop, she was at the curb in the back of a taxi with the window down. She did not call out to him. She had noticed before that he would see pretty much everything even though he never seemed to be looking, and she spoke up only when he looked at her.

"The cookbook I told you about, I read it over the weekend," she said, the rain blowing in her face. "Would you care to test me?"

"Me?"

There was no way he could turn down an offer like that without getting out of character. A man surviving on warmed up Spam out of a can ought to be ready to bend backwards, even to kill, for a free hot meal out of a cookbook. Besides, the rain was beginning to seep under the back of his collar, and he had no doubt that in this weather, his apartment was going to be worse than just damp and clammy. His hands would stick to soggy grime on anything he touched.

"Are you sure?" he said, hesitating a touch too long, and the cabbie lost it.

"Sure she's sure. Hop in, man."

Rainy rush hours were top money makers for cab drivers,

and Teeple gave in. He rounded the taxi trunk to the roadside back door and got splashed by a passing car—wondering whether Verhagen could have had a hand in that.

"Thanks," he said, bumping shoulders with Beth as he dropped into the back seat, trying to keep the wet bottom of his trousers away from bare skin. "Thanks for the invitation."

Sensing his discomfort, she gave him a touch too much of a smile as the taxi pulled off the curb and plunged into the jittery flow of rush-hour traffic. She seemed to be having sudden doubts of her own.

"It's just shepherd's pie," she said, still smiling.

"Oh."

"Baked ground beef in mashed potato crust."

"Great."

They rode up Broadway, all the way to 42nd Street where they turned right towards the high-rent part of town, and Teeple assumed she lived in some neat but cramped little pad in a good neighborhood. He pictured a studio with a Murphy bed, a kitchenette in a closet and a little table for two where one would not be able to lean back without knocking a picture off a wall or something. Her salary could not have been that much different from his.

So when the taxi pulled up in front a high-rise just off First Avenue with a smartly uniformed doorman standing under an elegant awning over an elaborate Tudor-like entrance, Teeple's heart sank. At that address, the apartment was bound to be so tiny that they would not be able to pass each other without apologizing. They were just off the UN Plaza, within sight of a row of soggy flags sticking to wet flagpoles in front of the United Nations building, and when the doorman stepped out from under the awning with a large umbrella, Teeple did not think it could be for them. But it was.

"Evening, Miss Gray."

Using the umbrella like a mother hen would use wings, the doorman herded them into a cavernous marble lobby where a smartly uniformed porter took over.

"Nice to have you home safe and dry on a day like this, Miss Gray." The porter led the way inside the elevator to punch the top-floor button so that Miss Gray would not have to lift a finger so high, then stepped back to frown disapprovingly at her escort's wet trousers until the door closed. Teeple appraised his behavior at a particularly generous seasonal bonus from Miss Gray—equal to at least her month's pay at the dreary olive green government office that suddenly seemed light years away.

Beth's top-floor apartment was a penthouse with white carpeting, high ceilings and tall windows that made her look small and almost humble as she lead the way in. She turned on the lights without groping, smiled affectionately at a lone calla lily on a grand piano, and led the way to a group of leather armchairs in front of a fireplace. When she lit the fire, the lighter worked at first try, and she had no trouble closing the grid. She lived here all right.

"Make yourself comfortable," she smiled shyly, as if she was not quite sure whether he liked it here.

"Let me guess," he said, raising an eyebrow. "You got a raise?'

"No."

"But?"

"What can I offer you?"

The glow of the fire and the smell of burning wood made Teeple forget his wet trousers, and he stood up to move over to the tall windows. A sight to behold.

On one side, the peaks of the midtown skyline dominated by the Chrysler Building were cut off by rain clouds, while the rain-splattered windows on the other side of the room looked down on the wind-swept East River and the Midtown Bridge. Clouds hung low over the top of the bridge girders, and it was both cozy and magnificent to see it all from so high up without clinging to anything for dear life. On top of that, the cozy sense of comfort was rounded off by the sight of a row of liqueur and wine bottles lined up neatly on a polished chest of drawers next to the window. No peach brandy, though.

"Wine?" Beth opened a bottle of red and poured two glasses she had taken out of a backlit mahogany cabinet.

The glasses looked and felt astoundingly fragile, and she held hers the un-American way, by the stem. Also, she stood and sat like someone who had been taught manners as a child, which certainly had not been apparent when they first met in the IRS cafeteria. Her natural habitat was obviously here.

There were old-fashioned oil paintings in ornate gold frames on the walls, not mixing well with a random and ostentatiously plain display of cheaply framed photographs by the piano—not a single one of them family oriented. The people in the photographs looked Beth's age, some ugly, some merely ordinary, all of them badly dressed and in all sorts of street rally situations; not quite the types that wore a flower in their hair, but close. They did not belong on a wall by a polished grand piano, unless of course Beth kept them there to make a statement. Because in all the photographs, she herself wore boorish lace-up boots with jaggy rubber soles, no makeup, no smile.

"Was it world peace or human rights you marched for?" Teeple said, careful not to sound disapproving.

"You don't believe in any of that, do you?"

"Do you?"

"In a way." Expecting a derogatory remark in return, she excused herself to escape to the kitchen.

She reappeared a few minutes later carrying a hot clay pot in padded kitchen gloves. No apron, though. She must have cooked the whole thing before going to work and only had to warm it up now.

They ate at a shiny mahogany table that had also been set beforehand. A red candle in the middle of the table matched the color of the place mats, and the napkin rings were ingenious little flower holders with water inside that had kept small clusters of jasmine blossoms fresh all day.

The plates had delicate silver rims, the cutlery was polished, the shepherd's pie out of the hot clay pot was excellent, and Teeple reached for a second helping.

"I dreamt about this last night," she smiled, her even white teeth sparkling in the candlelight. "I dreamt you ate a lot and I hadn't cooked enough."

"I'd have had nightmares myself if I knew about this."

"Is the pie bad?"

"I'd have worried what to wear."

"Your shirt's always clean." Beth took a moment to make up her mind to put down her fork and place her hand on his, the one holding the knife.

"You like putting yourself down, don't you?" she said softly, and when Teeple did not reply, she drew back, picked up her fork again and they finished the shepherd's pie in silence.

By the time they were done with the dessert, an apple pie that she had taken out of a local bakery carton, the candle on the table was almost half way down, and they moved to the sofa under the framed photographs to have coffee.

"Sorry," she smiled when she saw Teeple looking at the photographs again. "Would you prefer to sit somewhere else?"

"No. I . . ." The last thing he wanted was to hurt her feelings. She seemed much too vulnerable for someone wearing clumsy lace-up boots in street marches. "It's just that I'd have never guessed."

"That I'm into changing the world? What are you into?"

"Shepherd's pies."

"That was dinner." She folded one leg under her on the sofa, keeping the other, the one that made her limp, stretched out on the white carpeting. "There's got to be something that makes you get out of bed in the morning."

"My bladder, mainly."

She smiled back to show she understood defensive humor. "In other words, whatever you believe in, you prefer not to discuss. You don't wear your heart on your sleeve."

It was a statement, not a question, and Teeple could not help thinking of Danny Craig's notorious reason for not wearing his heart on his sleeve—it would jump off every time a wiggly ass passed by, hoohaha. But he would not go into that now. Beth seemed curiously vulnerable on the subject of social justice, as if it had something to do with the dilemma of her working in a dreary job in a dingy, olive green office while playing house under high ceilings on immaculate white carpeting on Manhattan's Upper East Side. Her story seemed to be long and complicated, and Teeple's time was up.

It was no longer raining outside, and the window panes facing the river were dry now. On the city side, the clouds had lifted, revealing the giant clock on the Daily News Building on 42nd Street, and the calculation was simple. It was nine o'clock, and he had 35 blocks south and 2 blocks crosstown to walk home. With a good minute per city block, he was going to be sitting by the phone at his damp and dirty den well before 22:02 hours sharp, the time Verhagen set for emergency contacts.

"Should I call downstairs to get you a cab?" she said when he stood up to go.

"Not on my salary," he smiled, and she accompanied him to the elevator.

"Have a nice walk." They shook hands, and she waited for the elevator door to close on him.

Down in the street, he pulled the flask out of his back pocket and took a swig. If she was looking after him from behind her panoramic windows, she could see him all the way to Second Avenue, and he carried the flask open in his hand for a while before he downed one more slug. Then he screwed the cap back on and put the flask in his pocket.

As far as he was concerned, he saw no need to tell Verhagen about this. He had stayed in character, which, under the circumstances, was all that mattered.

12

The next day at the office, they greeted each other as old friends, both careful not to overdo it.

"Well," Beth said later in the afternoon when they were for a moment alone by the water cooler. "Do you like stew?"

"Yes."

"Great."

"You sure?"

"Positive."

Again they took a taxi after work, again he let her pay for it, and again the dining table was set. The place mats were green this time around, with a green candle in the middle, and there were violets instead of jasmine in the napkin holders. And like the shepherd's pie the night before, the stew was precooked. Her new cookbook must have been exclusively on prefabricated meals.

After dinner they again sat in the opposite corners of the sofa under the ugly photographs, and she made sure not to go on with their discussion from the night before.

"Actually, I meant to ask you," she smiled to confirm that

beliefs and convictions were out of bounds for the rest of the evening. "That flask in your back pocket, what's in it?"

"Brandy."

"You should have told me you prefer it to wine."

"Not to yours." He took the flask out, unscrewed the cap, and held it out to her.

"Thank you." She took a sip and handed it back. "You like peaches?"

"Don't you?" Teeple leaned back, holding the flask in his hand. He did not put the screw cap back on. "You got to be quite a housekeeper to manage all this on your salary," he said.

"Maybe that's why I was kicked out of Stanford." She leaned forward to reach out and take the flask out of his hand. "These days, I guess, an educated woman is not supposed to be a housekeeper. Who knows."

"Cheers to college dropouts," he said as she took a sip and licked the peach flavor from her lips. It seemed to be growing on her, bringing a twinkle into her eyes, and the freckles on the bridge of her nose made her look like a girl ready to climb a fence to steal peaches from a neighbor's tree.

It was outright spooky how calm and comfortable he made her feel. She wanted him to come again. Soon. Tomorrow, if it was up to her. He was so easy to talk to — a wounded bird not prone to whining. How refreshing, for she had never told her own wounded-bird story to anyone for fear of being whined over. She had not even told her father — not everything, at least. And she for sure had not told her last date, the one with the flabby handshake, shifty eyes and sweaty hands. Teeple was so hugely different from the young men she had met at school, in street marches and online dating, and she would not return the flask to him yet. She just held it in her hand as if it were a teleprompter for a woebegone life story.

"Actually, what happened at Stanford, I financed twenty gallons of gasoline for my boyfriend and his comrade in arms. They were both broke but determined to help the poor by burning symbols of greed." She took another sip and when she handed the flask back to him, their fingers touched. "The geniuses used the whole canister I bought them to burn the logo on a Microsoft building in downtown Hartford. A night watchman got hurt trying to evacuate a bird's nest in a nearby tree, and they got to suffer for the good of the people more than they'd planned. The judge was an old, conservative fart and slapped them with six months in state prison each. I got away with a thousand hours of public service."

It had become a routine by then not to wipe the flask neck as they handed it back and forth, and Beth took a few, quick, nervous sips before she told Teeple about the way she had dealt with her punishment. She was doing her best to sound facetious, but all she managed was to smile while telling a sad story.

To work off her 1,000 hours, she took an unpaid teaching job at a public school that opened her eyes to yet another social injustice. She could not believe that something like that could be happening in America, teachers demanding no academic achievements from underprivileged students. She found it preposterous that a teacher should be scared to flaunt authority in the classroom. Had her teachers ever been scared of her? What nonsense. She was going to have none of that and would insist on teaching poor kids the same way she had been taught herself. She would not think twice before pointing out her students' shortcomings for their own good. She would let them flunk exams whenever they deserved it. And worse still, she was determined to teach them manners — the straw that broke the camel's back. A bunch of outraged, masked students caught her in the ladies room with her panties around her ankles and broke her shins with a crowbar.

One leg was not too bad. The other had to be put together with a titanium plate and screws, and when she woke up after the surgery, the school's legal advisor stood by her bed with a writ of spoliation.

Her case had made the news while she was in surgery, and the school board, eager to look wise and compassionate on a local TV station that specialized in sob stories, found her guilty of driving her students to violence by hurting their pride. She was ordered to apologize to those she had called underachievers, as well as to their parents and to the American people in general. She refused, and when she threatened to get herself a lawyer, too, the school principal visited her at the hospital with a legal team from the district attorney's office in tow.

"Tell you what, dear girl," they told her. "We'll close both eyes to your racist attitude and let you keep the screws in your shin free of charge. In return, you promise to stay out of public education."

She, of course, refused that, too. A legal wrangle followed, until her father stepped in and forced her to sign whatever they threw at her and be done with helping the underprivileged for once and all.

"My dad's no believer in charity at all costs," she shrugged, feeling her cheeks with a hand. They looked hot, and she turned the flask upside down to show it was empty. "To a self-made man like daddy, the only way to learn anything worth learning is the hard way. He never doubted the screws in my shin were good for getting me on the right track."

A telephone rang somewhere, and she stood up.

"Don't go away," she told Teeple.

She went to answer the call in another room and closed the door behind her. He could hear her talk, but could not understand the words. The longer the conversation dragged on, the shorter her answers were, but it obviously was not up to her to hang up first.

By the time she came back to the living room, the big hand of the clock on the Daily News Building stood at three minutes past the top of the hour, and Teeple stood up to go.

"No taxi tonight either," he said with a hand on the door knob, but she did not smile back.

It had obviously not been a good phone call, and Teeple was still thinking about her and her problems when he walked out of the building. He could not get her story out of his mind. Yet, even with that kind of distraction, he would not overlook a car parked at the red curb by a fire hydrant on the opposite side of the street. It was a gray Honda compact with one man inside, and he made sure to keep looking straight ahead.

At the corner of Second Avenue he turned south, and the gray compact pulled away from the fire hydrant to follow him. It kept bailing in and out of the flow of traffic at fire hydrants and in private driveways, never letting him get further ahead than 100 yards, and he wondered what would have happened if he had decided to walk down Third Avenue that was a one way in the opposite direction.

At 34th Street, the conspicuously clumsy shadow appeared to be satisfied that Teeple was on his way home and turned off the avenue. The gray Honda disappeared in the westbound traffic towards Macy's and the Empire State Building, and Teeple was fairly sure no one else was tailing him — at least not that obviously.

He got home shortly before 10:00 and sat down on the threadbare sofa next to the phone. The people next door were not arguing tonight, and the silence made the place feel almost cozy. His neighbors were either smoking pot elsewhere or had ODed while he was out, which was fine with him either way.

At 22:02 hours sharp, he dialed the local number Verhagen had made him memorize, let it ring four times, and hung up on the fifth.

13

In the morning, Teeple kicked off his threadbare bed blanket at the crack of dawn and got up with more alacrity than usual. In view of the bumbling tail from the night before, he needed extra time to make the meeting he had set up by the five-ring phone call before going to bed. The chances were that the man in the gray little compact had been so obvious just to have him relax.

So, to start with, he would not as much as glance over his shoulder when he stepped out of the building and turned to walk towards Third Avenue. Then, a few yards before the corner, he made an abrupt about-face, as if he suddenly remembered something, and walked to the opposite end of the block, against the one-way traffic in the road. No one could have followed him by car, and he used the Union Square subway station to shake off foot surveillance, if any. He took an uptown local to 34th Street, got out, switched to the express platform to wait on the uptown side, then abruptly hopped on a downtown train just before the doors closed and rode it all the way to Houston Street.

He arrived five minutes early at the coffee shop on the corner of Houston and Mulberry, but Verhagen was already waiting for him in a dark corner in the back, clutching a fancy espresso cup in his arthritic fingers. It was a fashionable neighborhood around here now. The glum turn-of-the-century warehouses had been converted into artist studios and luxury apartments, and the two of them were the only customers at the coffee shop at this time of day. Fashionable people did not get up early.

"A gray Honda compact," Teeple said as he dropped in a chair at Verhagen's table. "Could it be something you know about?"

"No." The old man smiled at a shapely young waitress who came up with a pencil and a pad. "Shall we make it a rush order?"

It was not quite clear to whom he was talking, and the waitress frowned.

"Don't do those around here," she said, curtly, and Verhagen was all apologies. So sorry, he had been talking to his friend here. And he did understand that no good food could possibly be served before its time.

Pacified, the waitress turned back to Teeple, and he ordered what seemed to come close to bacon and eggs: *Oeufs a la Bastille*, $35 a plate, French fries extra. When the waitress was out of earshot, he gave Verhagen the license plate number of the gray Honda that had followed him the night before.

"One guy inside," he said to round off the description.

"Would you recognize him again?"

"He made sure I knew someone was on to me, but not who."

"A jealous boyfriend maybe?"

Teeple looked up sharply, but Verhagen just kept on smiling.

"The girl's loaded, Hank. Daddy owns some pretty heavy industry. But then, I guess, you know that."

"No, I don't. Have you been checking on her?"

"Just to make sure Beth Gray's her real name."

"Is it?"

Verhagen shrugged. "She has a police record under that name. Two arrests for civil disobedience, one for inciting riots."

"Peace-on-earth riots."

"Hmm." As usual, Verhagen's thoughts were ahead of the conversation, and for a moment he looked like a man who had been grabbed by the sleeve to listen to an idle joke while chasing a bus. It took him a moment to let the imaginary bus get away and resign himself to taking it slow. "The point is, we are not playing it as much by ear as you might think, Hank."

"Whatever you say. Just do me one favor," Teeple said a touch sharper than he had intended. "Don't drag her into this."

"Nobody's dragging her into anything."

"You checked her out because you had nothing better to do?"

The waitress brought Teeple's *Oeufs a la Bastille*, a beautifully proportioned duo of overcooked eggs soaking in a watery green sauce, and Verhagen leaned back, away from the smell.

"A rich girlfriend might make it hard to believe that you wash your one and only shirt every day by hand," he said.

"What do you want me to do?"

"Maybe get behind with your rent or something." Verhagen put his elbows back on the table to make peace with Teeple's eggs. "You have been out in the field long enough to know that as often as not, it's the most carefully planned operations that take bum turns. Are you going to see her tonight?"

"Any problem with that?"

"No."

"Are you sure?"

"Go right ahead. It's perfectly natural. A fancy meal ticket."

"If you say so." Teeple watched the old man for a moment, looking for signs of displeasure. Then he glanced at his watch. "Anything else?"

"I'll check on the license plate number you gave me and let you know." Verhagen pursed his thin lips. "Which reminds me, that old girl friend of yours back in California thirty years ago? Wasn't she rich, too?"

"Why?"

"Just wondering what it is you have, Hank," Verhagen chuckled and kept on chuckling as Teeple stalked out of the coffee shop, leaving his eggs unfinished and the steep bill unpaid. Poor men with rich girlfriends tended to do that.

He arrived at his olive green desk at the IRS office just a few minutes late, with a coffee in one hand and a doughnut in the other. He had to take away the lingering aftertaste of a fancy breakfast and expected to see a frown from Beth's desk, but she was not in yet.

She did not show up by noon, and when he tried to look her up in the phone book, he only found out that she was not listed. He had a bad feeling about that, especially about Verhagen keeping his word to leave her alone. So, when she would not show up later in the afternoon either, he decided to drop by her place after work. He just had to be careful not to look and sound out of breath when he got there, and to kill time, he took a detour through what used to be Little Italy, now part of the neighboring Chinatown. The souvenir stores were selling traditional Italian knick knacks made in China, and the few remaining food shops that still bore Italian names had Chinese butchers chopping smoked duck, barbecued ribs and ginseng behind dusty displays of Italian cheese and salami. Big and small Chinese eateries had their doors and windows plastered with handwritten signs advertising cheap food, and Teeple stopped at a subterranean soup-and-noodles dive with a rock-bottom offer: complete dinner menu for $3.95.

The place was packed. So, he could not tell whether the navy-blue jogging suit with white stripes that had stopped by his table was on its way in or out.

"Hey, no kidding." The man in the jogging suit put a hot hand on Teeple's shoulder. "*Et tu Brute?*"

Teeple was having won-ton soup and had to bite off a string of noodles before he looked up. He did not remember the face, but the boisterous voice and the use of a stale Latin quotation were vaguely familiar.

"Hank, is it?" The man seemed to be deliriously happy about the encounter. "This dump's the best kept secret in New York. What are *you* doing here?"

"Eating."

"I thought you were set for life in Bosnia-Herzegovina." The man pronounced the name like someone who had been there. He was about Teeple's age, anxious to look younger. The fabric of his jogging suit was soft and readily adaptable to his deliberate body language, and Teeple, unable to place him, did not put his spoon down.

He kept on eating, but the man was not put out. He eased himself into a chair opposite and rearranged the toothpick dispenser and the soy sauce and mustard bottles in the center of the table to have a better view of Teeple's face hovering low over the noodle soup. "Sarajevo 1993. The Fourth of July bash at the American Embassy. Remember? Those two broads at the bar, weren't they a piece of work? One was the wife of the Cultural Attache, wasn't she? All Chanel, Gucci, no label was wasted on her. Man, was she all over you."

Teeple remembered that party because it was held in an air-raid cellar. A lot of people were there, with some of the women dressed to the nines even in a war zone, and one of them could have easily been the wife a Cultural Attache. Whether or not she was all over him was a matter of interpretation. He just could not put the story together with a face, and the man was determined to jog his memory.

"Ring a bell, Hank? I used to be a regular at the commercial section those days; remember me bugging them for import permits? Computers were hot merchandise those days. Anything over a megabyte of memory was classified." He took a toothpick out of the dispenser and began testing its breaking point. "Boy, were you a romantic figure those days. Some sort of a secret agent, right? True Hollywood."

"Oh." Teeple remembered him now—running around Sarajevo, telling all males with narrow hips and flat stomachs, no matter in what uniform, that they looked Hollywood. He used to be blond those days, though. Now his hair was pitch black, and under the harsh fluorescent lights of a cheap eatery, his hairline showed rows upon rows of infected looking implants.

"Wayne, right?" Teeple said, swallowing a mouthful of noodles. "Wayne Patton."

"Parton."

"Right." Now that rang a bell, loud and clear, and Teeple resumed eating. Wayne Parton used to be a shady character, the CEO or something of an outfit importing classified American computers to Yugoslavia, where it was no problem to repackage them for shipping to all kinds of places on the American black list.

"You left the place in '94, if I remember correctly," Wayne beamed, getting prouder of his memory by the minute. "The war lost its romance by then, didn't it?"

Teeple said nothing, working on his soup, and Wayne dropped himself a cue.

"I never asked you this before, but there were all kinds of rumors about you and the CIA back then. As they say, where there is smoke . . . anyway, what are you up to now?"

"I work for the IRS."

"Here?"

"Yes."

"In New York?"

"Uhmm."

"Jesus." Wayne knitted his eyebrows. They too were dyed, same color as the hair. "What can you be making? Thirty, forty grand a year? That calls for a hooch."

Wayne flagged down a waiter and ordered two glasses of plum wine. The waiter curtly told him they had no liquor license, and Wayne waved him off. He gave Teeple a quick sidelong glance, to check whether he had put the waiter's brush off together with his pretense of being a regular here, and broke the toothpick he had been toying with.

"Thirty grand a year's below the poverty line in New York." He brushed the broken toothpick aside and gave Teeple's forearm a playful squeeze. "And you know what?"

"No."

"I believe you." He let Teeple eat in silence for a while, then shook his head in a frustrated resentment of the world at large. "This country's going to hell in a hand-basket while we sit around slurping noodles. So, if you think I'm going to walk out of here and forget all this, wake up to reality, pal."

His hand on Teeple's arm felt eager and most anxious before he abruptly got up and almost toppled his chair. He caught it just in time, and patted Teeple on the back. "Meet me here tomorrow, bud. Say yes."

"Yes."

"Good."

Then Wayne Parton was gone, leaving behind just the broken toothpick, and Teeple finished his noodles before he took his ticket to the cashier at the exit.

On his way to Beth's place, he stopped at an Internet cafe to get off an e-mail message to Verhagen. He formatted it as an address book entry for Wayne Parton, Sarajevo 1993, and used a PoP address that would self-delete after one hit.

He made it to the lobby of Beth's building by eight, hot and windblown from walking all the way. Neither the doorman nor the porter recognized him, maybe because this time the bottom of his pants was dry, and he called her apartment on the house phone. There was no answer and he did not leave a message. And since by then he'd had enough of walking for one day, he took the subway home.

The building smelled like a sewer as usual. On the bright side, though, the people next door were quiet again, and he fell asleep without pills. He dreamt of Wayne's hair implants. Their unstoppable sprouting power seemed to have something to do with dark skies, flashes of lightning, and crashes of thunder. But no matter how much he tossed and turned in the flimsy rented bed, there seemed to be no point to all that, and in the tortuous way dreams twist logic, he realized that Wayne had not set a time to meet at the noodle place. It was only after he woke up that things began to make sense again. Wayne must have meant the same place, the same time.

14

The following morning, when Teeple got in the elevator in the lobby, Beth was already in, coming from down below. Strange. New York taxis did not take passengers into underground garages, and she had told him before that a car was a nuisance in the city and she had none. So, who brought her?

"Dinner tonight?" she smiled, as if skipping a day at the office or coming from the garage the following morning was no big deal. "My place again?"

"How about tomorrow?" he said.

"Anytime." She did not ask why, just like he had not asked who. They had not known each other long enough for that.

At quitting time, neither of them attempted to catch the same elevator down, and Teeple took a different detour to the Chinese noodle place. Punctuality was not supposed to be an underpaid slacker's trait. He arrived almost half an hour later than the day before, and Wayne Parton looked relieved to see him. The jogging outfit from the day before had been replaced with a pinstriped suit and a red tie that made him look like a corrupt politician ready to clear his name on TV.

"Just got in myself," he lied. The table was covered with broken toothpicks and shreds of a napkin, as if he had been sitting here for quite a while, fighting a nervous breakdown. "Do I have news for you, buddy."

"How bad?"

"You kidding me? I spread the word last night, got swamped with offers the first thing in the morning. Lemme ask you something." Again, Wayne put a hot, anxious hand on Teeple's arm. "What's the figure you have in mind?"

"You mean money?"

"What else?"

"I don't know."

"Come on."

"You tell me."

"You tell me what would make you happy?"

"A hundred thousand a year?"

"What?" Wayne looked sincerely flabbergasted.

"Fifty?"

"Come on, buddy."

"Forty?"

"A guy with your background? A hundred grand would get you hired by your neighborhood grocer who's up to monkey tricks with the tax on nutmeg. I'm talking major players here."

"You don't fiddle, do you?" Teeple smiled, and Wayne looked hurt.

"Hey, how long have we known each other? Would I be kidding you about something like this?"

"I don't know."

"The guy I'm meeting tonight will cough up half a mil for a job that shouldn't take more than a few months."

"Wow." Teeple had no problem sounding serious about that. Verhagen had told him to expect anywhere between $100,000 and $200,000, if they took the bait. You keep what you make, the old man had told him. Because after going through with this whole thing, there was no chance in hell Teeple would ever work for the government again. "Wow," he said again.

"I know," Wayne patted Teeple's back, looking worried about his silence. "I know half a mil's nothing to retire on. But hey, it's a beginning. If you do OK, the sky's the limit in the next round."

A waiter came over to take their orders, and Wayne glanced at his watch.

"Gotta skip the chow."

"I haven't eaten since breakfast," Teeple remonstrated, and Wayne heaved a sigh.

"The thing is, the guy I'm meeting tonight will want to know all about you." He tapped his watch as if to make double sure it was working. "No time to listen to your curriculum vitae while you choke on noodles."

Wayne dropped a dollar bill on the table, a compensation for not spending more, and got up to head for the exit. "Come on, Hank."

Outside, they turned to walk down a quiet side street towards the river. It was a nice evening, not too cold, not too hot.

"Now, let's see." Wayne took a notebook out of a pocket to write while walking. He was either used to taking dictation on the fly, or merely pretended to be writing down what he already knew. "You once told me you grew up out in the sticks."

"Did I?"

"On a farm in California, was it?"

"A ranch."

"Yeah. " Wayne checked his watch again. "Damn it."

"Sorry I was late."

"Don't keep apologizing." Wayne clicked in his ball-point pen and put it back in a pocket together with the notebook. "I'll be getting my ten percent one way or another."

"Ten percent of what?"

"Your year's pay. It's standard with employment agencies." Wayne shrugged. "Except that no employment agency would offer your anything near the kind of pay I have in mind. Are you listening to me, Hank?"

"Sure."

"To get you top dollar, I gotta convince my guy you did not join the CIA out of some kind of a patriotic fervor. Get my drift?"

"How will you do that?"

"By taking your word for it. What made you go into the spook business in the first place?"

"I don't know," Teeple shrugged, weighing the possibilities. Statistically speaking, men betray their country either out of disdain or for money, Verhagen had told him in one of their planning sessions back in Washington; both versions had been done to death in Hollywood, so let's stick to the truth for a change. "A steady paycheck, I guess," he said, casually.

"Right." Wayne was not opposed to that attitude. "The farm —sorry, ranch—wasn't doing well?"

"Not bad at first. The money I sent home helped my parents to hang on to it for a while."

"They lost the ranch two years later, right?" Wayne heaved a sigh of fake concern. "Look here, don't get sore. I already had a guy check the public records at the county registrar in Santa Barbara. What's aquatic salamandridae?"

"Newts. Slimy little critters with short legs and long tails that love warm mud."

"How would little critters with short legs and long tails push a cattle ranch into bankruptcy?"

"They lived in a lake on our property."

"Yes?"

"A girl next door found out they were on the endangered species list. She reported it to some commission, and a chunk of our acreage around the lake was declared off-limits to cattle grazing. After that, there was no way I could've pulled my parents out of that kind of hole on a government salary."

"No kidding." Wayne's face darkened with more sympathy. He knew the rest of Teeple's story. The ranch was bought by a rock singer, who turned it into a dope heaven for recording artists and a shrine for newt worshippers, and Teeple's father never got over that. Died a couple of years later.

They reached the East River at South Pier, and sat down on a park bench on the embankment. The Brooklyn Bridge was looming overhead, and on the river a tug boat with a string of overloaded barges in tow was chugging laboriously against the outgoing tide.

"That girl, the newt hugger," Wayne said, out of time for a more circumspect wording, "was she a nut case?"

"She was young and fell for Fitch bullshit."

"That guy?" There was a distinctly fraudulent note in Wayne's surprise. "You mean Richard Fitch?"

"Yeah."

"Man . . ." For a split second, though, Wayne's dismay sounded true. He seemed to be pursuing some distant memory of his own. "Women. Go figure. Were you sweet on her?"

"I was twenty and she was Miss California, almost."

"I hear you." Wayne got up to flag down a cab. "How do I get in touch with you? Or is that something you don't ask an ex-spook?"

A taxi pulled up, and Teeple rattled off his phone number, which he suspected Wayne had known for a while.

"I'll be in touch." Wayne got in the taxi and stuck his head out of the window. "That's what friends are for, ey?"

Then he was gone, and Teeple wondered whether it had been Wayne in the gray Honda the other night. Most likely not. He seemed to have worked his way up some fly-by-night outfit and might have had a bunch of gofers under him.

The chances were that a backup of sorts was still hanging around, but Teeple could not see anyone to fit the role. There was just a busload of tourists lining up in front of the Maritime Museum, men in rubber boots were hosing down the sidewalks of the fish market, and a young couple on a park bench stared at the river in a genuine post-fight stupor. They were much too young to fake lovers' hell. They had the real thing to deal with—which, in turn, made Teeple think of Beth's cozy little dinners for two that had turned out to be more than just misery seeking company.

15

The following day, Wayne called Teeple at work, sounding brusque and competent, as if someone were standing next to him with a stop watch and an efficiency checklist. He spelled out the arrangements loud and clear and fast: the Lincoln Center fountain at seven sharp. Tonight. Got it? He hung up before Teeple could confirm he did get it.

The meeting sounded like a big deal and, suspecting that the famous New York landmark might be crowded, Teeple arrived a few minutes early to allow extra time to find Wayne. But it was Wayne who found him, sounding out of breath.

"My guy's got this thing about punctuality. Nothing to worry about, though," Wayne shrugged, looking worried as hell. "You just kick back and look cool. Leave the squabbling to me."

"All right."

"I've asked for four hundred thou for a job that's gonna take you three months on the outside. OK with you for starters?"

"When will you want your commission?"

"Have forty grand on you?"

"No."

"You pay me when you get paid. I know where to find you."

They walked a couple of blocks up the less frequented Columbus Avenue, to a small movie theater with a badly lit marquee. There were either letters missing in the short list of performers or the names were very foreign.

"The biggest names in the business," Wayne explained. There was no one inside the ticket booth, and he led the way through a scuffed swing door and down a dark staircase into a basement auditorium. It smelled of mold and stale cigarette smoke, and they slipped into two of the many empty seats in the back.

"That's him," Wayne whispered. "The guy on the stage."

The guy on the stage was a stand-up comedian, fat and unkempt, who sounded as if he picked this line of work after a couple of relatives laughed at his jokes over a family dinner. His gig was a drawn-out monologue about a fat guy eating rotten meat because he thought that worms were a high-protein diet, and his body language was painful to watch. With a heavy foreign accent, he rhymed worm with squirm and diet with riot, and a handful of unkempt enthusiasts in the front row gave him a frantic ovation to show they could tell a smart guy when they saw one.

He did three curtain calls, throwing kisses with stubby hands that were held away from his body by fat cushions under the armpits. When it finally became obvious he was not coming out for more, Wayne got up and led the way backstage.

"His name's Reza," he whispered in Teeple's ear before they entered a "No Admittance" door off a dark narrow passage. "No last name, nothing. Remember that. Just Reza."

Reza was still out of breath, wiping his face on a dirty rag in what looked like a unisex dressing room. Still basking in the memory of a standing ovation, he lit his post-performance joint, and as a cloud of hairspray from the next makeup table drifted close to the match, Teeple stepped back a little, just in case. Was this the guy ready to cough up close to half a mil for a job that shouldn't take more than a few months?

Fortunately, the drifting hairspray was not combustible, and Teeple moved closer again when Wayne introduced the comedian as the guy he had spoken about so highly on the phone. "What did I tell you about this man? The toast of the town."

Sweat was pouring from Reza's forehead, down his cheeks and into his thick beard, and in the daze of post-performance euphoria, he took Teeple's handshake for a heartfelt homage.

"Stand on your head and they'll love you to death," he said, and Wayne chuckled, fraudulently.

"Man, they sure loved you."

"Give them fun and they'll say you're A-one."

Backstage, Reza's English was much less accented, and Wayne gazed at him with oily admiration.

"Reza's the first Muslim comedian this side of the Atlantic," he explained to Teeple. "I guess you know that."

"No."

"Ow, come on." Wayne could not believe Teeple wouldn't play the game. "You read the papers."

"Mr. Teeple's no slouch to beat us to the punch," Reza said, and Wayne made sure to roar with laughter.

"That was good, man."

"Teeple, the spy from the C-A-I . . ." Reza mused, unable to control the flow of rhyming adrenaline. He was harmless. His motives for doing what he was doing, Teeple assumed, were either money or a favor that had nothing to do with the common good of an ideological clique. The comedian was no fanatic outside the realm of his own babbling humor. "Feeble Teeple, the fallen spy working on the sly . . . Who the hell cares."

Reza pulled himself together to bend his thoughts to the triviality of real life and dismissed Wayne with an imperial wave of a hand.

"You may go now, Wayne the pain."

Wayne backed out of the grubby, artistic vestry with a grin, counting his own coins of reward in his head, and Reza put a clammy hand on Teeple's shoulder. His face was still sweating, but he finally seemed to be coming out of the rhyming ecstasy.

"OK, man. Do you know what a dresser does?"

"What?"

"You'll be taking off my pants and putting them back on, starting tomorrow." Reza's hand on Teeple's shoulder was sliding downwards to explore the biceps. "Hope tomorrow's convenient for you. Because if it isn't, tough luck."

Teeple did not have to step back too far to get out of reach of Reza's short, fat arms.

"What are you talking about?" he said.

"You really don't read the papers, do you?" Reza gave a stage chuckle. He could tell this hunk was going to be difficult. But then, who said life was a bed of roses? "Variety did a whole paragraph on my tour starting tomorrow."

"Congratulations."

"Thanks."

They left the theater through a beat-up back door. There were no fans waiting outside, but it was a nice evening, and once they got out of the back alley, the air was dry and balmy.

"Wayne told me you live downtown," Reza sighed, getting to the inconvenient facts of life now. How could anyone live downtown? "You better stay at my place tonight. We have an early flight out of JFK."

"Where to?"

"If you read the papers, you'd know. Got your passport on you?"

"Wayne said nothing about going abroad."

"Wayne the pain," Reza shrugged. "Did he also forget to tell you that I'll be on that plane tomorrow with or without you?"

Teeple believed him. The comedian obviously had his marching orders and was not quite sure how to put it.

"Luckily for you, Teeple, my friend, you don't have to worry about packing a suitcase. You'll have plenty of my stuff to schlep."

"I'll still need my passport."

"Crap." Reza hated people who did not have their passports on them at all times. "Gotta take a cab to drop by your place."

"I got to take a cab."

"Oh, yeah?" The comedian also hated disobedience. But he obviously had no authority to jerk Teeple around at will, which made him feel insulted and turn nasty. "Is it your passport that makes you act stupid, or could it be a last-minute roll in the hay you don't want to miss? A broad with a big pad and a small limp? Nothing much to look at?"

They turned a corner. The comedian was on the inside, and Teeple hit him in the stomach. He had hit as unobtrusively as he could, without a back swing, but his fist continued picking up momentum even after contact with the top layer of the comedian's fat. It was like beating on a jellyfish.

"Ugh . . ." Reza took a moment to catch his breath. "What the fuck?"

"What time did you say we meet at the airport?"

Reza hesitated for a moment, then decided to leave bad enough alone. He was not going to apologize for either the limp or the broad being not much to look at, and they were even.

"The Royal Jordanian at Kennedy," he shrugged, trying hard to resist the temptation to add more insults. It took him a moment to stop himself from glaring at Teeple contemptuously. He was not going to blow this job just because he hated tall men with blue eyes. "Six-fifteen sharp. Be there."

"The first-class counter?"

"Up yours." The comedian looked disgusted with other people's jokes, especially when they were not rhyming. But the job of delivering Teeple on time and in one piece took precedence over artistic pride, and the finger he held up was not quite straight. "Up yours, my friend."

"Until tomorrow then," Teeple smiled back. He left the comedian standing in the middle of the sidewalk and hailed a taxi — to hell with the poverty-stricken image. He had to show confidence in Wayne's promise that he was about to start a new life on a salary that might soon let him hire a helicopter to fly to Beth's rooftop.

16

Beth had a visitor when Teeple got there. A neat, young man in a suit and tie sat with her at the coffee table by the fireplace, shuffling papers.

"We're about done," she smiled at Teeple, not bothering with introductions. Yet, obviously for the young man's benefit, she pulled Teeple down by his sleeve to have him kiss her cheek.

They had never kissed before. They had both been careful to sidestep silly, touchy-feely routines, and the quick brush with her skin now felt like a blast of fresh wind that in turn blew in more misgivings about his new job—a dresser for a sweaty, fat comedian that was not funny.

"Something the matter?" she frowned a little.

"No."

She was not convinced, but let go of his sleeve. "You know where the drinks are."

The row of liquor bottles on the chest of drawers next to the river-side window had been augmented with half a dozen or so different brands of peach brandy, and Teeple could not help smiling. Had she gone shopping especially for him? Was it why she skipped work the other day?

He poured himself a fragile snifter that made peach brandy taste ever so different from the usual quickies out of a travel flask. And as he sunk into the overstuffed kidskin armchair by the window, it suddenly struck him. This place was not just squeaky clean and immaculate, it was soul cleansing. After decades of slogging it out in cheap hotels and short-term rentals in bad neighborhoods, dirt and mediocrity became something he had learned not to dwell on—making it hard to believe now that the squirming multitudes in the dark streets way down below the window were something he had ever been part of.

Against the backdrop of a dark sky, the inside of the apartment reflected in the window panes, and he could see the neat young man at the coffee table handing papers to Beth to read. She, in turn, would put them aside with barely a glance at the contents, and after a while the man gathered the pile into a briefcase, got up, and disappeared from the reflection in the window pane.

A door opened and closed somewhere, and a moment later Beth came back alone to refill his glass.

"My fault," she said. "I should've seen it coming."

"Seen what?" Were things getting complicated?

"My father had you checked out," she said.

"Oh." Sipping brandy in a kidskin armchair closer to the clouds than the earth, Teeple found it hard to believe that anything could be the matter up here. The sheer idea that bad things could happen to a man cuddled in the lap of luxury made him smile. "Is he coming with a shotgun?"

"No."

"Then, did he need my address to send flowers?"

"He just needed to know how much education you had." She sat down on the floor by Teeple's feet and did her best to sound amused. "Education is a sore subject with daddy. That's why my mother left him."

"Was she from a farm?"

"My mom was a Harvard graduate, a doctor of some kind of social science and proud of it. Every time she and daddy had an argument when I was little, she would call him a school dropout, and he'd bring up what he called a colossal difference between knowledge and wisdom that nerds and academics would never understand. I sure didn't understand it myself back then, but I liked the way he handled mother's tantrums about higher learning. They were divorced by then and he had nothing to lose. So he'd wait for her to run out of breath before he slipped in a quote from some ancient poet who said nasty things about educated fools, and they'd go on arguing for hours. A savage fuss about knowledge and wisdom, can you imagine that?"

"Not me." Teeple shrugged. "I never finished high-school."

"You didn't?"

"No."

"Are you sure?"

"Oh, yes."

"Wow . . ." Beth's eyes opened wide and, gradually, her face broke into a slow, bright smile, "now I get it."

"Good."

"This gotta be why my father's attorney came over tonight to tell me: the old man's willing to forget his list if Mr. Teeple is on mine."

"What list?"

"Résumés of suitable men."

"Mine's not that great."

"Because you were fired from your last job? That's a badge of honor in my daddy's book." Beth kept smiling, her teeth sparkling as she looked up. "No man worth a damn stands a chance in a government career. You don't argue with daddy about that. To him, getting fired from a senseless, dead-end drudgery is a sign of wisdom."

"You told him about me?"

"Didn't have to." Beth shrugged, glancing down at her bad leg. "After my — the accident I told you about the other day — he made it his business to know all about the people I meet."

"Doesn't he trust your wisdom?" Teeple was finding it increasingly difficult not to speculate how much her inheritance was worth. Probably a lot. On the other hand, she might have been plain crazy.

"Do I sound crazy to you?" she smiled.

"Just what you say."

"Sorry." She got up to refill his glass and went to sit at the piano.

She started to play, and Teeple leaned back to watch her hands on the keyboard. The music she played brought back memories of Roni's mother's gramophone—except that Mrs. Pitt, the Santa Ynez Valley snob and a snotty bitch according to some, played that kind of music only when she expected important visitors.

Live hands on a piano keyboard in an everyday situation honed the effect of a grand tune to a point where the rest of mankind blended into the wallpaper, or whatever it was on the walls here. Verhagen the spymaster, Wayne the crook, Reza the comedian—they all suddenly seemed far away and out of focus, and Teeple wanted Beth to go on playing to keep them there.

Wishful thinking took over his senses like some hazy ephemeral cure for painful repercussions of real life, and he did not hear the music stop until he saw her standing in front of him, her fingers no longer stroking piano keys but his hair.

"Actually," he said hoarsely in a halfhearted defense against what was coming, "I found a new job."

"I thought you were not looking."

"I wasn't."

"Is it out of town?"

"Yes."

The fingers in his hair froze.

"Why . . ." She caught herself in time. She would have hated to sound like a wife. "We'll miss you at the office."

"For all the good work I did?"

"That too." Her fingers in his hair were moving again, and she was so close that he could hear her heartbeat.

She bent over him, and the closeness took his breath away. The palms of her hands were warm and pliable on his face, as were her lips, as was her breath that felt like an early morning wind from an open range when the grass was still wet but the long-stem poppies already began turning their brittle petals into the rising sun to dry . . .

In the bedroom, though, the crisp bed linen smelled of lavender, and when she turned off the lights, the touch of her musical fingers on bare skin popped Teeple's heart into his throat — making breathing difficult, not unlike gasping for air, which at his age was a damn scary emotion.

* * *

In hindsight, though, the memory of a would-be heart attack in Beth's bed made Teeple all but worried about his health. On the contrary, it made him feel soundly annoyed when he met Reza at the Royal Jordanian Airlines counter shortly after dawn.

The comedian was at the end of a winding economy-class queue, arguing with a porter half his size. He thought it outrageous to be charged for half a dozen suitcases the same rate per piece like some tourist with one knapsack. He was a performing artist traveling on business, he told the porter, and he also knew his rights both as a consumer and an American citizen.

He gave the man two $1 bills, take it or leave it, and looked to Teeple for approval and friendship. He needed a friend in case the porter was bringing back reinforcements.

"I hate blacks," he told Teeple, looking around nervously.

Teeple picked up the smallest suitcase from Reza's pile to carry as his own and let the comedian take care of the remaining five, pulling and pushing them one by one every time the queue moved. By the time they reached the check-in counter, Reza was sweating and took out his frustration on the agent that was doing her best to smile.

With a haughty disdain for little people, he tossed a crumpled envelope on the counter, missed, and the girl had no choice but to go down on her knees to pick up the two tickets and the frequent flyer card that spilled onto the floor. She was very young, not quite sure how to handle the situation, and when she got back on her feet, she took her time to compare Teeple's passport photo with his face. There were not many Westerners with American names accompanying this airline's frequent flyers on eastbound flights, and she meekly turned to Reza as if Teeple were a child traveling with his father.

"Is Paris his final destination, too?"

"It better be. He's my dresser."

"Your what?" The girl went from confused to apprehensive.

From Paris the flight continued on to Damascus, where all kinds of bad guys had access to incoming passenger manifests, and Americans were naive. Judging by Reza's behavior, his dresser most likely was a wacko, too, maybe some crazy do-gooder bent on bringing democracy to the Middle East, and she would be in a lot of trouble if he got whacked the moment he stepped off the plane.

She insisted on Reza's detailed explanation in Arabic, which he did with a great deal of excessive, angry gesticulation. He kept on pulling down imaginary pants and putting them back on until the girl was satisfied that he was some kind of a Hollywood celebrity ostentatiously traveling in coach with a servant to spread American culture abroad. She issued JFK-PAR tags for their luggage and dutifully brightened up to wish them a pleasant journey. She sure was glad to have no part in whatever this odd couple was going to Paris for.

Le Château

17

A bored French immigration officer came to life when Teeple and Reza emerged from the arrival gate. After eight hours on a plane, the comedian looked even meaner than his passport picture, and the officer took his time to run a cross check with the rogue gallery on his computer screen.

"You two trravelink togetheer?" he asked Teeple in English, and it was only after his nod that he stamped Reza's passport and let them through.

"Asshole," Reza said, and Teeple looked away. After six hours of elbow digging on the plane, a dig and a grunt every time the comedian thought one of his jokes scored with a dutifully cheerful flight attendant, he could not stand looking at him.

At the arrival gate, they were met by a fiery-eyed man in a chauffeur's uniform holding a handwritten sign with Reza's name. The two greeted each other in English and let Teeple trot behind them to a white Rolls Royce parked in a no-stopping zone in front of the exit. It had ominously tinted windows, and a blond policewoman took care to keep her distance while writing a parking ticket. She finished by the time Reza's pile of suitcases was loaded in the trunk and came closer only to hand the slip to the chauffeur, who swiftly stuck it into the opening of her blouse.

They drove off laughing, leaving the policewoman to grope in her bra with one foot in the gutter. They were having a blast without being careless. Just in case the dumb blonde was calling for a backup, the driver made sure to get away fast and swung onto the expressway onramp with screeching tires.

The last time Teeple was in Paris, the *Periferique* had been just a disjointed succession of four-lane roads through the outer suburbs. Now it was a continuous freeway circling the city through an endless succession of underpasses and tunnels, and it took him a while to get his bearings. They were not headed for the center of Paris.

In Neuilly, they bypassed the turnoff to Chatellet, and turned into the setting sun towards Chartreuse and Orleans. The world brightened up as grim suburbs gave way to a gentle, rolling countryside, and in the front seat, Reza and the chauffeur ran out of conversation. They turned to furtive smoking, and Teeple tugged at the glass partition. It would not close, and he punched a button in his elbow rest to open the window.

It set off a warning light in the dashboard, and the chauffeur spun around to give Teeple a dirty look through the billowing smoke. Reza, who found it difficult to turn his bulk in a car seat, said it was all right, and the window remained open.

"Just a crack," the chauffeur barked to establish his supporting role in the chain of command.

Outside, against the setting sun, grazing cows were casting long shadows over the meadows, and the pastorale scenery was punctuated by patches of forest and by small villages looking snug and sleepy in the cleavage of rolling hills. The air streaming in through the just-a-crack open window smelled of hay and cow dung, the digital speedometer in the dashboard read a cocky 200, and by the time it got dark, they were a few hundred kilometers southwest of Paris.

Overhead road signs, lit with bluish iridescent tubes, were swishing by like ghostly summer lightnings, and the chauffeur would not ease up on the gas pedal even while lighting one cigarette from another. He only slowed down in the transition to the Bordeaux freeway, where a highway patrol car was lurking on the shoulder of one of the transition ramps.

"Where are we going?" Teeple said, suppressing a temptation to open the window all the way and wave to the police car to help him get on the next plane back to America.

"Oooh, where are we going, ey?" Reza and the chauffeur exchanged insider snickers. The smart guy in the back was getting worried, wasn't he? "Have a nap, Teeple. You'll need it."

The Bordeaux freeway was a toll road, and after they picked up a ticket at a drive-through booth, the roadway ahead looked deserted. The French preferred low-cost transportation to a super speedy one. A three-lane road with an immaculate surface was a costly luxury that made driving feel like flying between two perpetual reflective lines that pierced the darkness at the length of the high-beam headlights, and, after a short night in Beth's bed and a long day on a plane, Teeple dozed off.

Drifting in and out of sleep, he lost all track of time. His wristwatch was still on New York time, so when they finally stopped to pay the exit toll, he did a quick calculation. It was still before midnight here. The exit was called Poitiers, and the chauffeur had a brief staccato argument in French with the toll collector. Teeple did not understand a word, but Reza seemed to understand enough to look disgusted.

Past the toll booth, the limo swung onto a dark country road, and for the next few miles Reza and the chauffeur kept on commiserating with one another on toll collectors' stupidity in general. Not to worry, though; something was gonna give soon. The Frenchies were about to sing a different tune, they agreed with one another as they turned into a narrow dirt road and stopped in front of a tall, wrought-iron gate between two massive brick columns.

A red and yellow sign on one of the columns called for *Accès interdit*, prohibited access, while an elegantly understated brass plate on the other column identified the place as *Château de la Bataille de Poitiers*.

"Ever heard of it in America, the Battle of Poitiers?" Reza wheezed over his shoulder, taking the trouble to turn his massive bulk sideways to quiz Teeple about the part of European history he himself had obviously been couched in.

He was about to drop another derogatory remark about American education when the gate in front of the hood began to open and the chauffeur stubbed out his cigarette.

"The window," he snapped.

"Shit." Forgetting the history quiz, Reza stubbed out his cigarette, too. "Shut the window, Teeple."

They drove into a manicured park with the chauffeur clutching the steering wheel with both hands as if he were trying to lift the front wheels to atone for the crunch of tires on loose gravel. After a mile or so, the gravel path ended at another wrought-iron gate between two massive columns, this time with no signs on either of them.

Again, the gate opened without a living soul in the headlights—except that this time they drove in at a crawl and immediately stopped to wait.

"Keep your hands on your knees," Reza snapped over his shoulder.

The gate closed behind them with a squeak and a click, followed by a moment of riveting silence before a couple of black jumpsuits popped up in front of the hood with machine guns at the ready. Two more approached from the sides, and a civilian with a holstered side gun knocked on Reza's window to examine his papers. He stuck his head in to check the backseat and, insolently ignoring Teeple, snapped his fingers at the jumpsuits in front of the hood to step aside.

"You know the drill," he told the chauffeur. "Don't make us come after you."

After 100 or so yards of a humble, crunching crawl on more loose gravel, the headlights fell on a gray medieval facade with tall windows and goblins squatting on the ledgers. The chauffeur, a picture of humility and concentration now, found a gap between two pampered flower beds and pulled up at the bottom of a sweeping, artfully curved staircase flanked by elaborate balustrades.

Reza, his cockiness conspicuously missing, too, got out to open Teeple's door and give him the final pep talk in a hoarse, wheezing whisper.

"Don't blow it, asshole."

Some of the windows on the upper floor of the chateau were lit up, but the nape of Reza's neck seemed to be under pressure emanating from the dark ones. He would not quite straighten up even when a gust of wind blew the spray from a nearby fountain in his face.

The fountain spout was held in a simple-minded, pornographic manner by a petrified faun, and Teeple could not help a double take.

"Don't stare," Reza hissed. He relaxed only when the irreverent crunch of Teeple's footsteps on gravel ceased at the bottom of the sweeping staircase.

On top of the staircase, a blond servant in a red jumpsuit with a blue sash opened a massive, medieval door into an entry hall lined with two rows of marble statues. And again Teeple could not help a double take. The statues had their stony crotches covered with authentic-looking pubic hair.

At the end of the eerie alleyway of enhanced classic nudity, another servant opened another massive door, and Teeple and Reza entered what looked like a cross between a church and a bathhouse, except that there was no swimming pool anywhere in sight.

The mosaic tile floor depicted a medieval battle scene, and in the middle of it—surrounded by tiled images of swishing sabers, poised rapiers and detached body parts—stood a short, balding man in an impeccable white suit.

In contrast to the bloody carnage on the floor, his whites looked immaculate, as did his suave poise. He gave the impression of an eccentric interior designer poised to show a whimsical house to potential buyers, except that Reza would not greet him as such. The fat comedian, his eyes on his shoes, slithered forward with sagging knees to kiss the man's hand.

Then, murmuring some sort of a laudatory chant, Reza backed out of the room through a side door, and the man in white held out a hand, making it clear he did not expect Teeple to kiss it.

"Welcome, Mr. Teeple." His hand was soft and warm, a match for his fleshy lips and cheeks, but not for his piercing dark eyes that were also at odds with the British club tie he wore. "I am doctor Walid el Zyaad, and you must be weary at the conclusion of a long journey."

"Is this it?"

"Indeed."

A servant appeared from somewhere, his suede slippers shuffling soundlessly over the floor mosaic, stopping on the head of a medieval warrior who was in the process of impaling a fierce enemy, who in turn was about to lop off the head of a wild-eyed man in shining armor, who of course was up to something astoundingly brutal, too. The mosaic was a complex, ancient work of art on the subject of violence breeding naught but violence, and doctor Walid el Zyaad looked perfectly at home in the middle of it.

"We shall talk tomorrow," he smiled mildly, and Teeple all but expected to hear a gong marking the end of the audience. He caught himself just in time not to play the game. People like Zyaad despised pushovers. Never give in to a push, no matter how magnanimous, Verhagen had warned him in the blue and orange dump in Washington, where the word magnanimous had had a wholly different meaning.

It seemed that Verhagen had had no idea about the identity or the whereabouts of Teeple's final contact. Zyaad looked civilized even in the epicenter of a floor mosaic depicting a savage medieval carnage, and Teeple decided on a watered-down version of Verhagen's suggested get-acquainted routine.

"Am I going to work for you?" he said, his free-man-and-American-citizen voice echoing in the humbling milieu with an ungracious simplicity.

"Yes." Zyaad smiled back, looking disappointed. The man should have been coached not to speak before spoken to. "Any objections?"

"Not right now."

"Thank you." Under the cathedral-like ceiling, the echo of authority had the unmistakable effect of a final statement, and when Teeple would not move, Zyaad had no choice but to suppress irritation. The man was a guest in his house. "Is there something else? You desire a woman tonight?"

"No."

"A young man, maybe?"

"No, thank you."

"Well, then." Zyaad nodded to the servant to take Teeple away, no ifs or buts this time around.

The man grabbed Teeple's sleeve to hustle him out through a side door and down a long, bare corridor at the end of which he opened a door into a simple, hotel-like room—a non-Moslem one. It had wall-to-wall carpeting and paintings with people in them.

The queen-size bed had been turned down, with fresh pajamas laid out on a down blanket and a pair of slippers on the floor. There was a faint smell of incense in the air, and Teeple opened a door onto a balcony and stepped out.

At a distance that was hard to judge at night, the moon was touching on the rim of a low hill next to the silhouette of a lone tree, and the sound of cicadas and distant cow bells accentuated rather than disturbed the silence.

When he returned to his room, there was a trolley heaped up with packages in gift wraps, with another servant standing by.

"For the guest of the house," the man said, gruffly. English was not his mother tongue, politeness was not his racket, and the trolley had not been his idea. He left it standing in the middle of the room and opened a walk-in closet with a long row of beautifully pressed business suits and starched shirts on evenly spaced hangers.

"Every morning, you dress new," the man said, his accent most likely Russian. There was a touch of prickly superiority in his little blue eyes that turned into an outright prison-guard smirk as he pointed to the open door of a spacious bathroom stocked up with a generous supply of fresh towels and an impressive lineup of toiletries. "Every morning, you wash, shave, and smell good."

Not bothering to ask if there was anything else, the man sauntered out of the room, locking the door from the outside, and leaving Teeple alone with the trolley full of gifts.

He picked a package from the top of the heap. There was a dose of Caviar inside, probably the real thing. Verhagen had warned him about that. They'll shower you with gifts the moment you walk in; it makes them feel in the right when they screw you in the end.

Another package contained a snake-leather watch band, and he put it down on the coffee table next to the caviar. Then, leaving the rest of the packages unopened, he began to get ready for bed. He was dead beat.

18

When Teeple woke up, the sun was shining into the room and it took him a moment to remember where he was. The first thing that came to mind was Heaven. The chateau was on a hill, and the valley down below was filled with fluffy fog lapping against the edge of the terrace outside his room.

Heeding the butler's command from the night before, he showered and shaved, then opened the walk-in closet to have a closer look. The shirts were all white, but he had a choice of color in suits. He picked a gray one, with a pair of black shoes. He had never owned a really expensive pair, so the first steps were an eye opener. Good shoes felt snug and light and put a spring in his step even on thick carpeting.

A digital clock on the bedside table read 8:30, but the door was still locked. So, assuming he was not expected to go down for breakfast or something, he turned on the TV. At this time of day, it was mostly cartoons and news, in French of course, and he flipped through the channels until he heard English. It was CNN, with Larry King in red suspenders interviewing some dull-eyed teenage rock star. The English was soothing, even though in the morning sunshine, King's makeup looked like a death mask as he kept on agreeing with his adolescent interviewee that youth was the lifeblood of show business. The conversation bounced back and forth between senile and stupid, and Teeple was glad to shut it off when he heard a key in the lock.

Another blond and blue-eyed servant in silks and suede slippers slithered in with a breakfast tray and set the table on the terrace.

"Milk for your coffee, sir? Sugar?" English was the man's mother tongue, and it was all very civilized. The tablecloth was immaculate, the silverware sparkled, the choice of marmalades was extensive, and the croissants were still warm.

A few minutes later, Zyaad walked in without knocking. Again he wore a white suit, single-breasted at this time of day, smelled of rose water, and carried a yellow legal pad under his arm.

"Now then." He looked down on Teeple with a vaguely facetious smile. "Even though you chose not to rise to greet me, I can tell your clothes fit. Consequently," he nodded to the servant to pull a chair so that he could sit with his back to the sun, "considering that your sizes check out, we'll make do with just a spot check on the rest of the basics."

"You call the shots."

"Indeed I do," Zyaad smiled, watching Teeple put a dollop of peach marmalade on his croissant. One more piece of information that checked out: addiction to peach flavor. "Your basic training took place at the Farm, I take it?"

"Most of it." Making sure to speak with his mouth full to bolster the image of a simple cowboy, Teeple gave Zyaad the officially secret location in southern Virginia. It had already been given away in several books written about the CIA by disgruntled employees and converts to peaceful coexistence. "Explosives training was in Georgia, survival in Grace, Idaho, jungle warfare at Fort Sherman in the Panama Canal Zone. Want the exact locations?"

"No, thank you."

It was obvious that Zyaad was anything but a professional interrogator steeped in the latest debriefing methods. His tone was politely conversational, and he kept his hands well away from the yellow notepad he had brought with him, as if he were willing Teeple not to come up with anything he would be forced to write down.

"Your first assignment was where, Mr. Teeple?"

"Paris."

"Your first trip to Europe, I'd imagine? How exciting."

"A dream job."

"A dream job in terms of being able to do your best for your country?"

"I was twenty-five. The asset I was running was just a gofer at the Soviet Embassy, but what did I care. I was happy to be working on my own. In nineteen-seventy-four, the Cold War was going our way and there were not enough senior officers to handle Russian defectors."

"So you also traveled alone?" Zyaad pushed the yellow pad a touch further away. "Without supervision?"

"Without a chaperone, yes; but not alone. My cover was a cocky Yankee with a pocket full of dollars, bringing girlfriends to the City of Light to shop for French lingerie. The dollar was king those days, over five French francs to a greenback."

"How much did your Russian source get paid?"

"It was not my job to handle payoffs. All I knew was that the man delivered, because I was in Paris every other week."

"Always buying lingerie for the same girlfriend?"

"The rule was never to use the same cover twice."

"Hmm." Zyaad leaned back with a facetious smile, but his voice was serious. "Your uncle was being good to you."

"Who?"

"An uncle on the eleventh floor in Langley. Because a fairy godmother, I dare say, would not be that generous with disposable girlfriends."

"What are you talking about?"

"About a CIA rookie who lucked out in the City of Light. It's hard to believe it happened just like that, isn't it?"

Teeple took his time to butter another croissant. Zyaad was fishing, and refusing to nibble at his bait would not do.

"Had I ever had an uncle in the Firm," he shrugged, "I wouldn't be here today. Nor would I've been sent to Nicaragua after my Russian in Paris was blown. I went from the Champs Élysées straight to a grass hut in the jungle, from French lingerie to combat boots and sweaty fatigues crawling with ticks and leeches."

"Sorry to hear that."

Teeple shrugged. "That wasn't the worst of it. My job in Panama was tracking Communist agitators that jumped off Russian freighters in the Canal Zone to cross to Nicaragua on foot. Instead, I spent most of my time ducking the American press. They loved the Nicaraguan Sandinistas and did their crappy best to blow my cover."

"Was that the reason you broke a fellow countryman's nose?"

"How do you know that?" Slowly, Teeple put down the remainder of his croissant, wiped his fingers on a napkin, and sat back. "I was under the impression I was here to help you fill out your 1040 tax form?"

But Zyaad did not blink. "Your bar-fighting skills might be an indication of how good you are in general."

"In general, tax evasion tricks don't need a tough guy. It's white collar crime. Six months in a resort jail max. What you're leading up to can land me in San Quentin for life."

"Are you asking for a raise?"

"You raised the bar."

"How do I know you can jump that high?" For a moment, Zyaad looked offended, then made peace with speaking to an American. "We'll talk money later."

"When?"

"After you tell me something I don't know. Now," Zyaad frowned at his notepad and, with a sigh, pulled it closer. Back to work. "Did the New York Times ever sue you for the broken nose?"

"I don't know. A day after the bar fight, Operations yanked me out of Nicaragua and tucked me away at a top-secret tracking facility in the South China Sea to keep an eye on the Chinese Navy sneaking around Taiwan."

"Hmm." With another sigh and a frown, Zyaad took out a slim mother-of-pearl pen to make a note. Then he wiped his fingers on a handkerchief and sat back. "A boring task at best, I'd imagine?"

"Slow. Nine out of every ten blips were tourist ferries that could do no more than five knots. They were subsidized by the Chinese government to skirt Taiwan's territorial waters, and every now and then one of them was ordered to cross the line to rattle our cage. The war ships never came closer than twenty miles, the range of their guns."

"In other words, you had plenty of time to keep an eye on the commercial traffic as far as Hong Kong and Singapore."

"I had nothing else to do."

"But then, why particularly there? Why not Manila or Yokohama, or some other place like that? Who told you to zoom in on the Malacca Straits? Your uncle in Langley?"

"Ow, come on."

"I'm listening."

"The Malacca Straits pirates were front-page news those days. The media drooled all over them. Noble fighters for social justice, brave knights of an awakening self-awareness in southeast Asia, that kind of crap. It was my chance to get back at the New York Times for Nicaragua. I had plenty time to learn how to hack into shipping companies' computers to prove that the Malacca Straits pirates were not stealing from the rich to give to the poor. They stole from the rich to give it back to them plus interest plus a pile of laundered cash. I filled half a dozen portable hard drives with copies of letters of credit and phony insurance claims for merchandise presumably stolen from commercial freighters in the Straits."

To accentuate his annoyance with Zyaad's continuous references to an uncle or a fairy godmother on the 11th floor in Langley, Teeple leaned forward to throw his body weight behind putting that kind of nonsense to rest for good.

"Had I ever had that uncle you're hallucinating about, I'd have gotten a medal for the Malacca Straits mess instead of a reprimand for misuse of government hardware to play computer games."

"What happened to the portable hard drives?"

"Government property. They each got an archive number, and I was told that with my fixation on voodoo theories, I would do well on a remote island in the Caribbean instead of the South China Sea."

"Which one?"

"None. Someone in Langley must have looked at my stuff in the meantime, and I was sent to Bosnia-Herzegovina where there was a shooting war going on."

"Are you trying to say that someone was hoping for you to get killed?" Zyaad was being facetious, but Teeple pretended not to notice.

"When that war ended and I was still around, they sent me to the second best place to get shot, Somalia. Plenty of voodoo there, they told me to cover up for the real reason."

"More coffee?" Zyaad pointed to the coffee pot, but made no move to pour it. "Was it in Mogadishu you came across some of the cash that had been laundered in the Malacca Straits?"

"Mog."

"I beg your pardon?"

"That's what Mogadishu is called down there. Mog."

"Is it?" Zyaad watched Teeple thoughtfully for a second, then took a cell phone out of his pocket and punched a key. And, while the phone was dialing a stored number, he got up to go and lean on the railing on the other side of the terrace.

The fog down below the château had thinned out by then, and about half a mile down the mild slope, Teeple could see a group of rooftops. Four of them, fenced in as a package. He could not see the fence mesh at this distance, but the tops of the posts were bent inward, as if they carried barbed wire. They made the place look important.

Also, he could finally see the cows whose bells he had heard the other day. They were grazing in the meadows below the chateau, providing an eerie backdrop for Zyaad's throaty conversation on the phone. He was using different vocal cords in a different language, but the moment he snapped the phone shut, his voice mellowed back into his regular, well-oiled English.

"It's too late in Washington now. We'll have to wait 'til morning to check out the Mogadishu end."

"Do *you* have an uncle in Langley?" Teeple smiled, lamely, but Zyaad did not smile back.

He ignored underlings' jokes as a rule. Laughing along with hired help bred familiarity that never amounted to anything but slackness. He just picked up his yellow pad with the single, solitary note and abruptly rose to his feet.

They broke for lunch, and after Zyaad left, someone again locked the door from the outside.

19

The following morning, there was no fog in the valley below the chateau. The clouds were high and it was raining. Teeple could hear cow bells, but could not see the cows huddled under trees in the rain.

A couple of veiled women in black habits barged into his room while he was in the shower, and by the time he stepped out with just a towel around his waist and his hair wet, the bed was made and the women watched him like hawks to make sure he was not dripping on the freshly vacuumed carpeting. They wore the same suede slippers like the rest of the servants at the château, and their robes made them look like bats stunned by daylight. They polished the coffee table while Teeple dressed, brushed the armchairs, sprayed perfume, then gathered their brooms and buckets and slunk off.

Zyaad showed up a few minutes later. Again he carried a yellow notepad under an arm, but in deference to the weather, he wore gray and his mood was somber. With a curt nod, he dropped into one of the freshly cleaned armchairs, the one facing away from the light, crossed his legs, and heaved a sigh like a factory worker getting into position at an assembly line. This whole thing was a drag, but he obviously had no one else he could trust to do it right—especially in English.

"All right." He waved Teeple into a chair facing the window. "Where were we?"

"My pay."

"What do you need money for? You have all you need here."

"Do you plan to keep me?"

"Until you earned your keep." Zyaad shrugged. "To date, considering your transportation plus room and board, I'm in the red."

"To date, I haven't been told what I was hired for."

"All comes to him that knows how to wait." Zyaad let out another back-to-the-grind sigh. "That operation in Mog, as you call it, did it have a name?"

"It was given a crypt."

"A what?"

"A cryptonym to use in cable traffic."

"Such as?"

"Apocalypse."

"Were you in charge of Apocalypse?"

"I was it."

"Quite." Zyaad reached for his yellow pad. Teeple was beginning to put out a smoke screen, and he was not happy about that. Deliberate discrepancies and contradictions might force him to take notes. "Haven't you just told me you were sent to Somalia to do penance?"

"Yes."

"Yet your penance got a cryptonym?"

"Yes."

"In other words, instead of doing penance, you found yourself in charge of a top-secret operation."

"Not hardly." Teeple shrugged. "Calling that kind of operation Apocalypse was like doing an undercover probe into McDonald's and calling it Big Mac."

Zyaad smiled a little. He too was no admirer of governmental brain power, but that was neither here nor there. "Did Operations come up with the name?"

"Not by busting a gut over it."

"Hmm." Zyaad took a pen out of a pocket and put it on the pad as if it were a magic wand that would make notes all by itself. "Go on, Mr. Teeple."

"All I know is that a guy from Intelligence happened to take a package tour of the Silk Road with wife and kids. They had a lunch in Taldygorghanin, an old camel rest stop in Uzbekistan some fifty miles before the Chinese border, and he took a family snapshot against an old Red Army depot: a bunch of clapboard shacks run by a handful of sleep-walking Russians in dirty white coats. When he returned to work after his vacation, he showed the picture to his boss, who passed it on to the techs. The techs made enhanced close-ups and determined that now that the Soviet Army no longer controlled a fifty-mile radius around the labs, the padlocks on the shacks could be picked by anyone with access to a hair pin."

"Amazing." Zyaad needed no convincing to believe that government agencies did bizarre things; he had no doubt about that. Yet, goofy shots often find the bull's eye. "In other words, someone came up with a cryptonym that had nothing to do with anything except giving the shop away. Why?"

"Beats me."

"When did Operations give you the name of the Russian mule bringing enriched plutonium from that Taldygorg-something to Somalia?"

"I told you, Operations didn't know beans. All they had were blow-ups of rusty padlocks. The Russian mule's name I got from a gardening interest group from Michigan, a bunch of old ladies who were in Somalia to turn the Sahara nomads into water-well builders and lettuce growers. The old ladies were hell bent on teaching them to eat vitamin-rich food and live in peace with their neighbors. They just could not believe their ears when the naughty roaming men told them they spat on lettuce and had no intention of living in peace with nobody. They had the bomb and could kill anybody anytime they damned pleased. The old ladies were shocked and wrote about it to their congressman, whose aide passed it on to Langley. It eventually landed in Operations, and a couple of months later, I was ordered to look into the rumor."

"Was your source still in place down there?"

"That was the problem. The old ladies came down with diarrhea in the meantime. It put a damper on feeling noble in a developing country, and they left before I showed up. My luck was that one of them had a niece at the local UN Mission, who put me in touch with people who knew people who thought something funny was going on. A red-headed albino by the name of Kropotkin, an ex-KGB hit man, who had been hiding in Somalia for years, was suddenly coming to life in the Bakara Market—an A-1 retail outlet for the big trade in arms, drugs, women, you name it. There were precedents of human rights abuse there, so I got the nod from Langley to go ahead and spend a small fortune on videotaping Kropotkin's hangout. Operations figured that in a case like this, should CNN start screaming about an invasion of privacy, a sob story about a violation of some poor sucker's human rights would get even the CIA off the hook. Other than that, it was just a long shot in the dark. The asset I used to smuggle in a camera was iffy at best, the rathole had just candle light, and the only 400 ISO film I could get down there was a couple of years past expiration date."

"Yet," Zyaad smiled conversationally, "I'm told you got a Hollywood quality movie out of it."

"Kodak came through. The film was still good, and when I saw the playback, I thought some joker slipped me a copy of a TV sitcom. Real artistic stuff—a flicker of a candle, a freckled hand shoving aside a camel blanket over a hole in a wall, a huffing and puffing white guy lugging in a banged-up suitcase tied with a rope. Kropotkin.

"His matted red hair was wet, and his sweat was dripping on the lid of the suitcase as he untied the knots. There were half a dozen steel cylinders inside, about six inches in diameter each, and the way he took them out one by one, they seemed damned heavy for their size. But the buyer, a big black guy in a Playboy T-shirt and jogging pants, was pretty cool about it. He offered $1,000 American for the lot, and Kropotkin went ballistic.

"'You goddamned stupid or something?'

"'Stupid because I no buy cat in bag?'

"'You buy atomic bombs, damn it.'

"'The which you say to me.'

"'The which you look see for yourself, if you can read.' Kropotkin was pushing his luck. The little Russian looked like a starved rat in front of the black guy, an old pro who would get a bigger kick out of slitting a throat rather than acquiring weapons of mass destruction, but he did not care. He was so mad that he grabbed the big guy by the Playboy logo on his T-shirt and pulled him down to look at the engravings in the bottom of the cylinder.

"'Write it down, damn it.'

"'Write the what?'

"'The specs.'

"'Huh?'

"'The fucking numbers, engraved in fucking carbon hardened steel, idiot. Write it down. Does your customer have the equipment to check it out?'

"But the big guy could neither read nor write and was getting real mad. 'My customer has more equipment than you dream.'

"'No kidding.'

"'My customer has millions, you asshole.'

"'Oh, yeah?'

"'Yeah.'

"'You're making it up.'

"'Making the what?'

"'You're lying.'

"'You're lying, you bare ass sucker.'

"'Up yours.'

"'My customer owns a bank.'

"'And I own the world.'

"'You own not a pot to piss on. My customer owns the Emirates Bank.'"

Teeple fell silent and Zyaad tapped his notepad with the blunt end of his pen.

"Have you doctored the tape?"

"Didn't have to. The original soundtrack was good enough."

"How clear were the words Emirates Bank?"

"As clear as the rest," Teeple shrugged. "Am I getting worth whatever it is you plan to pay me?"

Zyaad returned Teeple's stare absently, then heaved a sigh. "What is it you want?"

"Five hundred thousand. U.S. dollars."

"Hmm." Zyaad suppressed a yawn. "Might sound like a lot to you. It's hardly worth arguing to me."

"Then we have no problem."

"You'll get your money."

"When?"

"What else do you know about the Emirates Bank?" Zyaad was drawing a succession of little circles on his notepad now. When he got to the end of the line, he put the pen down to survey the damage the doodling had done to his hands. There was an ink stain on one of his fingers, and he took a silk handkerchief out of a pocket to wipe it.

"Was the name Blewitt mentioned on that tape," he said, rubbing his finger.

"Who?"

"You know who I am talking about."

"No."

"Right." Zyaad put the silk handkerchief back in his pocket, gathered his notepad, got up, and left the room.

Teeple expected to hear the door being locked on the outside as usual, but nothing happened. The latch stayed put, and he went to the window. There was no one in sight all the way down the barracks at the foot of the hill, and he waited a few minutes before he tried the door.

It was not locked. It opened on well-oiled hinges, and there was no one behind it.

On one side, the empty corridor led to a staircase; on the other it ended with a stained glass door that let in daylight. It was not locked either, and as Teeple sneaked through it into the open, he thought he should have made a note of the name Zyaad had mentioned just before he left. But he was not going back just to write it down. He had to remember it.

Blewitt.

20

After old Joe Fitch called him my boy over breakfast in bed, Buzz Blewitt started doing what was expected of him by seeking anonymity among the riffraff.

He called France from a phone booth at a gas station in Sunland, a small blue-collar town 20 miles east of Malibu, where no one connected to the Fitch family would ever be suspected of hanging out. Old Joe sometimes flew over the place on his way back from a meeting with the governor in Sacramento, but that was it. Blewitt was safe here and let the French phone at the other end of the line toot-toot without bothering to look over his shoulder.

In Paris, in a carelessly furnished apartment overlooking the elegant Jardine de Luxembourg, Jacque Petain answered the Sunland call as soon as she located her phone under a pile of newspapers and magazines on her coffee table. She heard coins drop into a public call box in America and brightened up. Her suitcase was packed.

"*Oui?*"

"What *wee*?" Blewitt muttered stupidly for the record and for good measure banged on the phone casing to get his coins back—a confused old man who had called Paris instead of a cousin in Bakersfield.

At the Paris end, Jacque hung up and went to freshen up her makeup in a none too clean bathroom. She had no maid. There were piles of notes and drafts of political commentaries all over the place, some more sensitive than others, but none to be handled by hired hands. She had to cut corners in homemaking, but would not consider shortcuts in doing her face. She took her time brushing on mascara while she called her pilot on the bathroom speaker phone to tell him to get his ass to the airport on the double. Then, putting on lipstick, she called a very unlisted number at the Château de la Bataille de Poitiers.

"Salut," she said when Dr. Walid El Zyaad himself picked up at the other end. "I'm on my way."

Her simple statement of fact set off a torrent of effusive praise for such welcome news, and by the time she could get a word in, her lipstick was on and she began brushing on lip gloss. It required stiff lips, yet she had no problem putting a feeling into her voice. "Of course, Walid. Yes . . . oh yes . . . me too."

From the toiletry cabinet, she picked a perfume bottle marked WEZ, Walid El Zyaad, dropped it in her handbag, grabbed a designer leather jacket out of a chaotic closet, pushed the pre-packed suitcase with a foot out into the hallway, turned on the security system, and locked the door behind her.

Out in the street, she hailed a taxi.

"The airport," she told the driver. "Orly."

The man gave her a casual glance over his shoulder as she struggled with her suitcase into the backseat, and she assumed he failed to recognize her either because she was out of breath or because he was a foreigner. There were very few Frenchmen who would not know her regular voice.

Jacque Petain was the voice of France. Her vocal chords had the ideal frequency range for even the most sensitive sound equalizers, while the right makeup in the right lighting would have a camera lens interpret her high cheekbones and aquiline nose as classic beauty. She was a TV producer's dream, perfect for screens of any size, format and definition, home or business.

Her family came to France from Palestine when she was just four years old. They had left the chaos of public funerals and street marches in Ramala in the middle of the night, with just a stray dog barking after them as they drove a stolen car to Beirut. There they squeezed with several hundreds of other refugees onto a rusty freighter with one toilet, and, inevitably, the Greek coast guard picked up their smell the moment they got near Cyprus. They were turned away at gunpoint, but a few days later they got lucky. Just as they ran out of drinking water, they managed to sneak into Malta from the north, knowing that the Maltese navy had their hands full with African rowboat refugees from the south.

For almost a year, the family was hiding in the slums of Apalea that were not that much different from home. They lived on charity and whatever the father made in odd jobs, mostly at night, until they saved enough to buy a forged weekend pass to Corsica, from where a hop to the French mainland was no big deal. They arrived in Marseille by a regular ferry, and once they stood with their two feet and two cardboard boxes each in front of the Ferry Terminal on Quai D'Arenc, they would not look back.

They made straight for the ghetto on the hillside above the harbor, where sewers ran in open gutters in crooked streets impassable to police cars and too dangerous for policemen on foot. For months they slept on rags and flattened cardboard boxes in stinky rooms without windows, while the father worked night shifts. The family's ultimate goal was America; but forged entry visa into the land of dreams did not come cheap, and the father had to work longer and longer hours, until the night he dragged himself home with a bullet hole in his chest and choked on his own blood by dawn.

Jacque was five then. Her mother took on jobs cleaning houses for rich Arabs who lived outside the ghetto, dispersed among regular middle-class French, and eventually she began to earn enough to rent a room with a window in the slums. But since she would not consider it an option to stop wearing a headscarf, she did not dare to take the Metro where policemen would ask women like her for papers. So, while her mother was either working or walking between jobs, Jacque—or Fatima, as she was called then—roamed the slums with all kinds of neighborhood kids who spoke all kinds of Arabic.

Some of the cleaner and less violent children had a TV at home, and she picked those as her best friends. She would absorb the sound from television speakers like a sponge, and by the time she was eight, she could switch from Arabic to French and back with remarkable ease and fluency. Her mother did not know what to make of that and asked the local imam for help. She did not want her daughter, she told the holy man, to sit on two cushions on the infidel's floor. The imam declared Jacque's linguistic skills to be a gift from Allah, the righteous and compassionate, and spoke about it to the local muktar, who in turn spread the word in the upper echelons of the Arab community. The word got all the way to Château de la Bataille de Poitiers, and at the beginning of the next school year, Fatima was provided with a French ID card that rolled her age back by two years so that she could enter a regular French school as a regular six-year-old.

Important men, including Dr. Walid El Zyaad, kept an eye on her progress from then on, and the local imam was ordered to give her mother permission to send her to school without a headscarf and to call herself Jacque.

By the time she was 10, the new name stuck, and at the age of 16—14 according to her official ID card—Jacque married a rock-band stage hand by the name of Petain, who had learned all there was to know about underage girls from his employers. He ordered Jacque to get in a bath tub and dye her hair in all the right places, and the shock of seeing her come out of the bathroom naked, wet and blonde all over, got him thinking. She sure was a piece of work. So, when a bunch of ugly, untalented punks like the rock band he worked for could make zillions, why not his wife. He spoke about her to a stage hand at the local TV station, whose wife knew the wife of someone in casting, and Jacque was given a screen test.

The test was routinely filed in a talent bank, from where a year or so later, a computer picked her to stand in for a vacationing weather man on the low-rated midday news—which was a lucky break. The rest was the will of Allah.

The weather report on her first day on the job was the best thing the people of Marseille had heard in a long time: a spell of spring-like weather was passing through the south of France in midsummer, and Jacque had nothing but the most pleasant temperatures and low humidity to predict. And, by the will of Allah, the day the regular meteorologist returned from his vacation, the weather turned hot and muggy as usual. The station was inundated with angry phone calls, unflattering mail and threats to stop paying the TV levy. Women's magazines picked up the story as a proof of a finer female feeling for weather and nature in general, and afternoon talk show hosts had a new heroine.

Jacque Petain became an instant local celebrity. A prominent marketing consultant was sent down from Paris to help manage the Marseille station's soaring sales of commercial time, and the local imam gave Jacque's mother permission for her daughter to have an extramarital affair. Jacque had no problem bedding the marketing consultant. She moved with him to Paris, and shortly after her 21st birthday, she did her first prime-time weather on a national network.

She was making plenty money by then, so her lawyer had no problem to hammer out an agreement with her estranged husband. She was to keep her married name, and he was to get paid to keep his mouth shut about her sleeping around.

After years of hiding in windowless basements, life in the sun became an obsession with Jacque. She had no scruples about any end justifying any means and soon became known for getting hard news before anyone else—a talent that came with the reputation of an unscrupulous bitch. Her name became a household word all over France, so no eyebrows were raised when she began dating important men. Her editors had 24 hours of news to deliver every single uneventful day, and since international terrorism was becoming an issue in Europe just then, it seemed quite natural that she should focus on dating senior officials in the DGSE, Direction Générale du Surveillance Extérieure, and the DST, the French Internal Service. She would often arrive on the scene of an antiterrorist razzia before the government assault teams, and suspicious minds began to dig into her background. She was in the ideal position to pass hunters' secrets to the hunted before she dropped them off on her news-starved editor's desk. But her defense was iron clad. As an upstanding member of the journalistic profession, she stood for the public's right to know.

To plain folks, Jacque Petain was a hero. To her critics, she was as unscrupulous as the rest of her colleagues, while to her bosses she was a guarantee of soaring advertising revenues. She would volunteer for assignments in all kinds of hot spots, often circling the globe in a couple of days or less. She could appear on the evening news in dusty hiking boots, ducking ricocheting bullets in the Hindu-Kush, while the morning news would show her in a low-cut cocktail gown smooching with Hollywood superstars.

So, a quick domestic outing in a single-engine Cesna was nothing to get worked up about. There was no secret police or paparazzi to watch her take off in a small, conventional plane from just a secondary runway at Orly.

21

Walking fast but not running down the grassy slope towards the cinder-block barracks, Teeple heard a single engine plane coming in for a landing somewhere on the other side of the chateau. He could not be bothered to search the sky for it. After sneaking out of a room that should have been locked, it was common sense to assume he was here on borrowed time, and his first priority was to watch where he stepped. The meadow was still wet from the rain the other day, and he had already slipped a few times on slick, clay-like mud.

Besides, the plane seemed to have landed by the time he was close enough to the barracks to figure out the fence. No mesh, no barbed wire. The concrete fence posts were bare and free standing, with just two small round openings per post, and he had to get even closer to make sure there were no laser beams to trip. It seemed that the lenses in the openings in the posts were merely harmless surveillance cameras, and he stuck a finger into one just as the plane on the other side of the chateau began taxing on the ground. He heard the change in the pitch of the plane engine—just as he heard footsteps right behind his back.

He smelled clothes soaked with cigarette and barbecue smoke and imagined a surly guard who had been dragged away from an after-lunch smoke to deal with him. He expected to see a mad-as-hell face, but when he turned around, all he saw was a fist coming at him.

He knew he was going down, but it was too late to do something about it; then all was still. The plane somewhere out there had finally come to a full stop.

* * *

When Jacque's pilot shut off the engine at the end of the simple airstrip at Château de la Bataille de Poitiers, a waiting golf cart sneaked closer and respectfully stopped below the cockpit on the passenger side. There were no paparazzi on Dr. Walid El Zyaad's closely guarded private grounds to document the great Jacque Petain's arrival, and even if there were, no one would have dared to entertain dark thoughts about her purpose out here. A celebrity of her caliber, who had appeared on television with the likes of Jacques Chirac, Bill Clinton and Princess Diana, would be above suspicion even if she were seen copulating with the Devil in the middle of St. Peter's Square at the Vatican.

The white golf cart took her from the landing strip to the chateau, where Dr. Zyaad was waiting in his private drawing room, all dressed up for the occasion. He wore his favorite Wahabi robe that made him feel particularly good. The gold-braided head dress concealed his receding hairline, and when Jacque walked in, he sprung to his feet with the ardor of a man endowed with the kind of hair he had always dreamed of. He had been smoking a water pipe, and the bubble in the crania of his skull was pulling him upwards, making him feel as if his feet were hardly touching the floor.

"Greetings, my roaming swallow." He spread his robes to embrace her, almost knocking down an open laptop on the coffee table.

"*Salut*, Walid," she nodded curtly to hold him down to earth.

"*Salut*, Emissary of Happiness." Zyaad gathered his robes

with one hand and, ignoring the laptop on the table, used the other to steer Jacque towards the adjoining bedroom. Along the way, he took one more quick pull on the pipe and exhaled dreamily to the ceiling. "Let us fly . . ."

He squeezed Jacque's shapely buttocks to push her inside the bedroom and, starting to undress on the go, he slammed the door shut behind him with his heel.

By the time they returned to the sitting room, barefooted and wearing just bathrobes, the laptop on the coffee table had gone into standby. Zyaad restarted it, and while the operating system was coming out of hibernation, he restarted his water pipe — an ancient invention that could be brought to life faster than the latest Microsoft software.

It gave him time for a couple of pulls before a slide show came to life on the computer screen. Pictures of ancient weaponry began scrolling in two-second intervals against an interposed neutral background, and Jacque's frown deepened with every new item. It was a catalog of artifacts dug out by a team of archeologists in the rolling meadows in the vicinity of the château, where a crucial battle between Christianity and Islam had taken place 1,300 years ago. She could imagine what the heinous instruments of death and mutilation, looking so harmless on a computer screen, could do to a human body on a blood-drenched battlefield, and Zyaad watched her with a whimsical smile.

"You disapprove?"

"Just the gore." Jacque shook her head in disgust at a picture of an axe with a blade artfully curved for the sole purpose of not jamming in bone marrow or between spine vertebrae.

With a smug smile, Zyaad punched a fast forward key on the keyboard to bring on a picture of a Neptune-like three-prong fork. There was a contemporary matchbox next to it for comparison, making the fork look mercifully small, almost cute, and Zyaad, feeling Jacque relax, slipped his hand behind her back.

"I want you to show this particular item on the evening news. It's a surgical instrument dating back to when the Christians around here used leeches as a cure for all." He moved his hand further down her back, but, with a crucial PR job on hand, he made do with merely pinching her buttock.

"Cut it out." Jacque pushed his hand away to follow the computer slide show. The photos were numbered, and soon the numbers went into three digits. "How many items total?"

"Enough."

"And the archeologists?"

"Big names from the Sorbonne, Yale and Harvard, all of them amply rewarded for their expertise." Zyaad smiled at her knee that slipped through the opening in her bathrobe as she leaned forward to have a closer look at the next slide: a saber with a gold handle covered with sapphires and rubies. "You like?"

"No."

"Might've belonged to the Emir himself."

"I still don't like it."

"The spark in your eyes tells me otherwise." Zyaad could eat this beautiful, clever girl. "Your eyes tell me you shall put your heart into bringing these artifacts to the attention of the public."

"Only because you insist."

"My lawyers need a platform to destroy the myth of a Christian victory in the Battle of Poitiers, a lie that French children are being brainwashed with in schools. We have to prove beyond the shadow of a doubt that Emir Abdul Rahman Al Ghafiqi's withdrawal was not the result of a military defeat, but his disdain for medieval Europe."

"You're pushing it, Walid."

"We must prove beyond the shadow of a doubt that the Emir could not stand the barbarians and their weather. The Christians themselves put the date of the battle on October 10. And you know how vile and ghastly the autumn can be around here. Before central heating, France must've been fit for no one but savages."

"Oh, man . . ." Jacque leaned back and closed her eyes. Zyaad was on his favorite subject, and there was no way to shut him up. The best she could do was to point out the folly of his obsession and zealotry. "I can't believe I am in this conversation; and I can't believe the trip you are on."

"Because you have doubts about me? Or is it because of your doubts about Europe being ripe for conquest now that central heating and electricity made it habitable?"

"Ow, shut up."

"I wish I could, if only to please you."

"You're out of your mind, Walid. The council will never accept your theory that the best way for *dar al-Islam* to forget America and focus on Europe is to make *dar al-Harb* prevail the easy way?"

"America is breaking under its own weight, my love. That continent is relegated to wretched mediocrity by its own doing."

"And if not?"

"Do I detect concern in the world-famous voice?"

"Nothing will happen to me if you're wrong, you know that."

"And I do thank Allah for it."

"Don't do it, Walid."

There was a knock on the door and a man in a black jumpsuit stumbled in, not sure where to look. He was very young, a boy really, acutely uncomfortable in an atmosphere charged with perfume, sex and adult depravity, and he spilled the beans right by the door.

"Trouble, effendi."

Zyaad frowned, but it was too late to shut the boy up without making Jacque more jumpy than she already was.

"Speak."

"The American man Teeple."

"Yes?"

"Tried to break into the barracks. The guards have him."

"Then what's the problem?" Zyaad dismissed the stammering boy with a fatherly smile and turned to Jacque to explain. "No need for alarm, my love. I sent the archeologists home a week ago."

"What about the old women, are they still there?"

"Don't worry about them."

"I asked if they are still in the barracks?"

"Yes."

"You *aaare* nuts, Walid."

"Doesn't that make me lovable?"

"I am serious."

"Your eyes sparkle when you are serious," Zyaad slid his hand under her bathrobe, "and you're irresistible when your eyes sparkle."

"Ow, please." Jacque stood up and went to the window to stare at the barracks at the foot of the hill. From up here, she saw no sign of the old women inside and could only hope that neither had the intruder. "Who is he?"

"No need to put a wrinkle into your forehead because of him, my love."

"Forget a wrinkle. I'll be putting my reputation on the line."

"And the old ladies thank you for it with all their hearts. You should see them down there, busy like the bees painting placards, competing for the best slogan to portray Islam as a religion of peace and tolerance. The first prize is hip surgery. For I need my army strong and sound."

Zyaad stood up and went to the window to seek reassurance and inspiration in the sight of the ancient battlefield out there.

"In the replay of the Battle of Poitiers, there will be no emirs fighting kings, no kings fighting emirs. The outcome of that battle will rest in the hands of silly little people who wield the power to topple silly little governments of the people for the people at the ballot box. It is disheartening to me to hear so many good men on the council demanding to fight the mother of all battles the old-fashioned way with bullets, rockets and nuclear explosives. That kind of victory parade will lead over scorched land."

"The council is convinced it's the one and only way."

"Are you?"

"All I know is that the majority on the council will stop at nothing to silence you. And I mean not just by making you shut up."

"Nothing but the will of Allah will make me shut up." Zyaad lapsed into an unguarded moment of sadness, and she came to sit by him on the sofa.

"I told you, you are crazy, Walid?"

"Because I love you?"

"That too." She let her knee slide out of the opening of her bathrobe all the way to cheer him up. Fine hair was beginning to show from the knee up, but she was not going to worry about that now. He never wore his prescription glasses in her presence and was not likely to notice that she'd have needed waxing before coming here. "Promise me just one thing, Walid."

"Anything."

"For the thousandth time, read the Koran again tonight. Read once more about *dar al-Islam*, the House of Islam, being destined to conquer *dar al-harb*, the rest of the world. That's what the council lives by."

"So?"

"So come off it."

"Have I spoken like a fool?"

"Just sounded like one."

"Have I said I question the wisdom of *Sura* that commands us to kill the unbelievers wherever we find them? Never. I never said that and I never will. I am merely trying to point out that the Koran does not mention any particular means to justify such ends in the times you and I live in."

"Are you going to try to convince the Council that we can make do with . . . with . . ."

"With an army of hags and witches?" Zyaad opened the bathrobe over her thigh a touch higher and, as she had expected, had not noticed the fine hair on her silky skin. He was into poetry now. "In a world gone berserk with the sappy notion of democracy, hags and witches at a ballot box are equal to the most valiant warriors on a sacred battlefield."

Zyaad was kneeling in front of her now, opening her bathrobe all the way. "Democracy, my love, is nothing but a breeding ground for mediocrity. A ground that can only be conquered with mediocre means."

"Amen." With a sigh, Jacque made one last attempt. The man had done so much for her since she was a little girl. "Do it for me, Walid. For my sake, forget this nonsense?"

"Are you asking me to forget reaching for the stars with my bare hands?" Gently, Zyaad pushed her knees apart, and she leaned back and closed her eyes. She had known him so well, a man who had been born into a position where other men kissed his hand. That was normal to him. He wanted more; he wanted to drive the men that kissed his hand insane with envy for getting his nose between the thighs of a woman that the rest of the world could only drool over on a TV screen. He was not complicated. He was simple; but he was also tenacious—and as such, Jacque was beginning to believe, he might have a chance to pull off something that less simple-minded men would consider stupid.

22

Jacque's plane took off at first light, and Zyaad showed up at his mahogany paneled office shortly afterwards. Her perfume was still lingering in his nostrils, and he had to pull himself together to focus on the handwritten note on his gilded desk.

To hell with Teeple, he decided as he read it and called in his secretary.

"Just give me the bottom line." On a morning like this, Zyaad's attention span was more than volatile and his patience paper thin. "Did Teeple actually set foot in the barracks? Talk to any of the old women in there?"

"Internal security would not lean on him hard without your approval, effendi."

"How does he look?"

"Our people performed their duty by the book. His wounds are superficial."

With the memory of Jacque's limbs and lips still permeating his senses, the last thing Zyaad wanted was to face a man smeared with blood. "Give him a bath and a clean shirt before you bring him over."

The secretary bowed and backed out, and Zyaad sat back to let his thoughts stray back to the promise Jacque had whittled out of him in the wee hours of the morning: trust no one, including herself. She had refused to put herself above suspicion for his sake, and his heart flooded with admiration of his own integrity, for he was not naive. He would never close his eyes to people's weaknesses just so that he could see them in a more flattering light, far from it. But if a man could not trust a woman in love, then whom? She was . . . oh . . . Magnificent — a lioness with the heart of a nightingale.

Smiling, Zyaad dozed off in his chair and needed a few moments to bend his thoughts back to the mundane facts of life when they brought Teeple in — looking better than expected. The only visible damage was a purple welt under an eye and a cut lip, still swollen but no longer bleeding.

"How did that happen?" Zyaad asked matter-of-factly.

"Somebody didn't want me to get close to the fenced-in barracks down the hill," Teeple shrugged.

"Fenced in? My workers have no intention to join the unions." Zyaad intended to fake a yawn, but it came quite naturally. After 24 hours in and out of bed with the voice of France, the effort of bending his thoughts to fences and cinder-block barracks made him feel dead beat. "Also, Mr. Teeple, as you most likely found out, there's nothing worth stealing out there."

"I wouldn't know about that." Teeple looked sullenly out of the window. In the front yard, men in green aprons were working on the flower beds around the fountain, digging out all the red and yellow flowers to replace them with blue and white ones. "Your gardeners, do they live in the barracks?"

"No." Zyaad watched Teeple thoughtfully for a moment, then decided that the man had seen nothing. "No, Mr. Teeple; the gardeners do not live in the barracks. No one does."

"Why the fence then?"

"A fence?"

"An electronic one."

"Hmm." Outside the window behind Zyaad's back, a sudden gust of wind drove a fine spray from the fountain over the gardeners' bent backs, and Zyaad raised his hands to his temples. "The wind's from the south. You know what that means?"

"What?"

"A splitting headache." Zyaad said something to Teeple's guards, then explained in English. "I told them to have my hairdresser put something on your eye."

The guards took Teeple away, and Zyaad sat back to watch the wind bend trees in the courtyard. With Jacque's unspoken confidence in his lucky streak still fresh in his mind, it seemed reasonable to assume that Teeple had seen nothing in the barracks and no change of plans was necessary. So, until the south wind died down, all he needed was just a couple of aspirins and plenty rest.

* * *

The wind blew for the rest of the afternoon and at night it whistled in the roof gutters and flapped the trim of the window awnings. It died down before sunrise, though, and Zyaad looked much better when he showed up in Teeple's room right after breakfast as usual.

He brought with him his hairdresser to freshen up the makeup on Teeple's purple eye. Then he suggested a walk. The morning was clear and fresh, with white clouds drifting slowly in a powder-blue sky, and they walked down the sloping lawn towards the cinder-block barracks, dressed in suits, starched white shirts and neckties.

The ground was not slippery any more. The south wind had dried it out, and when they passed the spot where Teeple had been knocked down by the guard the day before, there were no visible traces of blood anywhere. The trampled grass had recovered overnight, and Zyaad let him come as close to the barracks as he had been on his own the day before. And again it was impossible to tell whether someone lived in there or not. Behind the windows that he could see, nothing seemed to be moving.

"Archeologists used to stay here, piecing together a fascinating story for me," Zyaad said, turning to lead the way towards the open country, doing the talking for a change. "Let me show you."

They walked side by side down a two-rut path through the meadows, away from the barracks and the chateau. The sun was in and out of clouds, and every time a shadow moved in, the air turned chilly. Swallows kept on swishing low over the grass, swerving at the last moment so as not to bump into the men's legs, but Zyaad was not amused by the daredevil antics. He had a brooding, faraway look in his pensive, dark eyes.

At the bottom of a shallow valley before them, a narrow stream snaked through clusters of bushes and trees, and Zyaad pointed to the opposite hillside. In the crisp, clear air they could see it with amazing clarity.

"Thirteen hundred years ago, the French King stood up there, left of the pine grove on the crest of the hill. Twenty thousand men, ten deep, shoulder to shoulder. A mile wide front. The Emir's army was where we stand now, twice as strong as the King's and four times as willing to fight, aware that the Christians were trembling in their boots.

"The Emir had conquered Spain earlier that year and his reputation preceded him. The local bards compared his fury and cruelty in battle to a raging tiger, and the French King got to believe it when he heard of the spoils of war the Emir had carried across the Pyrenees. Wagonloads of silk, silver, pottery, gold . . . pots of gold."

Zyaad paused to reflect on ancient commodity prices, then leveled a derogatory finger at the opposite hill.

"The French King was broke. His horsemen were no match for the Emir's, his raggedy foot soldiers were sheep ripe for slaughter, but he was in luck. On the eve of the battle, there had been no moon. So, under the cover of a near-perfect darkness, the King sent his inferior cavalry around the Emir's camp to the back where the gold was stored. At first light, while the two armies faced one another across the stream at the bottom of the valley, French horsemen attacked the Emir's treasures in the rear, and the front-line soldiers were horrified by the Christian guile. They were proud men. They broke ranks on the battlefield to run back to protect the spoils of previous battles, letting the French come down the hill and fall on deplorably depleted defenses."

Zyaad fell silent for a moment to let Teeple's imagination work on hearing a medieval army thundering down the opposite hillside, waving spears and axes. In his own mind, the stage was set to perfection. So the sudden interference of a 20th-century automobile engine was highly improper. It came from the far end of the valley, where an ungainly gray truck had just rounded a bend and kept on laboring up the narrow, winding road towards the château.

Two more trucks appeared, and Zyaad reluctantly turned his back on the ancient battlefield before them.

"We go back now."

He sounded saddened by the untimely interruption that had forced the specters of a brave, penniless King and a ruthless rich Emir to dissolve back into the pages of history books to make room for whatever was coming at him in this life.

23

Ten thousand miles away and way out of earshot, the rumble of unidentified gray trucks on a bright, sunny morning at the Château de la Bataille de Poitiers had nothing to do with the din of a helicopter with California registration markings that was flying old Joe Fitch into a crimson sunset over the Pacific.

The old man was coming home from a working lunch with the governor in Sacramento, and over the parched slopes of the Santa Monica Mountains, the chopper took a couple of rough jolts. After a scorcher of a day, the hot updraft was unpredictable where it met the cool evening air from the ocean, and the pilot humbly apologized for the arrogance of the elements into the intercom.

"Are you comfortable, Mr. Fitch, sir?"

He hated flying the old man. The family doctors would come down on him like a ton of brick every time the boss insisted on getting into a chopper, and so would the family lawyers. A man of old Joe's age did not belong in a flying object. An air pocket could rearrange the brittle bones in a way no surgeon would ever be able to sort out. The pilot knew that better than anyone, and it made him bitter to have people yell at him just because they would not dare to stand up to the old man themselves.

Yet at the moment, the old man looked impishly happy in his special bucket seat as they cleared the hills and the lights of the sprawling shopping malls and real estate developments of Malibu appeared down below. Most of those were owned by local construction companies controlled by an incorporated movie studio that was a small part of a mammoth, multinational concern financed by the Emirates Bank of Riyadh.

It had taken Joe Fitch half a century to develop a financial model that was not taught at business schools, and he was not ready to break it all up just because it might spoil his son's chances in the upcoming presidential elections. From the business point of view, as a piece of property, the White House was a pauper accommodation in comparison with the real estate values below the jittery helicopter.

Some of the beach houses down there were being bought and sold for obscene amounts of cash as no bank in its right mind would lend that kind of money to the Hollywood crowd. None of his own banks for sure, old Joe grinned happily as the pilot banked to the north over the world-famous Malibu Colony. The grossly overpriced beach houses of the silver-screen superheroes and heroines were crammed so close together that their famous owners could read not only the marmalade labels on their famous neighbors' breakfast tables, but also the screenplays and casting contracts on their bedside tables.

The Fitch estate was a couple of helicopter minutes further north, where beachfront property owners were past the need of spying on their neighbors. They were old money who got their information from the old-boy network, and Joe had no illusions about them. He knew they would rather stick their little fingers into a revolving door than to throw their weight behind his son. They were the part of America he had written off, and he would encourage his pilot to fly low over their rooftops. It made him feel good to rattle the ornate old china in the old farts' cupboards, and he was most pleased now to see a bunch of media vans camped in front of his imported 16th-century English gate. Nothing would tick off his neighbors more than a bunch of leftist hacks so close to home.

His meeting with the governor today was hot news. The man hated the Fitches with a passion and a vengeance. For years he had called the their philanthropic concern for the poor a front for a blatant abuse of human intelligence, and tonight he had even started the dinner with a joke about the Fitches' ostentatious handouts that made the poor kiss their hands and hate their guts. So, it had been in self-defense that Joe struck back, reminding the governor of the Fitch family's pull with the trade unions that could shut down California key industries in time for the next elections. By the time the dessert was served, California peaches in Napa Valley port, the governor was all smiles and bows, and old Joe decided to have Richard break the story about the man's about face to the media in the morning. It would give the usual teams of TV wizards a whole night to build up to the upcoming announcement. And, most importantly, the media mob in front of the Fitch estate gate was going to stay put all night and drive the neighbors crazy by urinating on their lawns and crapping in their bushes—for there was no way they could do that on the Fitch property.

It had an eight-foot wall all around its 13 acres, the exact size of the grounds of the Windsor Castle in England, and the house itself was a replica of the original castle's residential apartments built by Edward III. The helipad was in a spacious back courtyard, which in the original royal version had been designed by the secretive Charles II, and in old Joe's 20th-century adaptation was out of reach of even the most powerful tele-lenses.

Wolsley, the butler, was waiting near the landing marker, bowing his white head to both the approaching rotor blades and the arriving master. A green-aproned footman lurked in the background to take care of the luggage, and a starched nurse stood close by with a wheelchair.

Gently and with infinite care, the nurse and the butler scooped the master out of his bucket seat and transferred him in one piece into the wheelchair. He seemed rather peppy today, and the nurse no sooner put a blanket over his knees than he sent her packing. He nodded to Wolsley to grab the push bar behind his back.

"Is Blewitt in yet?" he said when the nurse was out of earshot.

"Yes, sir."

"Damn." Old Joe bit his lip as Wolsley pushed the wheelchair onto the brick pathway towards the house. He could feel every single joint between the bricks. But he went back to normal breathing the moment they reached the smooth, Florentine mosaic floor in the entry hall, and Wolsley seized the opportunity to please.

"I took the liberty of setting up a table outside to take your evening pills, sir," he said, drawing a deep breath of the mild evening air to make the idea especially appealing. The temperature was just right for the master to sit on the terrace with a blanket over his knees.

"Good thinking," old Joe nodded, making Wolsley beam with pride.

"Will you see Mr. B now, sir?"

It had been a purely rhetorical question, for Blewitt was already on the terrace, standing by the baroque railing and looking troubled, and Joe Fitch was not one to stand on ceremony.

"What's up, Buzz?"

"It's Zyaad, sir." Buzz Blewitt waited with the rest until the butler was gone. He was taking no chances, even with a hearing-impaired case. "The man's hell-bent on doing his thing."

"Is he?" Old Joe did not seem overly concerned. "What's the bad news?"

"I don't understand, sir." The wrinkles on Blewitt's troubled forehead deepened. This was not the time for reckless bravado. The next move was going to separate bold risk takers from impulsive gamblers, yet the master appeared as unconcerned as a child in a sandbox. He was actually smiling.

"Having the jitters, Buzz?"

Out over the ocean, the moon had a misty halo, a harbinger of bad weather, but Joe Fitch was not superstitious even on the eve of a damned risky move. He had made plenty of those over the years, and they no longer gave him sleepless nights. An old gambler's safety was in his knack for delegating risk, and old Joe would not stop smiling at the ominous halo of the moon while talking to Blewitt.

"Are you thinking of hedging our bets?"

"Possibly. There's a woman involved."

"Zealous and ugly?"

"On the contrary. She used to be romantically involved with your son as well as with a man by the name of Teeple, who . . ."

"Who I'm sure is no one I know." Old Joe had heard enough. Petty complications and inconvenient detail were the kind of nuisance he had been paying Blewitt to deal with. "Well?"

"Yes, sir?"

"Life's not a bed of roses, is it?"

In the black, starless sky over the ocean, the moon was wrapped in its own halo like an impish phantom that was giving away no hints about the outcome of a dicey undertaking at dawn, and Blewitt bowed to his boss's wisdom even though for once he disagreed. Today's women were so different from the submissive male pleasers that old Joe used to know in his day. Dealing with a modern female, Blewitt suspected, was well beyond the old man's comprehension and, as such, beyond the proverbial bed of roses.

24

The old maxim about life not being a bed of roses was exactly what came to mind when Blewitt pulled up in Veronica Pitt's driveway on the expensive side of Hollywood Hills. Her house was set way back on a large lot, and the long path to her door was lined with meticulously trimmed dead rose bushes—as if she had been expecting him.

For Veronica Pitt was not your regular homeowner. To her neighbors, she was a pain in the neck that did not have her act together; to the local children, who would watch her house from a safe distance, she was plain crazy; but to Blewitt, she was all of the above and more.

Years back, after Richard 'Slick Dick' Fitch broke up with her, she had threatened to write an expose on the Fitch family. She had a fixation about what she called an inherent Fitch stinginess that made them go into politics so that they could force other people to part with their money in the name of compassion, and Blewitt was dispatched to deal with her. He was under strict orders not to give in to her tantrums no matter what, making the task a frustrating, yet not an altogether unpleasant demonstration of unconditional loyalty to his employer. She used to be a piece of work back then, a beautiful little thing, light on her feet like a butterfly, yet with all the right curves. He did not mind a bit driving her to and from prominent physicians and psychoanalysts who knew all the right pills to turn her vindictive thoughts about the Fitches into virtual journeys through the more ephemeral side of life.

By now, the pills had taken away most of her butterfly qualities, except maybe where her mental stability was concerned. In that respect, she was a butterfly in the funnel of a tornado.

Her house door was wide open, and the hallway was covered with cement-splattered tarps. Valuable antique furniture had been pushed carelessly aside, and two original Ruisdales in gilded frames, once given to her by Richard Fitch as a birthday present and worth several million apiece, hung casually on a wall, one of them more askew than the other.

The tarps made a wrinkled, dusty pathway to the living room, where workmen were doing something to the windows. The window frames had been ripped out, and the raw openings gaped at the hazy spread of Los Angeles down below. The house was close to the top of the hill, and in the smog hovering low over the Los Angeles basin, the high-rise clusters of Century City, the Wilshire Center and downtown looked like sepulchers on dirty skin. The brown haze thinned out in the direction of the ocean, though, where a vague trail of diffused light made one guess at the sun's reflection in the Santa Monica Bay. It was quite a view. Yet the workers were replacing the windows with a solid wall, and Blewitt picked one that looked as if he might speak English.

"Where is Miss Pitt?"

The man shrugged and went on ramming screws into drywall panels. But when he figured the visitor would not go away, he lifted his head to summon help.

"*Hola!*" he barked at the ceiling.

A minute later an athletic, deeply tanned man in a skin-tight cashmere top and loose silk pants came down the staircase with a cigarette in his hand, not looking at Blewitt. He was barefooted and had to watch where he stepped in this mess.

"Veronica's not receiving today," he said, casually.

"Are you the servant?"

"Me?" The man looked up to scowl, but changed his mind when he saw the visitor's eyes. It was not his style to flip out over dudes with disabilities. "Sorry, man."

"My name's Blewitt."

"Oh." The man stamped out his cigarette on a tarp and burned a hole through it into the oriental rug underneath. "I'm Ms. Pitt's private secretary."

He obviously had an insight into Veronica's finances, and to justify his presence in front of an envoy of the man who paid the bills in this crib, he straightened one of the skew Ruisdales on the wall.

"I'll tell Miss Pitt you're here."

"What's your name?"

"Hedley."

Blewitt made a mental note to make arrangements to get Hedley out of the way at once. He was going to need Veronica looking fit, or as close to it as possible, and cutting her supply lines had to come first. Hedley would have to be tucked away at a hospital with a broken leg or something still tonight, he decided as he watched the man bounce back upstairs three steps at a time. He obviously was just a dealer, not a fellow consumer, and in comparison with his jaunty stride, Veronica looked weak and tired when she appeared at the top of the stairs a good 10 minutes later.

She came down slowly, one step at a time, holding onto the railing. She wore a baggy sweater and loose, flowery pajama pants, and the old butterfly quality was gone out of her stride. Yet Blewitt saw a glimmer of hope. She had put on lipstick and combed her hair, and when she came closer, he could see the hair roots showed just a fraction of an inch of gray. She had been to a hairdresser fairly recently, meaning she had her moments.

Also, she recognized Blewitt right away.

"I wrote Richard about all this," she said, doing her best to sound annoyed about the mess around her, but the dilated pupils gave her eyes a benign, doe-like expression. "Three times, I wrote him."

"That's not what I came for," Blewitt said, but Veronica was not listening. There were health issues involved here.

"Sunlight gives me splitting headaches. It's all in my letters. The louse never replied."

"As I said," Blewitt repeated slowly and patiently to test the fragility of her current mental balance, "I have not come here about the construction work."

"Just about the cost, right?"

"No."

"That will be the day." Veronica shrugged an ostentatiously indifferent shoulder. "You tell Richard this from me. He should have thought of the cost before he junked me with the rest of his babes. Inflation's killing him now?"

"I wouldn't know about that." Cement dust was drifting by, and Blewitt looked around with meaningfully raised eyebrows. "Can we speak somewhere?"

"What's there to speak about? I told you it's doctor's orders to get rid of windows."

Blewitt made sure not to blink. Hell hath no fury like a woman scorned. Yet, considering that he was here to put a scorned woman temporarily back on track, the situation was not entirely hopeless.

"We need you," he said, watching the cement dust settle on his sleeve. "We need your help."

"Why me? I'm not the only one bleeding him dry."

Careful not to show impatience, Blewitt brushed the dust off his sleeve and lapsed into a meaningful silence. He was not going to ruin an expensive suit by getting into a discussion out here, and Veronica got the message. She, too, used to be meticulous about her clothes back in the old days.

"Come on up," she decided.

Her bedroom was an eclectic collection of flower patterns. Flowers were everywhere, on the wallpaper, the bed linen, the chairs, the window drapes and her pants. A white, garden-like picket fence cordoned off a sitting area lit with an eerie array of candles, and the air was thick with the smell of burning wax and weeds. An open paperback novel lay spread-eagle on a bedside table, the front cover staring at Blewitt like a rebuke for an interrupted moment of tranquility. The cover picture depicted in endearing colors a cute English-like cottage overlooking a very blue sea beyond a lush green garden overflowing with red roses.

Also, there were red roses on the upholstery of the armchair she waved him into.

"Things not going well for Richard?" she said, not really wanting to know. "Is he worried he won't make the White House?"

"That is up to the American people to decide."

"Right." She gave Blewitt the give-me-a-break smile his remark called for, but it would not stop him from pontificating.

"Whether Richard is or is not elected president of the United States, his lifelong beliefs and convictions will remain the same. Pretty much like back in the old days when they forged such a bond between you and him."

"What the hell are you talking about?"

"The people of this country will always admire Richard for what he is."

"The walking eagle? A bird so full of shit it can't fly?"

Letting her get that off her chest, Blewitt resorted to a first-grade teacher's stoicism. "What I am talking about is your old commitment to causes that were as important then as they are now. World peace, equal opportunity . . . "

No matter how somber Blewitt tried to sound, he could not get rid of the irking suspicion that the upholstery behind his back was making him look like a garden dwarf up to his ears in a bouquet of roses. It kept grating on his concentration, and he sat up to take it once more from the top.

"Great causes have a long history, like good people have a long memory. Your name and reputation still means a good many things to a good many folks out there."

"Name one." Veronica hesitated for a moment, then decided that under the circumstances a vulgar smirk was called for. "Or, maybe, are you talking about my reputation for servicing senators?"

But Blewitt pretended not to notice. "This time, your expertise is called for in a bigger way."

"How big?"

"Big enough."

"You don't say." Veronica looked for a smirk in Blewitt's face but saw none. The size of Senator Fitch's private parts could not have been further from Blewitt's mind at the moment, and she replied accordingly. "You wouldn't have the guts to come here to ask me to go canvassing for the son of a bitch, would you?"

"No." Blewitt suppressed a smile. He had been lucky. Veronica seemed to be with it today. The cement dust in the air must have reduced her need to inhale other substances, and he decided to strike while the iron was hot. "I came here to ask you to help us with getting a bunch of good people together for a cause that has nothing to do with presidential elections in this country."

"Huh?"

"The event that I came to talk to you about takes place abroad." Blewitt made a big deal out of the fact that a certain degree of sophistication was going to be required: no riffraff, no professional peaceniks, no freaks. He was convinced, he assured her, that something like that would pose no problem for someone like her. She used to know such a lot of intellectuals back east, did she not? In which case, New York was the place for her to start. What did she think?

She said nothing, but sat back and crossed her legs to listen. She had often wondered what had become of all the people she used to know in New York. Those days, of course, she would arrive at La Guardia in Richard's private jet with two bedrooms, a Jacuzzi and a personal beautician. Her friends would pick her up at the airport, and they would talk politics all night, while her beautician did everybody's hair. The whole gang used to be so voluble and articulate. They would have such a gas together, yet she had not heard from any of them ever since she lost her personal beautician and the use of an airborne Jacuzzi.

Her phone had gone dead the day Richard broke up with her, and she always wanted to believe it was him who had pressured her old friends into staying away from her. In view of which, of course, it would do her a world of good to actually hear it from them.

"Well?" Blewitt was smiling and, unexpectedly and utterly out of character, gave her a wink. He was more relieved than she would ever know. "What will it be? New York here I come?"

"Flying commercial?" Veronica's irony was no longer aggressive, signaling her willingness to come around with just token concessions. "Maybe a window seat for me?"

"The aisle seat will be reserved for your personal maid."

"Well . . ." Any maid was bound to be better than the lazy bum Hedley.

Knowing Blewitt, though, it briefly occurred to her that the maid might be a nurse trained to keep her off dope, but she promptly dismissed that notion. Her habit wasn't that serious, was it? At the moment, for instance, her head was perfectly clear and her mind focused. She had taken in pretty much everything Blewitt had said about her being expected to get together the best bunch of people she could think of to represent the United States at a peace rally in Paris. And why the hell not?

Welcome back to life, Roni.

She was getting off the wagon, ready to put her shoulder to the wheel again—like a prodigal daughter returning to the womb of a simple, honest, hard-working family.

* * *

And she still felt that way the next day in New York, sitting in the lobby of the Plaza while her new maid checked the two of them in. Her name was Heather and, if she were a nurse, Veronica gave her no chance to practice her trade. She seemed to have lost the urge, at least for now. Her head was buzzing with Blewitt's instructions, and the subdued hum of well-dressed, sober and good looking men and women at the Plaza bar together with the hustle and bustle of Fifth Avenue outside, made her feel she belonged—as if the old sense of purpose and urgency had never left the pit of her stomach. On your feet, old girl. Time to get back to work.

She put on a conservative gray costume, a Chanel with red trim, red shoes and a matching handbag, and the first old friend she called on in New York was an aging, out-of-work actress who clapped her hands like a little girl when Veronica told her about marching for a cause in Paris.

Oh, oh let's. The actress was ecstatic. It was going to be so much fun. Just like in the old days. The travel's all paid for, no? Hotels and everything? And the media will be out in force, won't it? Veronica answered all questions with a resounding yes and ticked off the first conscript on her list of prospects.

The second name on that list was a guy who used to be famous for his unerring aim with Molotov cocktails. In the meantime, though, he had become a respectable businessman, and when Veronica asked him to come back to the fold, he rattled off a long list of complaints about a consumer society that would give him no time off. He was very sorry, but when it came to marching for the old cause abroad, he was out. He had to keep up with the mortgage payments in his mean-spirited homeland.

The third name on the list was a high-profile TV anchorman, who in the end turned her down, too. Regretfully, a heartless employment contract required him to project an apolitical image. So, her first day of rallying up old friends was a mixed bag at best.

On the second day, though, she struck pay dirt.

Flip Farrel, an aging action-movie hero who had had three box-office flops in a row in the US, was being hounded by his handlers to get his face into the limelight abroad, like Europe or some other place behind the moon. So, when Veronica told him he was to show up in a high-profile street rally in Paris, he could not believe his luck. He swore on his children's heads he would do better than his frigging best. What was the budget for the spectacle? Could he bring a bunch of dancers bound to knock everybody's socks off? Pink tights, no bras, the works. Sex and world peace were like birds of a feather, he laughed hysterically; they both made you feel like a million every time you did something to uphold them, huh? He sounded sincerely desperate, worth his weight in gold. Having him on board was a guarantee of at least 24-point headlines, and Veronica went to have a three-martini lunch at the Four Seasons.

She had to muster her courage to see the woman she really wanted to see all these years. Blewitt himself had suggested that it would do her a world of good to go see Hillary Gray, for old time's sake. They had not seen one another in ages, and Blewitt had actually insisted she take the time off to drop in on the old girl.

He even found out the address for her—which, of course, she did not need. She recognized the old brown-brick high rise the moment the taxi stopped in front of it. The Tudor-like entrance was still the same, and she all but choked up when she stepped on the familiar flagstone sidewalk in front of it. She used to love Hillary Gray.

In the mid-'70s, Hillary had dumped a super-rich husband who objected to her participation in street marches while pregnant. He worried that tear gas was not good for an unborn child, and Hillary had a bunch of long-haired lawyers deal with such antiquated morality. On the day of her court hearing, her friends, including Veronica, blocked traffic in front of the court building, burned cars, and smashed shop windows, and the media was all over Hillary Gray when she appeared on the courthouse steps, very pregnant and vivaciously victorious. Front-page headlines called it the dawn of a new era, and her divorce settlement became the talk of the town. It included a Manhattan penthouse, hefty child support and a court order for the fuddy-duddy ex to keep out of her single parenting—for Hillary Gray was convinced that tear gas thrown by mean defenders of the status-quo would cause the child in her womb to grow its heart in the right place. Also, she wanted no relics of the old world order anywhere near when she gave birth—no doctors, no pharmaceuticals. She insisted on going all natural all the way and, with just the assistance of a Shoshone shaman, she had proven to the world how right she had been. She gave birth to a perfectly healthy baby that Veronica remembered like it was yesterday—a girl. What was her name?

Beth, was it?

25

Beth came home from work shortly after six. She had taken off her office clothes, slipped into her pajamas, and gotten her cookbook out. In the pasta section, she picked a dish that looked delicious on a full-page picture: cannelloni in garlic sauce. She read the recipe twice, put the open book face down on the kitchen counter for further reference, pried a handful of cloves out of a head of garlic, and got the chopping board out.

The garlic was not to be chopped too fine, the cookbook warned. It was to be done with a lot of tender loving care, which in turn sent her off daydreaming. Hank liked garlic, too. Wouldn't that be something if he suddenly showed up? Because cooking with tender loving care for two was no more work than cooking for one—thinking of which brought about the kind of a lump in the chest she was getting used to by now. Ever since he had left her bed in the middle of the night to catch a plane without telling her where to, thinking of Hank Teeple was on par with swallowing a golf ball.

At the office, his desk remained vacant for just a couple of days before a teenager with an acute case of acne was put behind it. Normally, her heart would have gone all out to anyone like that, but to see a stranger sitting in what to her still was Hank's chair made her insensitive to the poor boy's bleeding ulcers.

She waylaid the girl from personnel in the cafeteria and asked her straight out if she knew where Hank had gone.

"That weirdo? Gave us a day notice, imagine that."

"He must've had a reason."

"Oh, yeah?"

They were having hot dogs, and the girl licked a drop of ketchup off her finger. "How was he in the sack?"

Damn.

With her mind drifting in and out of a daydream, Beth had made a paste out of the garlic on the chopping board, and her fingers were drenched with sticky juice that brought tears into her eyes just as the doorbell rang.

She threw a dressing gown over her pajamas and ran to open the door. Her hand, still wet from the over-minced garlic, stuck to the doorknob, but she did not care. It could've been Hank standing in the hallway.

But no such luck.

It was a woman, nicely nipped and tucked and well put together — a fitting gray costume with red buttons and red trim, matching shoes and a handbag. She was heavily made up, her only natural-looking feature being dark half circles under the eyes. As for the rest, she must have had a facelift or something. It was hard to tell her age.

"Veronica Pitt," the woman introduced herself, as if the name should mean something.

"Yes?"

"You have your mother's eyes. No sisters?"

"No."

"Then you must be Beth." The woman thrust out a hand. "How are you?"

Forgetting the garlic, Beth shook the extended hand, and for a moment they stuck together.

"Are you a glue maker?" Veronica Pitt disengaged herself and wiped her hand on the back of her skirt. "Your mother and I used to be very good friends. Is she around?"

"She's down in Florida." Feeling bad about the sticky hand, Beth felt obligated to volunteer more information. "She moved over there because she felt that here no one had time to talk any more."

"Right as always. What a gal. I used to love her."

"Will you go down to see her then?" Beth did not want to be rude, but now that she had made it perfectly clear her mother did not live here anymore, she expected the woman to back off. "I'm sure she'd want to see you."

"What's that?" Forgetting Florida and her smoldering love for Beth's mother, Veronica Pitt leaned forward to sniff the air. "Garlic?"

"Yes, but . . ."

"I love garlic." Veronica's eyes opened wide without crinkling the forehead, and Beth changed her mind about the facelift. It might have been just Botox shots. Still, she wished Veronica Pitt would go away so that she could close the door and go back to the kitchen to do something about the over-minced garlic. But Veronica would not budge. "Your mother and I used to have such good times together. Did she tell you?"

"No. I mean . . ." Beth was determined to put an end to the conversation, but how? She could not bring herself to hurt people's feelings after they laid themselves open to ridicule. "I mean she told me, in a way."

"Would you know her address in Florida?"

Beth nodded, finding it increasingly more difficult to tell the woman to go away. She did not know how to say no to people who refused to listen to her, and Veronica's smile broadened.

"Have a pen?"

Not knowing what else to do, Beth stepped aside, and Veronica walked in as if she were doing her old friend's daughter a favor by entering a place that held great memories but looked so hopelessly middle-class now.

It was clean and homelike, with no sign of personnel to keep it that way, and Veronica hated homes where every inch had been wiped and dusted by the person she was supposed to treat as an equal. In the old days, this place used to be full of overflowing ashtrays, books, newspaper clippings, discarded placards and greasy fast-food wrappers.

"A lovely nest you made here for yourself," Veronica smiled, thinking fast. Beth would have to do. She had no time to go down to Florida.

She put her red handbag down where she could see it. She had to remember to write a check before she left, because judging by the lone calla lily on the piano, Beth must have been buying those a stem at a time and might find it difficult to pay for a New York - Paris round-trip out of pocket.

She briefly considered asking if Beth would see her father sometimes, but decided against it. It made no difference in her scheme.

"All right," she said instead, smiling sweetly to storm Beth's last defenses. "How can I help?"

"All I have to do is to boil spaghetti."

"All right, I set the table." Veronica Pitt kicked off her red shoes and went to the kitchen.

She expected someone like Beth to keep silverware in a neatly lined kitchen drawer, and that was exactly where she found it. The girl was so unlike her mother. Which was all right, too. People like Beth could be talked into anything; and, most importantly, if Beth had a boyfriend, he was not likely to be a bully bound to make a fuss about her going to Paris. A girl like Beth Gray was as likely as not to be in love with some little muddler that did not matter one way or another.

26

Turning their backs on the ancient battlefield where the specter of a French King was poised to overrun a ruthless Emir's weakened defenses, Teeple and Zyaad set a fast pace back to the château.

The sun was out of the clouds now, and by the time they entered the courtyard, there was perspiration on their foreheads. Three gray trucks with Paris license plates stood in the middle of the yard, one of them with its front wheels in a flower bed, and there was no one around. No drivers, no guards.

"Take the back entrance to your room," Zyaad said, flatly. "You remember where it is."

Teeple took the same back door he had sneaked through the other way the day before, and again there was no one in the corridor. But as he approached the door of his room, he could smell cigarette smoke.

There was a man lying on the bed with his shoes on, smoking. He must have been here for a while, for there were cigarette butts on the floor. The air had a fuzzy bluish tint, and Teeple stepped forward to open the door to the balcony.

"Hey!" The man barked, dropping cigarette ashes on the pillow, but Teeple kept on going for the balcony door.

"Secondhand smoke's bad for my health."

"Don't be funny." The man might have been smoking rotting weeds, but he was no slouch. He switched the cigarette from one corner of his mouth to the other and whipped a knife out of somewhere. Or had it been the other way round, the knife first, the cigarette second? Teeple could not tell. It had happened that fast. One moment the knife was in the man's hand, a split second later it stuck in the window frame at Teeple's eye level, about six inches away from his face.

"Sit," the man on the bed commanded. He had barely moved throwing the knife, and Teeple backed off to where he felt the edge of the coffee table against the back of his knees.

With his eyes on the idiot, keeping his hands away from the body and careful not to make a sudden move, he let his eyes flick sideways to locate the nearest chair. And when he looked back at the bed, he was faced with three black holes. Two pitch-dark eyes were staring at him over the muzzle of a gun, and he froze. Look them in the eyes and you know, he remembered his father saying when they were in doubt about putting down an old horse. When you see nothing, it's time.

The man on the bed looked brain dead. So, in a way, Teeple was not surprised to hear the gun in his hand fire.

It stung like hell.

A heat wave surged through his body, and he saw something stick out of the hot spot in his shoulder. A dart.

He heard the door open behind his back, but his head would not turn. The neck seemed to be encased in a stiff rubber collar, yet he could feel hands under his armpits. Other hands grabbed his ankles to yank the feet from under him, and there was nothing he could do about that. They carried him down a flight of stairs, bumping a hip against the railing. His hip. He heard the bangs, but they did not hurt, and he tried to remember the name of the paralyzing agent used in hospitals to prevent the body from resisting a respirator. What was it called? Something that paralyzed muscles without making them stiff. He could remember reading somewhere that if not dispensed properly, the stuff could cause a critical rise in body temperature, which must have been why he felt on fire.

The hands under his armpits and around his ankles were rough and laborer-like, but the men's faces left no doubt about their aversion to hard labor. They looked disgusted with Teeple's weight. Out in the courtyard, they tried to swing him back and forth to throw him onto a truck, but couldn't get the momentum right. The ends of his body would not sway in sync, and he heard the men swear in an unintelligible language he seemed to understand. One, two, three . . . They finally got the swing right, and as he landed on the truck bed, he saw his rib cage catch on a nasty-looking, rusty fixture. But he felt nothing; not even a tickle.

A few minutes later, more men climbed onto the truck bed to sit on benches along the sides, trapping Teeple's prostrated body in a ring of black boots. The pungent smell of leather and shoe polish made breathing difficult, and he tried to breathe through the mouth. It made his inert tongue slide back, and he began to choke.

Boots moved, men laughed, and hands turned him over on his belly to have his tongue slip back out. By the time he stopped coughing, the truck ground into gear and moved. It seemed to be turning around, and the centrifugal force made Teeple dizzy. Then he passed out.

* * *

The next thing he knew, there was a wet cloth stroking his face and neck. It felt like a woman's touch, except that he could not imagine what Beth would be doing here — wherever here was.

It was pitch dark.

The paralyzing agent seemed to be wearing off, and he was beginning to hurt because he could move now. His legs were there for him from the knees down, and he felt his arms all the way to the elbows. With some patience and a great deal of endurance, he could even touch his eyes. He was blindfolded.

"Don't overdo it," a man said close by, and the wet cloth stopped stroking.

"Might need a bit longer," said the man with the wet cloth.

"You think?"

"He's not done yet."

They sounded like a couple of homey Americans discussing a roast in the oven, then the blindfold lifted. It had been pushed up Teeple's forehead, scraping the old welt under his eye. Was he bleeding?

Not that stains would matter here, he thought as he stared blankly at the dirty ceiling overhead. It had not been painted in years. Wires dangled out of an opening where a lighting fixture had been ripped out, and daylight was coming in through a small window that Teeple's bare feet were pointing to. He could see an overcast sky through it. Or was it dirty glass?

In that kind of light, the walls looked as bad as the ceiling, and there was no furniture. He was lying on his back on an elevated platform in the middle of the room, and the two Americans stood close by looking down at him.

The one with the wet cloth wore an olive green uniform with a badge on the sleeve. The other one was a civilian with a razor-thin smile and steely gray, mocking eyes that were out of sync with each other. He was cross-eyed. His thin lips stretched a little, and a corner of the mouth moved sideways as one of his eyes rested on Teeple's face.

"Can you move?"

"What?" Teeple cleared his throat and, giving an arm a try, his elbow slid off the edge of whatever he was lying on. The hand dangled, and the uniformed man bent to lift it and put it back up, flashing the badge on his sleeve right before Teeple's eyes. The writing on it seemed to be in French, but Teeple could not be sure. At a close range, his eyes were still out of focus; or out of something.

Judging by the color of the uniform, though, the man could

have been either a janitor or a park ranger. Where the hell did they have national parks in France?

"Do I keep the doctor on standby?" the park ranger said.

"If you like." The cross-eyed man did not care one way or another, and the park ranger started to leave.

Through the open door, Teeple could see colorful toys scattered on a dingy floor in the next room. Two children sat by, but were not playing.

"Have water around here?" Teeple said, hoarsely. He was parched, but the cross-eyed man gave no indication he had heard him. His mismatched gray eyes watched Teeple with the curiosity of a nasty little boy observing a fish that had jumped out of an aquarium, making him wonder how it would ever manage to flap itself back in.

"My name's Blewitt," the man said, and Teeple remembered embedding the name in his memory after Zyaad mentioned it.

"Where is he?" He tried to move his head to look around. Because if Zyaad were here, a servant would soon be bringing water in a silver carafe, with ice and silver tongs on the side. He missed the man. "Where's Zyaad?"

"On the rack."

"The rack?"

"A figure of speech. We need to make sure his case has merit before the tribunal convenes tomorrow."

"How about water?" Teeple lifted his head a little higher. He was naked and hot but not sweating, and his ribs were beginning to hurt where he had seen the rusty fixture on the truck bed dig in—none of which made a difference to Blewitt.

"How many job tickets did they give you at the unemployment office back in Washington?" Blewitt wanted to know.

"Five, six, I don't know." The pain behind the eyeballs made Teeple groan. "I don't remember."

"Four. You'd been issued four tickets."

"If you say so." The body heat was getting worse, too, and Teeple tried to look for the wet cloth the park ranger had been wiping his face with. "Listen."

But Blewitt wouldn't listen. He had a different agenda. "Three times you were sent on a wild goose chase by a man chewing on toothpicks. The fourth time around, that man was replaced by a woman with a neat hairdo, a string of pearls and an intelligent face. Didn't she make you wonder?"

"I don't remember pearls."

"Come on, Teeple. Our generation had been brought up to judge people the politically incorrect way, by their looks. Don't tell me the woman didn't look out of place to you behind a government office counter."

"I don't think I'd recognize her again."

Teeple heard voices in the next room and saw Blewitt turn his head to listen, too.

A child screamed somewhere. Then it screamed again, a telephone rang, and a moment later the man in the park ranger uniform came in, walking backwards. He was retreating before Zyaad, who had pushed inside the room spearheading a small pack of armed little people wearing black hoods.

Had Teeple not known how short Zyaad was himself, the size of his soldiers would not have been overly suspicious. But since he also knew the look of an MK14 assault rifle in the hands of a grown-up, it was obvious to him there were children under the black hoods.

He tried to sit up, but the pain behind the eyes made his head spin. The room wobbled, walls began to circle and the lights went out. His lights.

* * *

When Teeple could see again, maybe seconds, maybe hours later, Zyaad was leaning over him, unshaved and wearing no tie. At a closer look, his shirt looked as if he had slept in it, his manicured hands were restless, and Teeple fully expected him to start with excuses for both the disheveled appearance and for meeting here like this. Ramshackle pads were not Zyaad's natural habitat.

Yet Zyaad seem to be in no hurry to leave. His boy soldiers

had taken off their black hoods and rolled up their sleeves to wipe Teeple's body with wet rags smelling of rubbing alcohol.

"It's cold in here," Zyaad said, testing Teeple's awareness of the outer world. "Do you feel it?"

"I'm too hot for that."

"Get up and walk."

"Where to?"

"Back and forth, barefoot." Zyaad nodded to the boys to help Teeple stand up. "Put his underpants on."

"They took them," Teeple said before he thought of it. "The park ranger and the other guy, Blewitt."

"Blewitt blew it." Zyaad smiled a little. "But I don't think he pinched your underwear."

"What happened?"

"Your drawers are on the floor." Zyaad pointed to a bundle of clothes in a corner and looked on critically as the boys dressed Teeple to make him look more presentable. Then, seeing no need for further refinement, Zyaad stepped forth with a couple of pills in one hand and a glass of water in the other. No silver carafe, no silver tongues. He seemed resigned to roughing it. "Blewitt would've let you die, you know that?"

"Is that good or bad?"

"He's scared." Zyaad waited for Teeple to swallow the pills. "I'll need you the first thing in the morning, bright eyed and bushy tailed."

"What's in the morning?"

"Your big day."

Teeple could not remember Verhagen's plan calling for bright eyes and a bushy tail on a big day, but could not worry about everything right now. His breath was still wheezing, and he tried to breathe through his nose. It made the pain behind his eyeballs worse, and he went back to wheezing.

"Where am I?" He turned towards the dirty window, but the boys jerked him back.

"Let him," Zyaad commanded, and the boys let go of Teeple with the alacrity of crack soldiers. They would not move a finger as his knees buckled, and the uncoordinated body crumbled onto the floor.

He seemed to be getting better, though. He could feel the chill of the floor now and made it back on his feet on his own. Even the pain behind his eyes was becoming bearable as he leaned on the window sill to look out.

There was a decal on the window pane, and he could read the writing: Paris St. Germain Soccer Club. It was askew, and the glass was so dirty that the panorama of dilapidated buildings behind it looked like a black and white photograph of Europe in ruins after WWII—except for the satellite dishes in the windows and present-day cars parked along the curb.

People sat on the hoods of the cars and on door stoops, and the buildings cast shadows over a potholed roadway. There was not much traffic here. Some kind of a flag hung limply from a roof gutter on the other side of the street, while down below on the sidewalk, a bunch of girls in hipsters were swaying dark bellies to music blasting from a radio in one of the parked cars. The car was old and dirty and its license plates ended in 75— just like the rest of the plates on all the other old bangers down the street as far as Teeple could see.

He was back in Paris.

Paris

27

The International Conference on Peaceful Coexistence (ICPC) at the Ritz was expected to stir up passions Paris had not seen since the French Revolution or the student riots in the 1970s. For days prior to the conference, the French media had been on high alert, the great Jacque Petain of *Radiodiffusion Télévision Française* leading the charge.

Every day, radio and television would bring all kinds of developing stories and breaking news about Christian thugs closing in on the City of Light and enlightenment, and Jacque Petain wielded firsthand knowledge of extremists bent on exploiting the questionable French gospel of the medieval Battle of Poitiers. She was not quite clear as to what was supposed to be exploited which way, but her overall sadness over an orchestrated attempt to distort French history was so compelling that all over France people rose to the challenge.

Feminist organizations joined forces with the environmentalists to organize candlelight vigils all over Paris, while the radical left hooked up with the communists to trample down anyone indifferent to the ideal of peaceful coexistence. Noble ideals came at a price was their motto. Blood had to be spilled and sculls bashed to make people see how love and understanding could change the world if given a chance.

The silent majority, however, did not want blood in the streets, and since the primary Parisian taxpayer, the tourist industry, was worried about delays in the tight schedules of sightseeing buses, the *Conseil General* chose to be on the safe side. A press conference was called at the *Palais du Justice* to make an emotional, citywide appeal for calm and goodwill, while gendarmerie detachments in riot gear were being secretly mobilized from as far as the Seine-et-Marne and Ile de France districts.

So, when on the day of the Peace Conference the Christian thugs failed to materialize, the gendarmes, encased from head to foot in mean black helmets, bulletproof jackets and fire-resistant pants, were ticked off. In Place Vendôme, the anticipated hot spot of the riots, they were faced with the rank and file of chirpy old ladies in bright-colored summer dresses and wrinkled stockings throwing flowers at them.

Some joker, they figured, had organized hundreds of buses to bring in senior peace enthusiasts from all over Europe — including the good old ladies from the cinder-block barracks at the Château de la Bataille de Poitiers. Those arrived with homemade placards praising Islam as a religion of peace, and they kept waving them at TV cameras just as the nice Dr. Zyaad, who always paid for their jolly bus tours, had told them to.

There were rumors that Jacque Petain herself was going to hit the streets to do a report for the evening news, and the gendarmes threw in the towel. They moved their water cannons and tear gas supplies to the other side of Boulevard Hausman, where they also unbuckled and un-Velcroed the riot gear in order to slip into something more comfortable.

They reappeared in the sunlit Place Vendôme in freshly ironed, powder-blue shirts and smart peaked caps to help the old ladies on pedestrian crossings, which in the end proved to be more dangerous than an all-out racist rally.

Pedestrian crossings or not, wild-eyed drivers in old bangers threatened to run down anyone trying to keep them out of the drive-up lane to the Ritz entrance. They all claimed to have a higher dignitary in the back seat than the next guy, and the gendarmes retreated onto the sidewalks, where they got yelled at by the organizers for not risking their lives in the roadway. The Grand Mufti was expected to arrive any moment.

Consequently, when Teeple arrived, the last thing the frustrated gendarmes worried about was yet another old banger driven by a wild-eyed man in a robe and head gear. They did not give the car a second glance, not to mention taking the trouble to bend and look into the back seat where Teeple was hemmed in between two robed musclemen, hanging onto his arms and pulling his jacket out of shape. The gendarmes looked the other way as the car honked and wroom-wroomed its way towards the hotel entrance. The driver used the front bumper to push through the women's queue, then, with considerably more respect, pulled up in front of the men's entrance.

Teeple's guards dragged him out of the backseat and, pushing and shoving and swearing, they whisked him into the lobby. Waving a piece of paper that seemed to carry a mega weight, they shouted down the attendants at the registration booths. The leader and loudest screamer had one hell of a temper, and they encountered very little resistance even at the X-ray check point, where everybody was supposed to be thoroughly frisked for hidden cameras and voice recorders.

Teeple, wedged tight between two guards, was rushed past a swarming conference hall that looked like a department store on the morning of an annual sale and into a long, narrow corridor leading inside the murky bowels of the majestic old hotel. The closer they got to the back of the building, the more security guards there were in their way, but the magic piece of paper got them through to the end and into a rickety freight elevator.

The elevator smelled of food and dirty linen as it slowly ground its way to the top floor. It opened into the back of a grand ballroom — an impressive place even when entered through a delivery door. The walls and the high ceiling were decorated with carvings of flowers, cherubs and twisted garlands, and the sunlight coming in through elaborately draped windows reflected in the polish of a deserted parquetry floor.

On a closer look, though, the carvings on the walls were no carvings. They were plaster ornaments in need of a fresh coat of paint, and the parquetry floor was uneven and worn out. An enormous chandelier hung from the zenith of the vaulted ceiling, and Teeple could not help wondering how much a thing like that weighed. Several tons, most likely—which, in view of the cracked plaster, made it unreasonably hazardous to merely pass underneath.

Yet, it was exactly where his guards told him to stand. The whole ballroom floor was empty, but they wanted him right there under the center of gravity of the sprawling concoction of light bulbs and dangling crystal trinkets.

"Stand," they told him, and he knew better than to argue. There were ornate mirrors between the windows and he could see himself in several of them. In this light, the color of the welt under his eye seemed to be leaning towards blue and yellow rather than purple.

Two lecterns with Ritz logos stood on the sides, facing one another across the room, and Teeple's guards had an argument with one another as to where exactly their ward should stand. At first, Teeple thought they were quarreling about his position in relation to the lecterns. Then he figured they were worried about the chandelier, but not that it could fall on him. They ordered him to move back a few steps, to where death would not be imminent but merely likely if the whole thing came down.

"Stand here." They turned Teeple to face three gold-braided cushions lined up along the windowless back wall and stepped back to wait.

They were used to waiting, and the silence of the deserted ballroom made Teeple's ears ring as he looked around, wondering how much history tourist guides ascribed to this place— Louis XIV, Madame Pompadour, Napoleon, de Gaulle? He sure could not care less. A brooding shrine of yesteryear grandeur made the memory of Beth's spanking new kidskin sofa in the sky above New York seem like a fair alternative to a sinister adventure steeped in history—because something big was going on outside the ballroom windows, too.

In front of the hotel, a dense crowd had gathered around a tall, artfully wrought column in the center of the square, and when Teeple craned his neck, he could see the statue on the top of the column: a lone man in a short top coat and breeches. The swell of humanity made the column seem to be swaying, and it took Teeple a moment to turn his attention to a new arrival in the ballroom.

The stained-glass swing door of the main entrance had been opened by unseen hands on the outside, and Zyaad sailed in, looking like a sheik from the silent-movie era. He wore an immaculate white robe with a gold-braided head dress, blazing the trail for three gofers in black. They were shuffling in his wake with heavy boxes full of what looked like legal files, while Zyaad himself carried just a thin manila folder.

If this was supposed to be the tribunal Blewitt had talked about the other day, Teeple figured Zyaad was being ostentatiously defiant of the practice widely accepted by American lawyers to enter courtrooms lugging their own loads to make a favorably humble impression on the jury. But then, what jury? There was no jury box here—just three cushions on the floor and two unmanned lecterns facing each other.

Zyaad placed himself behind the lectern on Teeple's right, and his gofers put the boxes on the floor, almost kissing his feet in the process. He acknowledged Teeple with a faint smile of polite recognition, placed the slim manila folder on top of the lectern, and began to study its sparse contents.

Next to enter was Blewitt. He wore a blue suit with a bright yellow tie that matched the ballroom decor in spirit and concept, and his hands were tied with a rope the ends of which were dangling around his knees. He was accompanied by an inconspicuous character in a gray pinstripe suit with a deliberately muted necktie, and since they both looked uncertain where to go, Zyaad sent one of his gofers to play the good cop.

The man grabbed Blewitt by the dangling rope and, on a nod from Zyaad, led him to the opposite lectern.

Ignoring the indignity of being led like a cow to a milking stall, Blewitt looked straight ahead, acknowledging neither Zyaad nor Teeple, and the pinstripe suit followed every step of the way, establishing himself as Blewitt's lawyer.

The two of them exchanged a few words in a whisper, and the lawyer helped Blewitt lift his tied hands onto the top the lectern where he could keep staring at them. He hardly bothered to look up when a moment later, three bearded men with warped eyebrows filed in through the back entrance. They wore identical black head dresses and black robes with black belts. There were rhinestone-studded daggers dangling from the belts, and they were careful to hold the sheaths away from their loins as they plopped on the cushions on the floor, revealing gaudy sneakers.

They were young and tough, looking like a trio of punks picked at random at a street corner to serve as referees at a contemporary rendition of some ancient game in which they had no say. For it was not at their command that the chandelier suddenly lit up, controlled by invisible hands elsewhere. Reflectors lit the lecterns and made a circle of light on the floor where Teeple stood. He was close to the edge of that circle, and one of the guards stepped forward to poke him to move into the center.

The proceedings were taking on a life of their own, and Teeple half expected some master of ceremony to come up any moment to say it had all been a prank. Everybody smile at a hidden camera in the chandelier. For he had no doubt there was at least one of those in the mighty array of bulbs and glittering trinkets.

But the referees' stony stares suggested no flair for comedy. The one in the middle had a wire hanging from one ear and seemed to be listening before he opened the proceedings on an acutely somber note.

"The guy that called this tribunal goes first. No yadda yadda." The room had a hollow echo, and for a moment the referee looked startled by his own voice. Then he pulled himself together and nodded to Zyaad. "Take it away, man."

"Thank you." Zyaad smiled, doing his best to cope with what was quickly beginning to feel like quicksand. As far as he could tell, he had one up on Blewitt, whose hands were tied. Yet Blewitt's arrogant indifference to the rope hanging from his wrists made it clear he was relying on his lawyer to deal with the punks on the cushions. Had he, Zyaad, made a mistake by pleading the case himself? Had he overdone his anxiety about the secrecy and urgency of this case?

"In order to set the record straight before we begin," Zyaad cleared his throat and raised a hand to point at Teeple. "My interrogation of the here present ex-CIA officer had not been completed before the accused, Mr. Blewitt, showed up with a squadron of militia trucks on my property to remind me to get on with it. The council, he told me, demanded expediency."

Zyaad was groping for the appropriate poise behind his lectern. He could not possibly show disdain for the referees' stupid faces, yet he had to refrain from looking up once too often to the hidden camcorder in the chandelier — his one and only lifeline to his equals presumably assembled in some Bedouin tent in the Sahara or a cave in Afghanistan. He had to find a way to speak to a chandelier without looking like a lunatic.

"It is my contention that the accused has betrayed not only our cause, but our trust and our principles. He betrayed our holly struggle. He betrayed Allah." Zyaad's voice thickened, and he had to stop to prevent it from grinding to a choking halt all by itself. Obviously, under the circumstances, a droning ideological diatribe was not a way to go either, and he made do with just one brief, additional homily.

"Allah is my witness that in nearly half a century, I've never heard other than praise for the Emirates Bank of Riyadh. A praise for it's steadfast, worldwide support of our holy struggle — the very reason I turned a sympathetic ear when a few years ago, Mr. Blewitt contacted me with a scheme to further that worthy cause by exploiting the situation in the Malacca Straits."

No one said anything, and Zyaad ventured into more detail, ready to trim his sails should the referee with the earphone show impatience.

"It is common knowledge that vessels of Middle Eastern registry pay exorbitant insurance premiums in the Malacca Straits, because the Lloyd's of London chooses to consider the area a war zone. So, Mr. Blewitt's idea of finding a more reasonable insurance carrier made sound business sense. And his suggestion to use the Emirates Bank as the insurance underwriter was nothing short of genius."

Detecting no impatience in the center referee's face yet, Zyaad ventured into technicalities.

"Blewitt's plan to have the issuer of letters of credit underwrite the applicable insurance policies was a win-win situation in the Malacca Straits; like playing musical chairs with promissory notes. Mr. Blewitt asked for a fifty-fifty cut in the net increase of the bank's profit, and I concurred. The seemingly exorbitant sum of money was not more than merely a reasonable guarantee of loyalty in an operation spanning three continents, dozens of subsidiaries and a fleet of speedboats operating along the nine-hundred-mile stretch of the Straits.

"In an undertaking of that magnitude, Blewitt's loyalty had to be taken for granted, because I couldn't have possibly managed to breathe down so many people's necks in so many places at all times. Operational losses had to be anticipated, built in as incidental expenses. So, when at first a few million dollars went to waste here and there, I did not even know about it.

"It was brought to my attention only much later that several relatively modest sums of virtually untraceable cash, used to finance our American sleeper cells, were confiscated by the American Internal Revenue Service. Our people would routinely write off those monies as petty cash, and the ensuing minor political implications were regarded as a coincidence. So, it was only when an operation involving billions of dollars was blown without a single slip-up on my part that I began to suspect a mole in our midst."

Zyaad nodded to his gofers to pick up the cardboard boxes at his feet and carry them over to the referees.

"These documents represent a mere fraction of the effort that went into manipulating French politicians to relax their land ownership laws. The full extent of that undertaking would fill hundreds of boxes like these. In fact, in terms of money and effort, the endeavor was such that it was not only recognized but highly commended by the council itself." Zyaad made a faint, fleeting bow to the chandelier. "I acquired over a hundred thousand tracts of land in France, not one of them traceable to myself. The purpose was to relocate our brothers from city ghettos to the countryside — to make land owners out of them in order to attract spouses from the local population and thus become French citizens and voters in the European Union.

"No two of such parcels were adjacent, and no two solicitors that drew the individual deeds of trust knew one another. I made sure that no one could accuse me of buying up a country before I bought it. The deals were timed to close within one week, well before the local authorities realized what hit them — yet the French were a step ahead of us. They amended their laws in the nick of time, and we wasted huge sums of money on legal compensations in deals we could no longer get out of.

"I launched a thorough inquiry to look for the mole I was by then convinced had burrowed itself into our midst. Needless to say, I left no stone unturned, looking everywhere but in Blewitt's direction. Why? Because the Americans made sure I would not look that way. They leaked bits and pieces of misinformation about the French having been tipped off by a CIA agent inside the Malaysian government, and my people in Washington bought it. They fingered a cabinet minister in Kuala Lumpur by the name of Abdull Abdullah, an influential but not wealthy politician who had done a good job at keeping the Malaysian Navy out of the Malacca Straits.

"Unfortunately, Abdullah had a passion for blond women, demanding from them the same unconditional obedience he was accustomed to expect from his wives, which in view of his limited financial means made him a natural for the Americans to corrupt—a man for whom a journey was an act of mercy."

A journey? All three referees unanimously knitted their eyebrows, but only the one on the center cushion spoke.

"What?"

"Abdullah was liquidated."

"Killed?"

"Yes."

"Good."

"Before he was liquidated, though, Abdullah came clean. He admitted that his decadent sexual practices drained his financial resources and gave him no choice but to offer his services to the Americans. Yet," Zyaad paused to raise a pontificating finger, "despite the intensity of our interrogation, Abdullah maintained to the very end that the CIA had never for a moment considered his offer. He had all but begged to be permitted to lead them onto the money trail that originated in the Malacca Straits, but they turned him down with a yawn. The Americans couldn't care less. They did not want to be bothered. Why?"

Zyaad paused to drop his eyes in due humility. It was time to briefly flog his back.

"Without the benefit of the proverbial hindsight, I had not yet realized at that time that the Americans turned down Abdull Abdullah because he could not tell them anything they did not know. Back then, I was convinced that by cutting off Abdullah's moral dilemma, his penis, and stuffing it into his mouth, we had plugged the leak, and I went ahead with a carbon copy of the French deal in the Netherlands—a deal that went through without a hitch, thus confirming my belief that Abdullah had been the mole.

"I allowed myself to feel smug in false security until our people deep inside the American government found out that the CIA had known about the Dutch operation, too. The Americans let us get away with it only because most of the land we acquired in the Netherlands was below sea level and the Pentagon was confident that if the Netherlands went Muslim the democratic way, ten minutes of strategic bombing of the sea walls along the Dutch coast would fix any adverse voter imbalance."

Zyaad gave the referees the location of the folder containing the pertinent records, and they put their heads together. Written word was not their forte, and they granted Zyaad more time to speak.

"You're next," the center referee told Blewitt, who in turn nodded to his lawyer with an ostentatiously indifferent shrug. He could not care less how long Zyaad's tirade was going to take. He was ready to tear him to shreds any time. And to show he meant it, he turned to the window to alleviate the boredom by staring at the crowd in Place Vendôme.

It was growing by the minute — as he knew it would.

28

Elbowing her way through the crowd in Place Vendôme made Beth feel weak in the knees. It was hard to believe she had agreed to this—coming to Paris with Veronica Pitt. She hardly knew the woman, who had by now become so absurdly familiar. She had dressed for the occasion just like Beth's mother would—to offend, to arouse, to appease, and whatever else.

Mother had taken Beth to her first street rally before she was old enough to go to school. The occasion had required holding hands with a bunch of people to make amends for the calamity Beth's father had brought upon mankind, and Beth remembered mother sounding quite biblical when she called the smoke stacks of father's factories sepulchers on the face of Earth.

"Your father's name is written in black soot in the skies for all to curse," mother used to say, pointing upwards, and when Beth saw nothing up there, she had an explanation for that, too. "One day, sweetie, when you're old enough to get to know men, your eyes will open wide . . ."

Mother despised men. Yet when Beth was 10, a fat hulk with greasy hair and dirty fingernails began to call on them at the

New York penthouse regularly. He was a heavy smoker, dropping cigarette ashes all over the place, and would take off his shoes at the dinner table. He had smelly feet and kept saying the same things over and over again. He was into changing the world, and Beth used to hold a napkin to her nose until the man's after-dessert burp, after which he would pinch mother's behind and pack her off to the bedroom.

Beth hated to think of that time, the droning speeches underscored by a lingering foot odor that made her suspicious of making the world a better place long before she would openly admit to it. And it was the memory of Smelly Feet now that made her feel like holding her nose when the mob in Place Vendôme rose to wave placards at television cameras.

She was ready to cut and run to hide somewhere, but Veronica grabbed her hand to drag her deeper into the mayhem, and she gave in just like she had given in to her endearments back in New York. Veronica Pitt was a formidable persuader, grand and magnificent, making it perfectly clear that the slightest hesitation to fulfill her wishes would be an unforgivable affront to mankind. She was impossible to say no to.

So, Beth said nothing even when Veronica had dressed for the occasion in a breathtakingly preposterous fashion—a blazing red jacket, a tight white miniskirt and blue high heels—the colors of the French tricolor as well as the American flag. Mobs respond to visuals, Veronica had told her while putting the charade on at the hotel, and by the time the two of them reached the epicenter of the mob at Place Vendôme, at the base of an artfully wrought bronze column with a statue on top, Beth began to believe it. She recognized some of the faces there—batty Hollywood celebrities going bonkers over Veronica's outfit, with Veronica responding in kind. Laughing and shouting with delight, she let go of Beth's hand to hug and kiss and re-hug each and every one of them. They were here to make a dazzling statement, and no one paid attention to Beth and her baggy brown pants and clumsy hiking shoes meant for real marching.

She felt desperately alone in the boisterous cast of thousands, missing Hank more than ever. Because, in a way, it was by his doing that she was here. Anything was better than staying at home with just a golf ball in her throat for company, waiting for the doorbell to ring. And the more she thought of him, the more he looked like the one and only firm point in the universe, something to cling to in a deluge of mob madness that was pushing and shoving her further and further away from Veronica and her celeb friends.

Before she knew it, she was off the sidewalk with her bad leg in the gutter, where she bumped into a well-dressed young woman who, too, seemed disgusted to be here. The two of them found themselves face to face, almost rubbing noses in the push and shove. The woman said something in French, but when she figured that Beth did not understand, she switched to English without abandoning her French intonation.

"Don't the celebs look like mallard to you?"

She introduced herself the European way by her full name, Jacque Petain, and explained her presence here as just another day at the office. She was a reporter, she told Beth, and could write a 10-column essay on this kind of charade in any bar round the corner and be right on the money.

"*Alors.*" The woman took Beth's arm as if to protect her from the milling mob around. "Want to join me?"

"To do what?"

"Aaah. An American, aren't you?"

"Yes, but..."

"Would love to hear your take on all this. How about it?" Jacque Petain indicated knocking back a drink, and the screws in Beth's shin said oh-yes-please, as did her brand-new hiking shoes. She had bought them the day before at the airport, and they hurt like hell as she now pulled herself up on her tiptoes to look for Veronica.

She could see her running with outstretched arms towards a tall, good-looking man spearheading a wiggling and skipping array of girls in pink tights who carried matching pink banners calling for all good people to Make Peace Lovely. The man posed under one of the banners with Veronica, who stood out like a sore thumb in her Franco-American colors against a pink backdrop.

"The reason she is not singing the Marseillaise must be that she doesn't know the words," Jacque Petain snickered, following the direction of Beth's stare. "You know the bunch?"

"Some of them."

"Flip Farrell sure needs publicity more than a *pissoire*."

"What?"

"A urinal."

"Oh."

Again, Beth thought of Hank. He would say something like that. Maybe not quite about a urinal, just in general. He, too, despised mob hysterics. What was it he had told her? Two men alone won't agree on anything; add a third one and they'll all go to war to defend a collective opinion.

"Just a quickie, huh?" Jacque Petain took Beth's elbow to steer her towards the Ritz. "One Pernod never killed anybody."

"What?"

"A Pernod a day keeps the doctor away."

There was a sagging banner over the entrance of the Ritz, promoting the Peace Conference in three languages—Arabic, French and English—as the beginning of a new era, and Beth hesitated. Only women in headscarfs and burkas were going inside the hotel.

"I'm Catholic," she stammered.

"So?"

"I . . . don't know."

"*Allez*. Come on, you're with me."

29

From the lighted circle in the center of the ballroom floor, Teeple could not make out faces in the mob outside. Nor could he read the placards. His eyesight was not what it used to be. He could only guess what the slogans were about and took a moment to turn away from the window when he heard his name called inside the room. He was on.

"Mr. Teeple," Zyaad was saying, "what is your profession?"

"Clerk with the Internal Revenue Service."

Zyaad shot him a dark look. Don't do this to me. The clock's ticking. "Until recently, you worked for the American Central Intelligence Agency, yes?"

"Yes."

"Have you ever been married?"

"No."

"Are you a homosexual?"

"No."

"In which case," Zyaad smiled in preparation for a crucial fine point he was sure would be lost on the three sullen referees, but not on whoever was watching through the camcorder in the chandelier—unless, of course, it was a just secretary making a transcript. "In which case, Mr. Teeple, being neither a family man nor a homosexual, we may presume that for thirty years you have given your level best to your employer?"

"Well . . ."

"Lonely men tend to do that, you know?"

"If you say so."

"Modesty suits you." Zyaad was still testing the best way of speaking upwards without gaping. "Modesty also fits in with your refusal to believe in a guardian angel inside the Central Intelligence Agency."

"I told you, there was no angel."

"Right." Zyaad reluctantly turned to the referees. "As I pointed out in the transcript of my debriefing of this witness, the proof that he has not been aware of a guardian angel on the executive floor in Langley is threefold. One, in thirty years he had not made it higher than case officer second grade. Two, not one of the reprimands he had received for his resistance to politically correct changes within the agency had been erased from his record. Three—and I explain that later—his deceased colleague, Danny Craig, was also a personal friend."

The center-cushion referee suppressed a yawn, and Zyaad turned his eyes back upwards as if pleading for an absolution to a higher intelligence. The sight of the dumb punks on the floor was nauseating to him, one of the richest men in the world, but since he could not tell how much authority they had to cut him short, he decided to liven up his rhetoric with the common touch.

"It was in a bar fight, wasn't it, Mr. Teeple, that you broke a man's nose? Nicaragua 1971?"

"I told you it was."

"You told me you used a technique acquired in the hand-to-hand combat training at the so-called Farm back in America, yes?"

"Yes."

"Now," Zyaad briefly glanced at the referees. As he had

hoped, the mention of a bar fight and a broken nose had grabbed their attention, and he turned back to Teeple to capitalize on the momentary advantage. "You broke a bone with an acquired technique. But what about the motive for the swing? Can we say it came from the gut?"

"The man I had the fight with worked for the New York Times. They would print details of our operations down there as if they were charity benefits, and our men were being picked off by the KGB like fish in a barrel."

"How did you know the man in question was a journalist?"

"He wore his press card on a string around his neck because the hookers in Managua did journalists at half price. The other half was subsidized by the Sandinistas."

"Interesting," Zyaad smiled, knowing he had the referees' attention for a little while longer. Bar fights, shooting fish in a barrel, discount hookers, it all sounded like their kind of happenings, and he spoke more slowly now. "Absurd as it may sound, witness Teeple is not making this up. I had his testimony corroborated. In Nicaragua, newspaper reporters would indeed get fifty percent off from the local pimps with ties to the leftist government."

Zyaad paused to let the information sink in. Then, the groundwork in place, he proceeded towards the heart of the matter.

"So, to further establish this witness's credibility, I took the trouble to find the journalist in question to make sure his nose was still crooked. The man now teaches mail-order courses on journalism and was more than happy to talk to a live person when my investigator knocked on his door. He confirmed that after the bar fight, his newspaper was ready to sue, but Mr. Teeple seemed to have disappeared from the face of Earth." Zyaad smiled at Teeple almost affectionately. "Where on Earth were you hiding that not even New York lawyers could find you?"

"On an island in southeast Asia."

"Where you began to learn all there was to know about the Malacca Straits pirates, right?"

"Just indirectly, I told you that."

"It took you, you told me, a couple of years to get onto the money trail that led from the Malacca Straits to North Africa."

"I was transferred to North Africa a month after I sent in my report about the Malacca Straits business because no one in Washington wanted to hear about it. I told you that. Your guardian angel theory doesn't make sense."

"Yet, judging by what you told me about your activities in Somalia, you did not hesitate to risk your life to make a videotape of a back-alley deal in enriched plutonium. Who told you that the payment in that deal was to be made in cash skimmed from the Malacca Straits operation?"

"I don't think anyone made the connection at that time. The African section at Langley was too busy tiptoeing around human rights issues."

"How about your own people on the spot, did they know where that money came from?"

"If they did, they did not tell me."

"Well," Zyaad smiled and waited for a moment to give Teeple a chance to reconsider. "I do have a copy of that top secret video, you know that?"

"Sure."

"The 'Received' stamp on the archive folder is dated May 11, two days after the Russian seller had been scheduled to show up in Red Square to participate in the annual celebration of victory in World War II."

"There's also a date stamp on the tape," Teeple said for the record. He could not see where Zyaad was going with this.

"Are you talking about the little red figures in the lower right corner of each frame?"

"That date is May 5."

"Camera settings can be so easily manipulated."

"Not by half a dozen television networks setting their cameras wrong on May 9. Kropotkin's empty seat in the Red Square spectacle was two rows behind the Russian president."

"Proving what?"

"I don't know. You started this."

"Exactly. Kropotkin was found on a Mogadishu beach on May 8 on a heap of broken bottles and washed out plastic with a bullet in his head." Zyaad raised his voice without a glance at the chandelier. "The UN air-traffic control center that was set up to keep track of corruption in humanitarian help has a record of an American private jet entering the Somalian airspace on May 7, leaving on May 8. The passenger manifest of that particular aircraft has just one name on it. Have you ever known that name, Mr. Teeple?"

"No."

"No?"

"I told you. No."

"That name on the passenger manifest was Buzz Blewitt." Making sure not to gloat in Blewitt's direction, Zyaad looked pleased by the surprise in Teeple's face. He had managed to confuse his own witness, thus pre-empting the most obvious strategy for the defense: discrediting a prosecution witness by portraying him as a plant.

"Now, Mr. Teeple, correct me if I am wrong. You have been recalled from Somalia on May 10, two days after Kropotkin's body was found on a garbage heap, one day after he failed to show up in the Red Square in Moscow. Your flight from Mogadishu to Washington had a stopover in London, right?"

"Yes."

"At Heathrow, you were met by your people from the UK office and told that there had been a change of plans. You were not going home. You were to hop on a plane to where?"

"Singapore."

"Your presence was needed down there—an urgent mission for which you were assigned a cover. What was that cover?"

"Waste disposal expert."

"In other words, it was a covert mission. Your old friend, Danny Craig, had managed to convince your superiors at Langley that he had an idea where to find the merchandise from that Mogadishu deal. And he told you so personally on the phone."

"Yes."

"Did he call a spade a spade?"

"What spade?"

"Enriched plutonium. Did he refer to it as such on the phone?"

"I told you, I don't remember every word we said."

"But you do remember the type of phone security you used, don't you? Would you call it state-of-art technology?"

"No."

"In which case, what are the chances that in this particular case, you had not been issued the latest hardware intentionally?"

"In a government job, foul-ups are a way of life."

"With every foul-up having its own smoke screen?"

"It was not my job to worry about that. I was not a political appointee."

"Exactly. You had no idea about the smoke screen to protect an American presidential candidate, a candidate running on the tax-the-hell-out-of-the-rich ticket, a man whom . . ." Zyaad pointed a finger at Blewitt and held it there, "whom the accused had to shield with his body and soul from the slightest hint of suspicion of having a hand in an offshore tax shelter? Blewitt could not have possibly allowed my witness Teeple and his partner Danny Craig to bring to light something that would lead to a massive inquiry in Washington, an inquiry that was as likely as not to expose a part of the complex money-laundering web sponsored by the said presidential candidate's family."

Zyaad was aware he was getting carried away and took a deep breath to make it clear he was getting to the point now.

"With the American presidential elections around the corner, Blewitt's back was against the wall. He had no choice but to call in a favor—my foiled French deal. It was payback time, and the CIA had to choose between Danny Craig, an insignificant little pawn making his hands dirty in a little job, and Buzz Blewitt, a man with easy access to the ledgers of the Emirates Bank of Riyadh."

It was time for a wrap, and Zyaad once more raised an accusing finger at Blewitt, but lowered his voice to seek revenge with the humility of a religious man.

"For a man like Blewitt, death is too merciful, purgatory is too benign, hell's fire is not hot enough."

"Objection!" Blewitt's attorney stepped forth to place himself between Zyaad's accusing finger and the man he was paid to defend.

The attorney was a religious man himself, but the pay was good enough to keep his family financially secure even if he himself should burn in hell for siding with the infidel.

31

"Dr. Zyaad is right," Blewitt's attorney began, humbly. His client's hands were still tied. "There have been arbitrary write-offs on the Emirates Bank's books. My client is not disputing that. No business is immune to information leaks. A damage caused by low-level indiscretions has been an indivisible part of the cost of doing business since the beginning of time. Neanderthal females would betray the whereabouts of prime tribal hunting grounds to desirable enemy hunks; Hun warriors infatuated with the glitter of Roman armor would betray their brothers clad in rags; Judas betrayed Jesus for near to nothing."

His unaccented American voice was pleasantly modulated, seeking semantic flaws in the flowery syntax of Zyaad's closing statement.

"In view of Dr. Zyaad's poetically enhanced perception of justice, it is my contention to translate his words into everyday language. Hell's fire is a cruel and unusual punishment for minor bookkeeping irregularities—especially . . ." he allowed himself a lingering hint of a patronizing smile, "especially when mundane monetary loses would not cause the plaintiff to get behind with his mortgage payments. A great wealth such as Dr. Zyaad's has indisputable advantages when it comes to making ends meet. Yet, most unfortunately, a great wealth as often as not goes hand in hand with an all-consuming ambition."

Done with the ephemeral, the attorney put on glasses to consult his notes.

"Dr. Zyaad stands to substantially increase his already more than substantial net worth if he can prove that the Emirates Bank had been an instrument of treason to the Muslim cause in my client's hands. Speaking of which . . ." looking over his spectacles, the attorney turned a facetiously rueful eye to the referees on the floor, "speaking of which, can we get the rope off my client's wrists?"

There was a moment of silence as the center referee listened to his earphone before he shook his head. Request denied.

"A wise decision." The attorney made sure not to sound facetious yet. "My client has no need to gesticulate about straightforward evidence. He is not here to challenge the fact that his employer, the illustrious Mr. Joe Fitch, owns fifty-one percent of the Emirates Bank. That figure is a matter of public record. It is written in black on white in official documents—documents that also show beyond the shadow of a doubt that every single share of the remaining forty-nine percent is owned by Dr. Zyaad. In other words, Dr. Zyaad is officially second in command."

The attorney smiled benignly at the three referees on the floor.

"What is not a matter of public record, however, is the fact that Dr. Zyaad is not accustomed to playing second fiddle no matter what. It is a state of mind that has to do as much with the arithmetic of forty-nine against fifty-one as with the infamous medical condition called megalomania."

"Hey!" the center referee frowned at the attorney. He did not know about courts of law, but he could tell a guy spoiling for a fight when he saw one. "You a shrink or something?"

"Merely an attorney at law, sir," the attorney bowed humbly.

"A simple man in possession of simple, straightforward evidence. Dr. Zyaad paid a total of twelve million dollars to twelve prominent archeologists to dig in the fields and meadows in the vicinity of his château near Poitiers. For Dr. Zyaad is obsessed with a dream—a dream of unearthing a proof that in the year 732 of the Christian calendar, Emir Abdul Rahman Al Ghafiqi's retreat after the battle of Poitiers was merely a strategic maneuver to get away from the harsh European winter. According to Dr. Zyaad, the Emir chose to withdraw to the more temperate climate of his homeland to wait thirteen hundred years for central heating and electricity to make Europe more habitable for a conqueror—the conqueror this time being Dr. Zyaad himself.

"As every psychologist will tell you, megalomaniacs are blinded to rational thought. Men suffering from delusions of grandeur live outside reality. When they cannot get what they want, they convince themselves that they want what they can get—as a result of which Dr. Zyaad acquired himself a witness that would play in his hand."

The attorney took his time to turn to Teeple, but the eye contact was swift and abrupt, like a gear that had engaged at full speed.

"Mr. Teeple, you sold Dr. Zyaad your life story for money?"
"What else."
"Can we say you needed money desperately?"
"You can."
"Has your dead-end job with the Internal Revenue Service in New York been driving you to despair? Or was it the deplorable living conditions at . . ." the attorney consulted his notes, "let's just say at your shabby residence in the mean streets of lower Manhattan that in the end convinced Dr. Zyaad of the honesty of your determination to betray your country?"
"Zyaad never asked me where I lived."
"Then, can we assume, you gave your address to Dr. Zyaad's scout while playing at a has-been on skid row?"
"That man knew I had a job."
"The term skid row was just a figure of speech, sir," the at-

torney smiled pleasantly. "A joke, if you will, Mr. Teeple. We know you told Dr. Zyaad's scout about your employment. Your aim was not to fake destitution, merely an all-consuming unhappiness about your present living conditions that were in so stark a contrast with what could have been."

"Like what?" Teeple had no problem to sound bored with the gibberish.

"Had things not gone wrong for you thirty-something years back, you could have had it all: a fairy-tale life on a picturesque cattle ranch in California, sheep, chickens, horses, a bunch of kids and a beauty queen for a wife. What was her name, Roni? Or was it Veronica? Veronica Pitt?"

Teeple glanced at Zyaad, who still looked confident the attorney was either going to shoot himself in the foot or to talk himself into a corner.

"She was a piece of work, wasn't she?" the attorney persisted, and Teeple shrugged casually.

"She was all right."

"All right? Is that all?" The attorney paused to make sure everybody understood it was time to stop tiptoeing in the tulips. "She was out of your league, Mr. Teeple. She dumped you for a better man and exposed you to ridicule from your peers that made you, understandably so, leave home and swear revenge. For thirty years you waited for a chance to get back at that better man. So, when that chance finally materialized in the megalomanic ambitions of Dr. Zyaad, you volunteered to trick this mentally unstable man into helping you destroy Richard Fitch's chances to become president of the United States."

"What?"

"You are not a paid informer, Mr. Teeple. You are a volunteer. The jig's up. You're not doing this for money."

"You got that one right," Teeple grunted, sullenly. "So far I haven't been paid a dime."

"How much money were you promised?"

Again, Teeple glanced at Zyaad who seemed to be torn on that issue. He did want Teeple to come clean. Yet he was beginning to wonder what else the attorney was up to, and Teeple got the message. Lying about money now might complicate things later.

"Five hundred thousand," he said. "U.S. dollars."

"I'm sorry to hear that." The attorney paused to make sure all eyes were on him before he came to the point. "Because by the time I have finished with you, Mr. Teeple, your would-be benefactor will be in no position to pay anything to anyone. Especially not to a phony witness."

"Objection," Zyaad called out, a touch too firmly to keep his voice from breaking, but the referees said nothing. What the hell did they know about legal gibberish? They just kept up the stony faces, and Blewitt's attorney took over the role of a judge himself.

"Objection denied. For Mr. Teeple is as phony as they come." The attorney paused to make sure the courtroom was ready for the real bombshell. "I hereby call the real witness."

He let the implications of his statement dangle for a moment, then turned to the center referee.

"Someone here to fetch her?"

The referees looked up. "It's a woman?"

No one moved, and the attorney looked at Teeple's guards, who certainly were not taking orders from the sidekick of a man whose hands were tied, and an awkward pause followed.

Yet the door opened, powered by unseen hands on the outside, proving that whoever had been watching through the chandelier was not just a stenographer taking notes. A stenographer could not have possibly put together that kind of choreography: a spellbinding moment of total silence before the squeak of rubber soles on parquetry preceded Beth's solo entrance.

31

Beth was dressed for a street rally, not a ballroom, and the squeak of her jagged shoe soles stopped dead as she halted in the doorway, hesitating to step on a shiny dance floor in heavy-duty gear.

"Stand down, Mr. Teeple," Blewitt's attorney said, and, hearing the name, Beth's eyes froze on the back of the man standing in the spotlight in the center of the room.

"Hank?"

The center referee nodded to Teeple's guards who stepped forward and, not sure what to do next, grabbed him under the armpits to show determination. They jerked him backwards, paused for further instructions, and when no one said anything, they figured it was all right to drag him back to the back wall and have him stand there.

Blewitt's attorney approved of that arrangement with a nod and crooked a finger at Beth. "Step forward."

"Why?"

"Please."

"I . . ." To the best of her knowledge, Beth had come here for a drink. What was it called? Pernod? Was it a French custom to drink Pernod in a spotlight?

"Why?" she said aloud.

"Why not."

With her mouth slightly open and the soles of her boots sounding unnaturally loud in an ominous silence, Beth made a few limping steps forward to where Hank had been standing a moment before. In her old brown sweater and loose tweed pants, she looked out of place in a ballroom spotlight. With stunned curiosity, she first examined the most conspicuous figure in the room: Zyaad, standing at his lectern in flowing white garb, gazing back at her with a puzzled frown. Then her eyes wandered to the other side of the ballroom where Blewitt stood at an identical lectern, dressed up for an old-fashioned *thè dansant*. A stray ray of sunshine made his yellow necktie glow, and Beth reluctantly turned to the man by his side who did the talking. She disliked that one most.

"What is your name?" Blewitt's attorney wanted to know, and Beth glanced at Hank for guidance. The spotlight was in her eyes, and he looked away as if he could not bear the sight of her squinting.

"What's all this?" She pointed at a window. "The police are right there. I can see them."

"Of course you can." The attorney smiled with fatherly pride about her cleverness. He, too, had a daughter. "Do those brave gendarmes look to you as if they were rearing to storm the place and rush to your rescue while TV cameras are rolling? Even cops are smart enough to figure the media would crucify them if they dared to barge in on a peaceful religious conference."

Then, abruptly, the attorney's fatherly smile turned chilly, as if some warm molasses faucet had been suddenly shut off by some strict judicial decree, and Beth was beginning to understand. Hank was here on some kind of a trial in front of all these people.

"Who are you?" She glared at the three stooges on the floor, but again it was the attorney who answered.

"Who is who in this room is of no interest to you. It might even be to your advantage not to know. All I want you to understand is that if you agree to cooperate instead of fighting me every step of the way, I promise to be lenient to your boyfriend." The attorney turned his mocking eyes to Teeple. "For he is your boyfriend, isn't he?"

"We work together . . . worked, I mean. In an office."

"Do you? I mean, did you?"

"Yes."

"How old are you, Beth?"

It sounded like a harmless question, and she answered it as such.

"Twenty-three."

"Then Mr. Teeple is more than twice your age. He must've cut a pretty tragic figure behind an office desk back in New York to catch your eye."

"He's no tragic figure."

"Yet, I'm told, you wined and dined him as if he had not eaten in months and had to be fattened up or else. If that was not compassion for a soul in distress, what was it? A romantic attraction?"

Beth turned to look at Hank again. She did not want to say anything that might be taken against him by people whom she did not know for reasons she could not even begin to fathom. But he would not look up. He just kept staring at his feet, letting her grope in her own darkness. Why?

"I cooked for him because he needed warm food," she said, defiantly.

"But haven't you just told me he was not a tragic figure?"

"I said he needed warm food."

"Then how about the fine wines you plied him with? Were those meant to merely increase the nutritional value of the said warm food?"

"What are you talking about?"

"Empty wine bottles with costly labels were found in your kitchen refuse in New York, Beth." The attorney turned his fatherly smile back on to show that even though he was about to use offensive language, he meant no offense. "Tell me, how much does a girl with no office skills get paid in a crummy office job?"

Beth did not answer that, but the attorney was not upset with her.

"You probably don't even know, do you? You might not have ever bothered to look at your paycheck. Your father is among what, the ten richest men in America?"

"Not ten."

"A hundred maybe, give or take a few?" The attorney smiled and shook his head with phony compassion. "What a bummer to get disinherited, huh?"

"How do you know that?"

"A little bird flew in through the window and told me you were a bad girl in the past, Beth. Your father had been very upset with you, and his lawyers told you in no uncertain terms that he would only consider putting you back in his will if you married a man he approved of—a mature man with enough common sense to deal with your misguided infatuation with social justice."

Beth hesitated, then decided to say nothing. She was grasping at straws, hoping that if she let the attorney come down hard on her, he might have less time for Hank.

"Tell me, Beth, could it be that the inheritance issue was an incentive for the expensive wines for Mr. Teeple? Is it possible that you were fed up working in an office and figured that your father might approve of an old-fashioned G-man? A man to keep you out of trouble, so to speak."

Sticking to the theory that a mulish silence might deflect the attorney's attention away from Hank, Beth made no answer, and the attorney rubbed his hands. "Of course, there always is the possibility you fell in love."

"No." Breaking her silence on impulse, Beth had not quite managed to sound convincing, and the attorney mercilessly zeroed in on her insecurity.

"All the same, you followed Mr. Teeple to Paris, didn't you?"

"No."

"Yet, you are here?"

"I have not followed him."

"Then I shall rephrase myself. You came to Paris to keep an eye on him after you found out that she was going to be here, too."

"She?"

"She, the beauty queen. Has Mr. Teeple never told you about the girl on account of whom he left home thirty years ago?"

"Who are you talking about?"

"The woman whose shoes you wanted so badly to fill."

"What shoes?"

"Veronica Pitt's."

The attorney had made the 's' of the possessive sound like the swish of a whip, and Beth turned to Hank for explanation. But he still would not look at her. He seemed to be thinking hard about something, and she again sought refuge in defiance.

"What's all this about?"

"The lady that showed up at your door in New York a few days ago, how did she introduce herself? Had she rung your doorbell just to say hi? Hi, Beth, here you have me. Do something."

"Huh?" No matter how hard she tried, Beth was much too distracted to bring things into the right chronological order that fast. She knew the attorney had it all wrong. She just could not put a finger on the discrepancy and raised her voice. "You complicate things on purpose."

"Let's make it simple, then. What was her name, the lady that came to say hi to you in New York three days ago?"

The timing of the attorney's switch to a soft voice and a lingering smile was perfect. It made Beth sound like a trapped screeching owl struggling to duck daylight.

"What do you want from me?" Her voice broke, and in the abrupt silence, the attorney's soft-spoken self-confidence came across with a crushing clarity.

"I want you to tell us the name of the lady that brought you to Paris?"

"Why?"

"What was her name?"

"I..."

"What... was... her... name?"

The referees on the floor craned their necks like vultures watching a dead man walking, and Beth realized they were not looking at her. They were staring at Hank, and she had no choice.

"Veronica..." she said, hoarsely.

She had spoken in a whisper, as if she hoped against hope that no one was going to hear her, but the attorney kept his volume up.

"Veronica who?"

"Pitt."

"Louder."

"Veronica Pitt." Beth's voice trailed off, and the attorney paused to poise himself to go for the jugular.

"Veronica Pitt told you she was going to Paris, and you had no choice but to tag along to make sure Mr. Teeple wouldn't let you down on the little matter of inheritance. A hundred million dollars, I have been told; is that about correct?"

"You have it all wrong." It was all so absurd. Beth did not know Hank knew Veronica. And she had not asked Veronica to take her to Paris. It was the other way round. Also, she was not worried about money and did not know where to start to get the record straight. "I told Hank about the money before he went away."

"Oh?"

"I did."

"In other words, he knew before he came out here how much you were worth."

"I guess."

"You guess?" The attorney was still being patient, but not for long, his smile was saying. "You guess, or you know?"

"I know," she said, softly, afraid that if she lied, the consequences would be for Hank alone to bear.

"In other words, you knew he knew. Is that what you said?"

"Yes."

"Are you sure?"

"Yes."

"Thank you."

The attorney was grinning now, and it was too late for Beth to switch to lying. She would have lied her head off had she known what to lie about, but the attorney was no longer interested in her. He was talking to the chandelier.

"Only moments ago, Mr. Teeple told us he needed money so desperately that he would betray his oath of allegiance to his country and testify for Dr. Zyaad. He wanted us to believe that he had traveled half way around the world and risked a prison term at home for the meager reward of half a million. Would a man do something like that when he knew that so much more money was just waiting for his nod and the proverbial yes-word uttered in the comfort of his favorite armchair in a fancy Manhattan penthouse?"

The attorney was openly grinning at the chandelier now and could not resist veering away from law and justice to show a facetiously poetic vein.

"Let us hereby stand reminded never to underestimate the power of hormonal attraction, the one and only mistake Mr. Teeple and his handler had made in their brilliant scheme to discredit my client. Joseph Verhagen, the renowned spy master and believer in undiluted brain power, did not bother to include love in his formula of intellectually immaculate subterfuge and deception." Out of the corner of his eyes, the attorney saw Teeple push off the back wall and paused to enjoy the final clincher. He had been hoping for that.

"Leave her out of it." Teeple said, hoarsely.

"Isn't it too late for that?"

"She knows nothing. Let her go." Teeple said, aware of the attorney's widening smile but not giving a damn about it.

"Are you trying to tell us something, Mr. Teeple? Have you yourself and you alone been privy to the cunning subterfuge to discredit my client?"

"If you want to put it that way."

"Indeed I do." The attorney nodded to the guards to take Beth away.

They grabbed her under the armpits, and Teeple lunged forward. The lunatics were capable of anything; but he barely managed half a step before men were on his back, pulling him down.

A foot on the back of his neck pinned one side of his face to the floor, making him see with just one eye. The hardwood parquetry made the sore spot under his other eye hurt, and his barely healed lip opened up. He could taste blood as he tried to turn his head to look for Beth. The heel at the back of his neck pushed closer to the spine, found the right spot between two vertebrae, and he stopped struggling. The view from his free eye stabilized, and he could see the center referee listen to his earphone, draw his dagger and hand it over to one of the guards.

"What are you doing?" Teeple heard Zyaad cry, but could not see him.

He only saw the man with the dagger step over to Blewitt and slash the rope on his wrists, missing the vital arteries by a fraction of an inch.

The ends of the cut rope slid off Blewitt's wrists and fell on the floor with a silent, no-nonsense simplicity that finally made Teeple see the fancy trimmings falling off Verhagen's trick. The old man had had no choice. He knew Teeple was a chip off the old block, and the only way to make an actor out of the son of a man who could not play act even in horse trading was by giving him a script with a few pages missing. Verhagen needed a command performance to discredit Blewitt with a twist—a twist that would, in the end, do in Zyaad.

So, if Zyaad had been the fall guy from the start, the scheme had worked. The point of the exercise had been far beyond not just letting Danny's death go to waste in the wasteland of political correctness, and Teeple had no choice but to trust Verhagen on that.

Beth, on the other hand, had done nothing of that sort. Beth had been sucked in as a one-of-a-kind prop.

But lying flat on his stomach, pinned down to the floor with his face down, there was nothing he could do for her right now. He could not see her with his one free eye. He just saw the center referee pull the wire out of his ear and draw a finger across his throat to indicate that the court was in recess.

Everybody began to leave, filing out of Teeple's squashed field of vision one by one, until they were all gone and the heel on the back of his neck lifted.

Somebody was helping him stand up.

32

Outside the hotel, the peace rally in Place Vendôme was beginning to lose momentum. In the dissipating mob euphoria, Veronica Pitt's aching vocal cords brought about the inevitable disenchantment with a world she suspected had not been listening, and melancholy began to set in. Her exultation stalled, tethered on the brink of reality, and took a free fall to where she suddenly remembered Beth.

She could kick herself for not paying closer attention to the blond woman she had noticed out of the corner of an eye picking up Beth literally in the gutter. The two of them seemed to have bumped into one another as strangers would in a packed city street, and she would not give it a second thought at the time. Flip had still been so damned funny then, and they were all having such a good time.

It was only now that Veronica's darkening mood warped the image of a blonde stranger into a guaranteed non-blonde. That woman's hair was yellow. Even at a distance, it had looked bleached and brittle—meaning that the natural color had been much darker. Something Blewitt might've had a hand in?

What the hell was going on? Veronica was getting really ticked off. Beth was a dear old friend's daughter, and when she tried to call Blewitt, all she would get at his number was static. Either her cell phone didn't work in Paris, or the sonofabitch had blocked her calls.

"A problem?" Flip Farrell came up from behind to give her a rowdy bear hug. He, too, was hoarse and anxious to end the farce on a high note. "Wanna come with us to watch the spectacle on the evening news?"

"No." Veronica had to find Beth no matter what. She needed a phone that Blewitt was not blocking, and the mere thought of figuring out what coins one needed in a French phone booth made her furious. Damn public phones, damn Paris, damn Blewitt. She'd had it. She needed a hit. She needed a hit bad and fast, and Flip was getting on her nerves with his chit-chat.

"A gorgeous woman like you," Flip brushed her ear with his dry lips, "don't tell me you don't love to see yourself on TV."

They were all going to watch the tube at a chic bohemian pad within walking distance from the Ritz and, come to think of that, Veronica saw her chance. A bohemian pad, huh? Stuff would as likely as not abound at those cribs. Besides, she needed to pee.

Beth would have to wait.

* * *

Beth could not get rid of the crazy memory of Hank lying face down on a ballroom floor with a man's foot on his neck. She had wanted to put something under his head, a pillow or something, but the men that had her by the armpits lifted her of her feet and dragged her out of the ballroom. They locked her up her in a broom closet, and for fear of making things worse for Hank, she would neither scream nor bang on the door.

The broom closet smelled of wet rags and ammonia that after a while became not altogether unpleasant to breathe. And with nothing to look at except a sliver of light under the door, Beth lost track of time.

She might have been in the closet for an hour, maybe two, maybe longer. She sure had no idea what time it was when a key rattled in the lock. The door hinges squeaked, a silhouette of a woman appeared in a surge of light that made her squint, and the accent was familiar.

"'ere you are."

It was the well-dressed French woman Beth had been supposed to have a drink with. What was it called? Pernod? The goddamned, stuck-up con artist had lied through her teeth, yet Beth was determined to go on playing the game for Hank's sake. Did that make her crazy or what? Because in the hushed, carpeted atmosphere that the broom closet opened into, it also seemed utterly senseless to make a fuss about a botched happy hour.

The silent corridor was lined with silent numbered doors, and they took an elevator down to the lobby where a smartly uniformed doorman looked puzzled by Beth's smell as they passed by on their way out.

In front of the hotel, the sun was gone from the cobblestones and so was the peace rally. In the center of the square, the bronze man on the tall column looked lonely and neglected, sticking out of a hodgepodge of discarded candy wrappers, crushed Styrofoam cups, cigarette butts and abandoned placards. Everybody else was gone. Veronica Pitt, Flip Farrell and his hopping pink beauties, the benign police, the enthusiastic old ladies in their summer dresses and wrinkled stockings, they all seemed to have disappeared into thin air. Even the smell of mob was gone.

The renaissance facades around the deserted square had returned to their silent historical significance, and Beth could not see what else there was for her to do in Paris, except beat her head against historical masonry for letting Hank down. She had been left behind like all the candy wrappers and cigarette butts around her, discarded and spent, thankful for any company, no matter how dubious. What was the woman's name again? Jacque? Who cared.

The memory of the eerie kangaroo court at the fancy old ballroom had long been diluted by the broom closet fumes, and names meant very little to her right now.

"What was that all about?" she heard herself asking the woman who called herself Jacque.

They were crossing Place Vendôme in the direction of the Louvre, and the wind from the river began to loosen up the ammonia-induced congestion in Beth's brain and sinuses.

"Who were those clowns?" she went on, not quite recognizing her own voice.

"Pardon?" Jacque was suddenly struggling with her English, and Beth took a deep breath to give her frustration a belligerent ring. She was an American in Paris, the shrine of Western civilization for God's sake, not some third-world autocracy where people vanished without a trace. She had the right to know.

"Were they trying to convict Hank of something? What kind of scam was that?"

"Scam?"

"That's what I said."

"*Je ne sais pas.*"

"They were a bunch of lunatics."

"Yes." Jacque took Beth by the hand to lead her towards a taxi stand on a street corner. "Come on."

At the end of the row of waiting taxis, Jacque opened the back door of a black limo with tinted windows that did not have a taxi sign on the roof, and Beth hesitated. Was she going to let one woman fool her twice? But then, what good would a screaming fit do? Was she prepared to roam the streets of Paris alone, with just guilt about letting Hank down for company? Her boots hurt, as did the screws in her shin, and she had no money.

"I got to find Veronica," she said.

"All right."

"You know her?"

"No. Get in."

Jacque pushed her inside and squeezed in after her. In contrast with the filth in the street, the limo's back seat looked extravagantly clean and luxurious in the twilight of tinted windows, and Beth sank into the voluptuous upholstery with an unmitigated sigh of relief.

The limo pulled away from the curb and at the next corner plunged into the one-way traffic of the Rue de Rivoli. And as if the air conditioning had chilled out Beth's bad vibes, she began to take in her surroundings. There was a silhouette of a chauffeur behind a tinted glass partition, looking unflappable even when the traffic flow swept them into the maelstrom of Place de la Concorde. There were no marked traffic lanes there, and as the limo swayed from side to side to avoid collisions with cars that were coming at them from all sides like angry bees, Beth kept touching shoulders with Jacque in a sort of sisterly way that after a while broke the ice.

"Where is Hank?" Beth said, quietly, and it worked. Jacque got her English back.

"He's all right."

"But..."

"You'll see."

The limo weaved its way through the chaotic Place, crossed the Seine, and entered a maze of narrow cobblestone streets jam-packed with parked cars. There were very few pedestrians here, and as the limo came to a brief stop to negotiate a tight corner, Beth heard the door lock on her side engage, while someone opened Jacque's door from the outside. She tried to grab her wrist but missed.

"Goodbye, dear." Jacque slipped out to make room for a man in a business suit to take her place.

"Get going," the man told the chauffeur before he was quite in and slammed the door shut when the car was already moving.

He sounded American, but in the combined twilight of a narrow street and tinted windows, Beth could not make out his face or the color of his suit. It could have well been black or navy blue, but there was nothing ambiguous about his necktie.

It glowed bright yellow, bringing back the memory of how much she had hated the man's guts back in the ballroom.

Without his lawyer, though, Blewitt alone seemed all right. He stayed in his corner, careful not to gloat. Nor would he move closer—the reason for which, Beth assumed, might have been her smell. Yet he did not seem interested in conversation at a distance either, and she wondered whether he, being an American after all, could possibly know where on Earth Veronica had been all this time.

33

The chic bohemian pad where Veronica and her buddies had gone to watch the evening news after the Peace Rally was a walkup in a shabby tenement off the Rue de Rivoli. It belonged to a cute young starlet by the name of Cherie, a giggling doll who collected famous butt imprints in her sofa, and since the still fairly famous Flip Farrell had been so conspicuously deferential to a crazy American woman dressed like the French tricolor, she invited her, too. She could tell that Madame Veronica, a red-white-and-blue sour pickle who would not see forty again, was *seulement* business to him.

"Who the hell's she?" she whispered in Flip's ear when Veronica disappeared in the bathroom the moment they arrived at the apartment.

One could hear a pin drop behind the walls here. The old renaissance building had been remodeled after World War II, when cheap building materials were not soundproof, and they heard Veronica pee behind the partition.

"Be nice to her, OK?" Flip muttered, lowering his voice to a whisper. It stood to reason that if they heard what Veronica was doing in there, she could hear what they were saying about her out here. "The old girl might be worth your while."

"Oh, yeah?"

"She's Richard Fitch's ex."

"Who is he?"

"You kiddin' me?" The peeing behind the partition ceased, and Flip lowered his voice another notch. "Never heard of the next American president?"

"*O la la.*" Politics and politicians bored Cherie to tears. They were oh so blah.

"Before you get on a high horse, *ma soeur*," Flip muttered with a mock French accent, sliding his hand behind Cherie's back and pronouncing "Fitches" as "*Fitchees*". "*Les Fitchees* own *tres grandes* movie studios."

"In Hollywood?"

"Where else."

"*Merde.*" Cherie pushed Flip's hand off her buttocks and got up to turn on the TV to overpower the sound of Veronica's further bathroom activities. As an aspiring pop star, Cherie had a signature stunt and all the responsibilities that went with it. She would hold powwows at juvenile prisons to keep kids away from drugs, and what she had just heard from behind the bathroom partition was a hearty snort—a bit too rich even for her. "The damned woman found my stash, damn it."

"Don't be a Scrooge. I told you, be nice to her."

"She'll get me busted. Imagine the headlines."

"Nah."

"Look at her."

Veronica came out of the toilet wiping her nose on a red sleeve, making it look as if some of the color had rubbed off. She threw herself on the sofa next to Flip, just in time for the evening news. The shimmering glow of the TV screen made her red-rimmed eyes look outright bloodshot as she opened them wide to make out the anchor woman.

Veronica Pitt had a knack for faces, and the bleached hair was the clincher. The evening news babe was the same phony blonde that had picked up Beth in Place Vendôme this afternoon.

"You bastard," she gasped.

She had meant Blewitt, but Flip could not know that and looked hurt. What had he done wrong? Was his fly open? But Veronica was not looking in his lap. Her eyes were glaring on the TV screen, and he was curious.

"You know her?"

"Everybody knows her," Cherie chimed in, remembering Flip's reminder to be nice to the ex of the next American president, who owned *tres grandes* movie studios. "Jacque Petain is, how do you say, the voice of France."

Ignoring Cherie's twitter, Veronica narrowed her eyes at Flip. "Where the hell do you know her from?"

"What?"

"Who told you? Blewitt?"

"What do you mean I blew it? What's the matter with you? I never saw the woman in my life."

"Shhh, you two." Cherie reached out to clamp Flip's lips with her red fingernails as pictures from the rally in Place Vendôme came on, with Jacque Petain's voice-over—in French, of course.

"What the hell?" Veronica demanded to know. The whole goddamned Paris was ganging up on her. "What's she saying?"

"She calls us, how do say, valiant warriors of peace," Cherie translated and clapped her hands as the TV camera singled out the three of them holding hands to form a human chain to lock something or other in people's hearts. "We look good, no?"

"Like hell I do." Veronica stood up to turn away from the image of rubbing hips with Cherie, who was half her width. "Got a phone? Any old land line."

"*Ce qui?*"

"A phone. With a wire?"

"*Qu'a-t-il dit?*"

"Wire... like... wire."

"*Aaah, oui.*"

Happily, Cherie led the way to the bedroom where the bed was not made and an old-fashioned telephone was half buried in a heap of crumpled Kleenex tissue on a bedside table.

"Sorry," she giggled apologetically, making a halfhearted attempt at straightening the bed blanket. Hollywood had been her dream ever since she was a kid in the suburbs of Lyon. Her father still worked in a textile mill there, and the guys in the canteen had been giving him a hard time about his daughter's occasional porn gigs to prop up a sputtering career. A solid role in a solid family movie, she was sure, would make everybody shut up; but she was beginning to have her doubts about Veronica's influence in Hollywood or anywhere else as she watched her rummage in her handbag. The would-be American president's ex-girlfriend pulled out what looked like a notebook, dropped it on the floor, picked it up, dropped the handbag, extracted the phone out of the heap of Kleenex, and took a shaky stab at dialing a number. It took her a while to get it right.

"Get me Blewitt," she growled when someone finally picked up at the other end. A pause. "How the hell do I know? Go get him, damn it." Another pause. "Don't get smart with me. I want Blewitt to get me out of here tonight." A short pause. "No, not tomorrow. Write it down. Now."

She hung up, threw the notebook into the handbag, missed, picked it up, picked up the handbag, and walked out of the shabby chic Parisian pad without a goodbye to either Flip or Cherie—especially not Cherie, whose stash she had in the bag, the whole thing. Blewitt had driven her to stealing from the poor.

The bastard was making her crazy.

He obviously couldn't care less about her once he had what he wanted—whatever that had been this time around. She really did not want to know. Something hot must have gone bad; what the hell did she care? She just had to kick the habit and think faster next time around, which was all but a piece of cake after 30 years of an on and off relationship with Richard Fitch. The Fitches and the Blewitts of this world made her want to puke. She could not live with them and she would not last too long without them, just like she would not last without whatever made her feel good—whatever feeling good was about.

At the moment, though, feeling good was not an option. The streetlights of the City of Light gave her a splitting headache, and she scuttled into the twilight of some kind of historic arcades where a few light bulbs were out. The mosaic pavement had tiles missing, the dark corners smelled of mold and urine, and her feet were killing her. Stiletto heels were not made for pounding historic pavements, and she sat down with her back to a wall to give the sonofabitch one last try.

She fished the phone out of her handbag, and having pulled out the stolen stash with it, the question was what to do first, dial or inhale? Why not both? This was an emergency. So, after she punched in Blewitt's number, she dropped the phone into her lap to have both hands free to put Cherie's stuff to work. All of it.

And what good stuff it was.

It hit the spot in a flash, making her forget she was sitting in a filthy niche of ancient masonry, with the latest microtechnology in her lap dialing Blewitt's number. It just kept on ringing, and she had to laugh when she saw Heather coming to do something about it. What a girl. A maid who never missed a beat. Always where she ought to be. Always on cloud nine.

Except that as for right now, the cloud Heather seemed to be walking on made it terribly uncertain whether she was just a maid rushing to her mistress's rescue or Archangel Gabriel riding a thunderhead to inflict banishment and damnation—for the phone in Veronica's lap kept on ringing and ringing, while Veronica was passing out.

34

When Blewitt saw Veronica's name on his cell phone display, he glanced at his watch and slammed the phone shut without answering. The old girl was being taken care of. One less thing to think about.

He put the phone back in a pocket and turned to Beth, who needed his attention much more urgently. In the twilight of the limo's tinted windows, she sat in her corner of the backseat like a bird with a broken wing, haunted by the memory of Hank lying on the floor with a man standing on his neck.

"He'll be all right." Blewitt told her, his lead eye focusing on her profile thoughtfully. He liked her, considering she was a woman. "Relax, will you?"

"Go to hell." Beth made it perfectly clear that she'd rather kiss a snake before she trusted a cross-eyed man. The way he'd had his attorney talk to Hank back at the stuffy old hotel was the pits—one American bashing another in front of a bunch of crazy armed foreigners. It made her sick just to think of it.

And to make things worse, the back of the chauffeur's head up front kept on looking unflappable while driving to kill time.

Wrought-iron street lamps were beginning to light up against the backdrop of a darkening mauve sky, and they crossed the Seine at least three times without getting out of the inner city. The incessant stream of headlights around them would halt for pedestrians only if they stepped into the light beams like fearless lion tamers, and every now and then, when Beth looked up from the frenzy on the ground, she would catch a glimpse of either the Eiffel Tower or the cluster of white cupolas on a hilltop popping up once on the left, once on the right. They had been driving in loops and circles.

Then, as if suddenly the time had come, the chauffeur got his act together and began to drive in one direction, heading up a straight, American-like avenue. There were no sidewalk cafes here. The sidewalks were lined with fast-food stands and dimly lit boutiques with steel bars in the windows, but the street signs, Boulevard Sebastopol, were unmistakably Parisian.

Further down the boulevard, the traffic began to slow down, until it came to a standstill before the portals of what looked like a gaudy castle but turned out to be a railway station. The blue neon sign *Gare du Nord* hovered over a melee of taxis, cars, trucks and buses that were double- and triple-parked along the bottom of wide-flung steps that led up to the base of magnanimous columns supporting a temple-like portal. The station had been built more than a century ago, when railway was a transportation of choice and privilege, and the outdated aristocratic grandeur stuck out like a sore thumb out of the fumes of snarled middle-class traffic. It was an ugly, bustling place where Beth hoped never to get stuck all by herself.

"This is where you get off." Blewitt told her, pushing something into her hand. She did not want to take it, but she was in a corner.

"What's that?"

"A train ticket."

"What for?"

"A train. Do you want to see him or not?"

"Hank?"

"Have someone else in mind?" Blewitt was holding out the ticket, showing some concern about her mental stability. "Did you hear what I said?"

"What?"

"Platform thirteen. You have a sleeper compartment." He thrust the ticket into her hand, and Beth heard the door latch on her side pop up. "Walk fast, keep your head down. If you need to take a leak, hold it 'til you are on the train. You have five minutes."

Clutching the ticket like a schoolgirl bringing home a bad report card, Beth got out of the limo with her heart pounding.

"Platform thirteen," she heard Blewitt calling after her, but she could not see him. He had been careful not to show his face in the open door. She just saw his hand pointing to the stairs.

Then the door slammed shut, the limo drove away, and for a moment she stared after it as if it were the last life boat of a sinking ship.

She was on her own, having no choice but to start limping up the mighty granite stairs towards the magnanimous entrance that at the moment looked to her like a gateway into a bad dream. At a closer look, though, the columns were not that impressive. They were just massive and old, splattered with graffiti and beleaguered with souvenir and fast-food stands.

Inside the cathedral-like main concourse, the flagstone floor was filthy, and Beth kept her head down not because Cross-eyes had told her so, but because she had to look where she stepped. She was glad for her heavy shoes, never mind they hurt. She felt blisters coming but, prodded by resounding loudspeaker announcements she did not understand, she ignored the pain and kept on limping into the dubious safety of a reserved train seat as fast as she could.

The departure of the Paris-London Rapid on *Voie* 13 was scheduled for 20:51. Cross-eyes had not been kidding. She was just about to make it.

A clock hanging from the trusses of the vaulted ceiling showed 11 minutes to 9:00, two minutes before departure, but the platform was not particularly busy. A lackadaisical station master was supervising the loading of the last mail sacks, a sweating coffee vendor in a dirty apron was scrambling for last-minute sales, and a couple of uniformed conductors vied for Beth's attention. There were very few passengers on this train.

Beth's compartment was in the first-class carriage, and she held her breath when the conductor showed her in.

But there was no one inside.

The bed had not been turned down yet, and the upholstery of the seats looked worn-out, with the initials SNCF elaborately stitched in dingy white head rests.

"*Mais regarder ici.*" The conductor, aware of the frayed ambiance, opened the door to a tiny bathroom to proudly show off a stack of clean towels. There was no one in the bathroom either, and it took Beth a moment to realize the conductor was talking to her in French.

"What?"

"No luggage, Miss?"

"No." She was about to ask about a tall, handsome American who was supposed to be here, but stopped herself in time. Cross-eyes had said nothing about Hank waiting for her on the train. He might have meant the train would take her to him, and the conductor couldn't have possibly known that. Besides, she had no money to tip him and sat down to stare out of the window.

She did not know that European railroad employees did not expect tips. So when she saw the conductor smiling at her, she just assumed that the smell of the Ritz broom closet was finally gone out of her clothes.

"Call me when you want the beds made, Mademoiselle."

The conductor left, closing the door behind him, and it took a moment for his last words to strike home. Had she heard right? Had he said beds? Was the plural something he had read off the passenger manifest, or had it been just bad English?

The train moved with a playful clank of metal. The locomotive was way up front, and Beth turned back to the window to watch the carriage slide past the platform like a snake slithering out of its old skin. Then the platform ended, and the train plunged into darkness to grope its way through a maze of switches and light signals until it found the high-speed Paris-London line and got really going.

The spliceless rail on massive concrete ties turned the ride into a smooth glide into darkness, and Beth sat back to put her bad leg on the opposite seat to think.

Think of what?

Where was she to start? Should she go back all the way to Hank's first day at the office, coming in late with a cup of coffee in one hand, the employee rule book in the other and a doughnut in his mouth? Or should she go back only as far as their first walk across the park, when it suddenly struck her that he was a wounded bird with a dark secret? Or should she take it away from the moment he had told her he found another job? She could not sleep that night after he left for the airport way before dawn. She was used to sleeping alone, but that night her bed had felt emptier than ever, and she got up to go to the kitchen to organize her spices in alphabetical order. Yet, fiddling with spice jars would not keep her from willing the doorbell to ring, and at one point, for the life of her, she could not decide whether oregano went before pepper or the other way round. For she could see him ever so clearly opening the door—except that the door of her apartment opened on hinges, and she now saw him coming in through a sliding one.

He had opened the sliding door of the train compartment just a crack to slip in sideways.

Then he flipped the lock latch and, when he looked at her, she could cry to see him smile. He was OK, not worse off than the bruise under an eye, and she felt the old golf ball pop up in her throat again—even though his entry had been far from grand. He had sneaked in like a man on the run.

But she did not care. Sneaking or strutting, a black eye or not, his smile made the tiny train compartment feel like a cathedral where the organ was suddenly playing her favorite tune.

"Thank God." The marching shoes made her bottom-heavy, but she felt like flying as she sprung up to throw her arms around his neck. He was so tall. She did not quite manage to get her hands round his neck all the way and held onto his shoulders as if she were hanging from a cliff.

"I am sorry," was all she could bring herself to tell him.

"What should I say?"

"Say you're not mad at me." She let go of his shoulders to grab his hand. She had to feel him for a moment longer to make sure she was not dreaming. "It was so horrible. A nightmare. I didn't know what to say. Who were all those people? What were they to you—like that cross-eyed guy that brought me to the station? I thought you two hated each other. His attorney made me so mad in that phony court room. Because it was phony, wasn't it? Were they all crazy in there? Was Veronica guilty of something? What was it about me filling her shoes?"

Now that Beth had taken the plunge, she wanted to know everything at once. Also, she wanted to tell Teeple she hardly knew Veronica Pitt.

"She just turned up at my door."

"It's all right." Teeple helped her sit down, taking a closer look at her face. "You're wearing makeup?"

"Just around the eyes."

"It looks good."

"Veronica did it for me for the rally." Beth did not want to dwell on the subject. She could not care less about eyeliner and mascara now. Because what had started as a dismal train ride suddenly turned into trekking the unknown with no one but Hank to lean on. "I was so worried because I didn't know what to say back there. That man Blewitt was so horrible to you."

"He's not now."

"Then you are not on the run?"

"Not terribly."

"But . . ." She could not decide what was more puzzling, Hank not being on the run or Hank buddying up to Blewitt.

Outside, the city lights had thinned out, and the train picked up speed. They were in the outer suburbs of Paris now, and the sight of regular people in regular clothes walking dogs and children kicking balls on brightly lit soccer fields turned the memory of men in floor-length garbs with rhinestone daggers into merely a passing shiver.

"I couldn't make heads or tails of it. What was going on back there? Who was the prosecutor? Who was the defense, the jury? Were you supposed to be a witness of some sort, Hank?"

"Some sort sounds about right."

She gave him a fleeting frown, then went back to her zillion questions.

"Those three men with daggers sitting on the floor, they looked so annoyed with me like I was . . ." She wanted Teeple to finish the sentence for her, and when he wouldn't, she went on. She had to know, one way or another. "Was I supposed to be a jilted mistress?"

A cell phone rang in Teeple's pocket. He took it out to listen, and Beth could hardly wait for him to take it off his ear and slap it shut again.

"Was I supposed to be an infatuated, silly girl, while you were the wise, mature man who made the mistake of letting me get infatuated? Like all that talk about me trying to fill Veronica's shoes."

"Forget it."

"How can I?"

"That's what I've been trying to tell you, but you're not listening. They duped us both, in different ways, but it came to the same in the end."

Teeple glanced at his watch. There was not enough time to go into detail before the next stop where, he had just been told on the phone, they should expect further instructions. But Beth was determined not to let bygones be bygones in a hurry.

"Is that why you and Cross-eyes are suddenly buddies? Has he apologized for all the insults? What about the man in the white garb you testified for, what was his name?"

"Zyaad."

"What happened to him?"

"His head's probably in a basket by now."

"A basket?"

"The one for heads."

"What?"

"The guillotine's back in fashion."

It took Beth a moment to figure out he was not joking. "Then, I mean, what about you?"

"What about me?"

"Why not you? Why not your head, Hank?" Beth was not sure what she felt like. Did she want to laugh or cry? "You lied for that man, Zyaad. Why not your head in a basket?"

She was beginning to sound frightened, but not falling to pieces. She merely seemed determined to understand how scary things worked so that she could stop being scared, and Teeple had to think ahead. Should they get separated later on, she had to know enough to make an educated guess where to run if she had to run alone; so, obviously, the truth was the only way to go.

"My head still is where it is because that's what I do for a living," he said.

"Meeting women? Like me?"

There was a knock on the door, and Teeple moved beside it with his back against the wall. Then he nodded to Beth to open up. It was only the train conductor, asking if he should turn down the beds, and she sent him away.

They were out of Paris by then. In the darkness outside, lights were becoming weaker and smaller and farther apart, and when Hank heard the conductor move on, he returned to his seat and picked up where he had left off.

"My job was to outsmart a bizarre ideology before the folks realized what a bizarre world they live in."

Beth did not understand, and Teeple reverted to less universal terms.

"Blewitt's on our side. Always was. I just did not know until this afternoon. I came to Paris convinced that he was the bastard

I was supposed to help get hanged. You heard what the attorney said about my motives."

"That's what I thought was so unfair."

"It was the only way to get things done." Teeple hesitated, remembering the photographs over Beth's piano back in New York. This was neither the time nor place to preach about a foolhardy strive for a better world. There were no simple answers to simple questions on either side of the issue, and he made do with just a shrug.

"In politically correct times, common sense is not for public consumption. Blewitt's a crook, but being on our side makes him the good guy."

Beth said nothing. She seemed taken aback by Teeple's abrupt, harsh reasoning, and he went on choosing his words more carefully. Under the circumstances, he had to speak softly to persuade rather than shock.

"Blewitt's boss made billions doing business with Zyaad. They had a pretty neat thing going. Just every now and then, Blewitt had to take time out and squeal on the Muslim cause to appease Washington. And when Zyaad got wind of that, Washington was in a bind. They could not afford to loose a source like Blewitt, but they could not get rid of Zyaad like in the old days, the simple way. America's no longer good at that. No one in the government is dumb enough to play at keeping secrets that the Washington Post might splatter all over the front page the next morning. Zyaad had to be terminated without a drop of his blood on American hands or soil. He had to be discredited to a point where he would get liquidated by his own people.

"I was sent to feed him a story he wanted to hear in order to confirm what he had suspected all along, that Blewitt had been screwing him coming and going. With my help to discredit Blewitt, he had the case pretty much wrapped up until you waltzed into the ballroom to discredit me and turn the tables—courtesy of the people who lied to us both because they knew I was a lousy actor. They needed me to get mad for real when you turned up as the ace up Blewitt's sleeve."

Teeple gave Beth a moment to think, but she did not need as long as he thought.

"An ace?" she said, much too calmly to sound unruffled, and Teeple gave her a concerned sidelong glance.

"A double twist," he shrugged. "An old trick, if you like."

"I like ace." She was fighting tears. "Now what? The ace's been played."

"I'm getting you out. We'll be fine."

"We?"

"Yes."

"You will be fine, Hank. And I'm glad you will." A tear slithered down her cheek, and she turned away from him to stare at her reflection in the dark window. "You did your job. As for me, I am a loose cannon."

"Come on."

"With my past, who can tell what I might do next. Blewitt can never be sure I won't blow the whistle, or spill the beans, or whatever you call it in the trade. I'm a walking time bomb. Run for cover everybody, a bleeding heart knows about a dirty trick."

"Would you shut up, please?" Teeple wanted to take her by the shoulders and shake her. Because what she had just said was not that farfetched, and the last thing he needed now was to have doubts himself—doubts that back in Washington, Verhagen had another densely handwritten page about getting them both out of this. "We'll both be OK, don't worry."

"I was so easy to dupe once. Why stop there?"

She was back to the subject of unrequited love, and again Teeple's phone rang in his pocket. And again, he just listened. Then he opened the window. A stream of damp night air rushed in, bringing in the smell of wet earth and grass, and the few visible lights outside were far away and far apart. The moon was out now, sprinkling the flat countryside with a bluish shimmer, and Teeple threw the phone out of the open window without turning it off.

"Zyaad's buddies got my number faster than I thought," he

said as he closed the window with a bang to confirm his resolve to get them both out of this alive. But Beth's capacity for rational thinking had been exhausted, replaced with nothing.

"I thought the deal with Blewitt was to protect you," she said, quietly.

"The deal was to give us a head start. It was the best he could do." The truth was bound to make things worse, but Teeple was no actor. And it was too late to become one now. "You just got to believe me, Beth. I was promised you'd be left out of it."

But Beth was not listening. She was crying, and all Teeple could do for her was to wipe her tears as the train began to slow down before the next stop. He had no idea whom they were about to meet, nor did he have Kleenex on him. He just wiped her tears with a finger and, getting too close to an eye as the train hit the station switchyard, he smudged her makeup.

35

The train came to a halt and Teeple, leaving Beth's smudged makeup alone, pulled down the window to stick his head out. It was a small, sparsely lit station with a flagstone platform and a broken clock under a black and white sign *Berc sur Mer*, a small seaside resort frequented mainly by the English. The Paris-London Express stopped there in summer, but after the end of the bathing season, nobody got off here and only a handful of passengers got on. A rowdy bunch of hooded teenagers piled up into a second-class carriage up front, and a lone woman in a pantsuit, carrying what at a distance looked like a duffel bag, climbed into the dining car in the middle of the train.

Teeple waited until the train got under way to make sure no one else got on, then he pulled his head back in and closed the window. Beth's face was dry now, with just her eyes redder than usual, and he waited for her to look up.

"When have you eaten last?" he said when she did.

"I don't know."

"Aren't you hungry?"

"Am I?" The last thing she wanted to talk about was food.

Her immediate need was more urgent than that. "When you said you did not know about me getting involved, did you also not know about the other things? Like heads getting lopped off?"

Teeple shrugged and held out a hand to help her stand up. "Come on. You got to eat something."

The train moved on, and he held onto Beth's elbow to keep her from bumping into the walls in the narrow gangway to the dining car. The tables had white linen cloths and napkins, but except for the woman in the pantsuit, the whole place was empty. Well-to-do tourists did not travel by train in Normandy at this time of year, and regular French passengers did not like to spend money on food they had to order from a menu written in four languages.

The woman in the pantsuit was sitting with her back to the entrance and raised a hand to wave without turning around. She could see them in a mirror. From the back, she seemed neat and not very young, and Beth relaxed when she saw her from the front, too.

In a starched white blouse buttoned up to the chin, the woman looked 40-plus, prim and proper, and most likely well off. Hardly a professional assassin that had been sent to help Teeple do away with a silly bleeding heart that knew a dirty secret. Also, she had a nice smile, even though she was not smiling at anyone in particular.

"Hello, Hank. Recognize me all covered up?"

She was the woman with the kinky shoes and black underpanties who had brought Teeple to Verhagen's place back in Washington. There was no trace of a D.C. hooker in either her voice or appearance now, and they shook hands. Her current accent was Midwest, the look was unmistakably corporate, and Teeple, remembering the tattoo in her cleavage, assumed it had been a removable one and was no longer there.

"Care to join me?" She pointed across the table, and Teeple steered Beth into the window seat. He took the aisle seat to prevent escape as the woman abruptly held out a hand to Beth. She introduced herself by the same name she had used with Teeple in the Washington bar.

"I'm Heather." She smiled at Beth's smudged makeup. "Allow me."

She pulled a crisp handkerchief out of a sleeve and deftly wiped the smudge under Beth's eye while talking to Teeple.

"Your cell phone, where is it?"

"In some meadow a few miles before the last stop. Hope the battery's still good."

"It won't need to work long. When I called you, they'd had a fix on it for at least half an hour." Still talking to Hank, she checked Beth's other eye without looking into it. The makeup was OK there, and she stuffed the handkerchief back into her sleeve. "I don't see why no one thought of that. If Zyaad all but owns France, why not the French Telecom."

"Owns France?" Beth butted in as if the present tense were finally something to feel good about.

"A figure of speech, dear."

"I mean is he still alive?"

"I wouldn't hold my breath." Again, Heather avoided Beth's eyes and Teeple put her behavior down to negative female-to-female vibes: a cool older woman finding it difficult to connect with a nervous young one sporting smudged makeup.

Heather, if that was her real name, which Teeple doubted, was good at whatever she did and her pay had made her frivolous. The diamond ring she wore was at least six carats, and the duffel bag in the rack above the table was Vuitton. So, assuming she was merely being full of herself in front of Beth, he left it at that, at least for the time being.

"No time for a meal," Heather decreed, expecting no opposition. She called a waiter and ordered a bottle of Dom Perignon, fast and with chilled glasses. It went right along with her six-carat diamond. "*Allez, allez.*"

The unshaved, swarthy waiter glared back at her in undisguised contempt. If he was one of Zyaad's sleepers, it was not unlikely he had been activated this fast, Teeple thought, and

Heather seemed to concur. Her eyes flicked upwards to the Vuitton bag in the overhead rack, and Teeple assumed she had a gun in there. It made him wonder how she figured to get to it fast if need be.

Fortunately, the waiter delivered the champagne with the sly humility of a professional building up to a good tip, and Heather would not look up to the bag again, not even when she lifted her glass in a toast.

She took a ladylike sip and checked her watch, a Cartier. "The next stop's just another little seaside resort. A little car, nothing fancy, will be waiting for you in front of the station as you get out on your left. A gray compact with French license plates."

Heather pushed a tagged car key across the table. The tag had the red-and-white Avis logo, and Beth commented on it before Teeple put it in his pocket.

"Maybe Zyaad owned Avis, too," she said, and Heather acknowledged the past tense with a fleeting smile. Yet she went on speaking to Teeple as if Beth were not there.

"The car's navigation system will turn on when you start the engine. Don't fiddle with it. It's programmed to lead you to a boat landing. When it tells you you arrived, you arrived. Leave the key in the ignition and go straight to the boat waiting at the end of a pier."

"A boat to where?"

"Good question." Heather was getting quite uneasy about Beth listening to all this, and it suddenly occurred to Teeple that female rivalry might not be the reason for that kind of behavior. Heather might have known Beth's faith.

"She knows everything," he said, putting an arm around Beth's shoulders.

"Hmm." Heather went on looking at Teeple, spitefully, making him realize that there was only one way to make it clear whose side he was on and how determined he was to stay there.

"We are getting married," he said, tightening his grip on Beth's shoulders.

But Heather did not bat an eyelash. "Congratulations."

"Thank you."

"Set a date yet?" Heather smiled, not really wanting to know.

"It's a done deal." Keeping the arm around Beth's shoulders, Teeple leaned his other elbow on the table. "No secretes between a husband and wife."

"None?"

"None."

"Right." Facetiously mimicking Teeple's urgency, Heather leaned forward, just like he had, and, finally and abruptly, looked Beth in the eye, not just at the eye makeup. "The boat will take you, the happy couple, over to England still tonight."

The train was beginning to slow down before the next stop, and Teeple got up to help Beth slide from behind the table. Then he reached out to Heather, but instead of a handshake, he held her shoulder down with one hand and pulled the Vuitton bag off the overhead rack with the other.

"I'll borrow this, if you don't mind," he said.

"If you like." Heather did not struggle. The waiter was watching from the kitchen, and she kept on smiling. "Even though I'm sure you'll find at least a sandwich on the boat."

"We might not like the condiments."

"Which reminds me," Heather took another ladylike sip of champagne, watching Teeple over the brim of her glass, "you'll have one more mouth to feed tonight."

"What?"

"There will be three of you getting on that boat."

The train stopped, and Teeple saw no sense in bitching about being told about an additional refugee in such an offhanded fashion. There was no time for that. And even if there were, what good would objections do? So, holding Heather's bag by the straps and Beth by the hand, he led the way out without a glance back.

The last step from the dining car down onto the platform was high, and to free his hands to help Beth step down, Teeple held the bag under his arm. It felt soft and flabby. There was no gun inside, and for a split second he thought he felt an impish grin in the nape of his neck; but when he looked up, there was no face behind any of the train windows.

And the premonition that all this was merely a part of some ad-hoc evacuation Plan B became even more acute when he saw the car waiting for them outside the station. Standing under a lone streetlight, the gray dented compact looked like just another flimsy prop in a makeshift scheme.

The door creaked and reluctantly opened only when Teeple tugged hard at the door handle. Inside, a slumping, colorful woman was sleeping in a semi-sitting position in the backseat, and he gave a start when he heard Beth's gasp behind him.

"Veronica?"

In the cut-rate glow of a public street light, the face in the back seat was deathly pale and sallow, and Hank threw the useless duffel bag on the back seat next to her. Then he leaned inside to pull up one of the pungent red sleeves to feel the pulse.

She opened her eyes, and Teeple remembered the look — unfocused when resting on him. Then the eyes closed again, as if weighed down by loose skin that made the face look like a crumpled old photograph from a distant past he had found in the attic while looking for something else. He all but shook dust off his hand as he let go of the wrist and squeezed into the cramped driver's seat.

The car was a stick-shift, and he quickly ran through the motions to refresh his memory. Clutch down, first gear, gas and clutch up. Where the hell was the reverse? He had to back out of the parking spot first.

"She looks sick." Beth whispered in his ear as he started the engine, and he did his best not to sound impatient.

"Let's hope it's nothing contagious."

The navigation device came to life, and he ground the car into gear, feeling like a truck driver hustling to deliver perishable goods before their expiration date. And it was only then that he noticed the smell of peach-flavored air freshener. Blewitt's parting joke? A mock wedding gift, maybe? Not likely.

Blewitt was not the just-kidding type, Teeple thought, trying to ignore the moans in the back seat. Veronica Pitt was swaying from side to side as if she were gathering momentum to rise and shine; but she went back to sleep as soon as he got out of the tight parking lot and onto a straight road to follow the direction of the arrow on the navigation monitor. The moans in the backseat turned into snores, and Beth went back to the marriage thing.

"That woman on the train, what was her name again?"

"Heather."

"I don't think Heather bought the wedding story."

"Why not?"

"Don't you really see any other way out?"

"Not without glasses." They were on a straight stretch, and Teeple put on his spectacles to peer at the navigation monitor. But Beth wanted a serious answer.

"I mean it, Hank."

"So do I."

Like the little car itself, the navigation was a cheap gadget designed for teenage entertainment and teenage eyesight, and Teeple had trouble reading the tiny screen even with his glasses on. "What does it say about the final destination?"

"*Plage du Soleil*," Beth said without leaning closer or squinting. "Beach of the sun? Is that where we're going?"

"Maybe we catch a quick swim. What does it say about the driving time and distance?"

She told him, and he calculated in his head. 35 minutes for 27 kilometers put the average driving speed below 60. They were going to drive on secondary roads at best. But Beth would not be sidetracked.

"Did you give Blewitt the same story about getting married?'

"Yes."

"Did he believe you?"

"Your inheritance made me sound convincing," Teeple shrugged. "Blewitt knows that all I have to go back to in America is unemployment pay and a mean reputation."

The road was narrow and bumpy, full of sharp turns, and he had to keep his eyes and mind on driving while discussing the pros and cons of a marriage of convenience.

"You better believe it, Mr. and Mrs. Teeple won't be invited to a lot of black-tie galas in Washington," he grinned and, pondering a future in which a suburban neighborhood barbecue would be the event of the year, took a tight curve too fast.

In the back seat, Veronica slumped sideways with a thud, and Beth leaned over the headrest of her seat to rearrange her curiously pliable body back into a sort of sitting position.

"How is she?" Teeple said, not really giving a damn.

"I don't know."

"Do you smell alcohol?"

"No."

"Then who knows what she's on."

Veronica's eyes were closed, but she was breathing, and Beth returned to the subject of marriage.

"Funny. I never thought of a wedding gown that way?"

"Oh."

"You decided to pull a bride's veil over my head to guarantee my silence rather than having me on your conscience. That's all you want, isn't it."

"What do you want?"

"Girl things." She shrugged. "Love, to name a few."

The headlights cut deep into the night ahead, and Teeple glanced again at the navigation monitor. The arrow was pointing straight ahead, no advisories, no warnings. They were on track and on time—provided he took no wrong turns in the dark, or worse. Cheap navigation systems made no allowances for a middle-aged driver's night vision, nor for the fact that at night the glow of even a flimsy little monitor lit the faces in the front seats with ghostly clarity. At 50 km an hour, a pot shot from the roadside would have no problem finding the dead center between his or, more likely, Beth's eyes. Or both.

But nothing happened. They reached Plage du Soleil right on schedule, and Hank leaned forward to peer down the main street ahead. It was one of the spanking new developments that would turn into ghost towns off season. A place where no one was nobody's uncle or brother or ex-wife, where strangers came on holidays to run around with other strangers in shorts and flip-flops, pretending to have a blast.

The beach must have been quite close. Drifting sand made desert-like ripples on the road, swishing against the windshield in erratic gusts, and every time a pebble hit the glass, Teeple winced. He could imagine a gunman slurping tea and nibbling on cookies while lying in wait in one of the deserted little houses on straggly postage-stamp lawns that lined the street like proud trophies of modest prosperity.

The destination was straight ahead and not far now, and Teeple had to finish what he had started.

"So?" he said.

"What?"

"Will you?"

"Marry you?"

"Yeap."

"Do I have a choice?"

"No."

"That bad, is it?"

"Worse. I'll keep on asking." Teeple gave Beth a sidelong glance. She looked sickly pale in the greenish glow of the dashboard and her voice was hoarse and weary.

"Even if my inheritance made the marriage idea believable, what guarantee does Blewitt have that a poor husband can make a crazy, rich wife keep her mouth shut?"

Teeple did not like the "poor husband". But he had been asking for it, and his answer was a touch too quick and decisive. "Fortunately Blewitt's not in charge."

He had managed to sound authoritative, even though the best he could do right now was to hope, pray rather, that somewhere out there in the darkness, way beyond the unseen dark sea, Verhagen was pulling strings on the other side of the Atlantic.

36

It was a bright, sunny afternoon on the other side of the Atlantic, way beyond the dark beaches of Plage du Soleil, and Lieutenant Mulvaney of the Washington, D.C. Police Department was way behind schedule. The mighty hub of a political and military superpower had its petty oddities, like a ballooning petty-crime rate, and the lieutenant often worked straight through lunchtime to deal with stolen purses and inconsequential dead bodies.

So, when a few minutes before noon, he was called to check on a relatively insignificant abuse of the law in the mean streets behind the big lawbreakers' shrine, the Capitol, he was not planning to waste a lot of time on it.

The body he found inside the little orange and blue walkup fitted the scene like just another dead partridge at a partridge shoot: a mean looking dude well over 6 feet, 200 pounds, a sweat suit, ski mask, the works. His big, coarse, stiff hand was still clutching the proverbial Saturday-night special that smelled of burnt machine oil, and the lieutenant needed no loupe or a psychobabble manual to put the cause of death down to an exchange of gun fire. He signed the appropriate forms, initialed the time sheet, and was about to hand the batch over to his sergeant to fill in the rest of the blanks when he noticed the party that had remained standing in the shootout.

She was an old lady with an immaculate hairdo and a neat string of pearls, and the lieutenant's eyes froze on a gun lying on a crochet coverlet on a chest of drawers that the old lady was resting a proprietary elbow on.

"You live here?" he asked, doubtfully. The place was a walk-up in a crummy old building, and the old lady's pearls looked real. Her dress was silk, her shoes were polished, and her arthritic hands manicured. "Do you own this place?"

"Oh no, sir." She sounded pretty cool, considering that they were talking over a dead body at their feet. "Not on my husband's pension."

"Where's your husband?"

"Out of town. On business."

"I thought you said he was retired."

"I said we couldn't afford to own this place on his pension."

The lieutenant bit his lip and glanced at his watch. Then he took the sergeant aside.

"Was the coroner in yet?"

"In and out like a bat." The sergeant lowered his voice, glad the lieutenant asked. "The time of death jives with the nine-one-one call. Both guns fired one shot. One bullet's in the dude's gut, the other in a wall."

"I want the ballistics, fingerprints, the works."

"You do?" Reluctantly, the sergeant ticked off a check box on the form on his clipboard. He was a conscientious man who did not like to waste taxpayers' money. "This whole thing's a cinch. The old dame squeezed the trigger in self-defense."

"Have you seen her hands?"

"Yeah."

"And have you seen the gun?" The lieutenant nodded towards the chest of drawers.

"What about it?

"It's a .35 Beretta, the James Bond kind. You don't get an arthritic finger through that kind of trigger guard in a hurry. I want you to check out the husband."

"You think he's any younger than her?"

"Shut up. Find out when he left town and how. I mean it."

"I can tell."

"So hop to it." The lieutenant wanted to hand this case over to homicide before it bogged down in its own paper trail and got filed among the irrelevant.

Back in his car, before pulling away from the curb, he turned on his laptop and typed in the name he had copied from the mailbox on his way out: Mr. and Mrs. Joseph Verhagen. It was a restricted site he connected to, and after recognizing the origin of the request, the server asked the lieutenant to reconfirm the password and his service code. He did that while driving, and the feedback popped up just as he reached Stanton Park. He read it while he was stuck in a gridlock.

"Shit."

He had heard the rumors about old ex-tough guys. Some of them could hardly walk by now and would do anything in their waning power to relive the old Cold-War glory days. As a rule, they worked outside the bounds of today's overly benevolent government agencies, and Joseph Verhagen sounded just like it. There were deletions in his resume that could have been done only on very high authority, and lieutenant Mulvaney put the chances of a random break-in at the crummy apartment behind the Capitol on par with those of a blind man stumbling into an empty bleachers seat at the Super Bowl.

Lost in speculation, the lieutenant jumped when a cacophony of horns behind him called his attention to an opening in the traffic ahead. He got going with a jerk and turned onto Massachusetts Avenue with screeching tires.

The avenue was lined with Richard 'Slick Dick' Fitch's election posters, and the poster eyes peered through the lieutenant's windshield at the laptop in the passenger seat. It gave him the creeps together with a few more horns for erratic driving.

At the next stop light, Lieutenant Mulvaney exited Joseph Verhagen's page, closed the browser, deleted the log entry from the history of accessed sites, and felt like washing his hands. But, being in a car stuck in Washington, D.C. midday traffic, he called his sergeant instead.

"Listen up," he snapped testily, feigning preoccupation with more important cases. "About the Verhagen case, forget what I told you. Use your own judgment."

"I hear you. Why?"

"Because."

Lieutenant Mulvaney intended to retire on a full pension. He would not be a burden to his kids just because he had once tried to do the right thing instead of a politically correct one. With Dick Fitch bound to be moving into the White House soon, political correctness was not here just to stay but to grow and blossom. A daily orgasm about brotherly love and devotion to the new president was going to be supervised by ruthlessly compassionate vigilantes, and the lieutenant knew he better started learning how to live with that or else. He had 20 years to retirement, and in the prevailing political climate, a government employee uncomfortable with a botched hit on a deluded, old-fashioned patriot working below the White House radar was not likely to last 20 days.

So much for that—and for the land of the brave and the free. Wasn't life supposed to be fun, damn it?"

It was a balmy, Indian summer day, and with the Verhagen case out of the way faster than he would have thought, Lieutenant Mulvaney figured he might have time for a late lunch.

Yet, no matter how hard he tried to be reasonable, he was not having as much fun as he figured was due to a smart guy who had just made up his mind to stop feeling guilty about going with the flow. Because, at the end of the day, the sun was going to go down whether he condoned it or not, and with Slick Dick's posters smothering lampposts all over America, lights might not be coming on anytime soon.

37

There were no street lights in Plage du Soleil. The place was strictly a summer paradise, occupied only when days were hot and long, and Teeple turned on the car's high beams to make out what looked like a traffic accident ahead. It turned out to be just a pile of scrap metal posing as artwork in the center of a roundabout, and, distracted by a few loose pieces banging in the wind, Teeple took the curve too fast, bringing Veronica back to life in the back seat.

She began to mumble, working herself up to swearing about crazy drivers, and Teeple had to turn up the volume of the navigation speaker. The last thing he wanted was to miss a turn. Fortunately, the digital voice merely insisted on driving straight, and he doused the headlights. With precious little chance of oncoming traffic, the moonlight was good enough.

Three hundred meters to destination . . . a hundred . . . fifty . . . arrived at destination.

The road ended in a deserted parking lot by a small marina basin. There was no one around, and by the time Teeple turned off the engine, Veronica, confused by the sudden calm and quiet, toned down her disapproval to mumbling under her breath.

On the water, several sail boats were rocking in their moorings, the wind whistling in their bare riggings, and the only sign of life Teeple could see was a boat docked at the end of an adjacent pier.

The boat's navigation lights were on, reflecting on water, but there seemed to be no one on board and Beth didn't like it.

"Look like an English ferry to you?"

"A ferry to England doesn't have to be English."

"It's so small."

"Transportation's been nationalized in France." Teeple made a lame attempt at a smile. If he could not trust Verhagen now, he might as well sit down and wait for whoever was about to catch up with them. "Let's get going."

The car was a two-door sedan, and trying to pull Veronica out of the back through the constricted opening between the folded driver seat and the door frame, Teeple heard fabric rip. He let go of her arm before the whole bright red sleeve came off, and she bounced back into the backseat as if she had been sitting there in a blob of chewing gum. It was obvious that even if he managed to get her out somehow, the listless body was unlikely to have the use of its legs, and the boat was far away.

The beach was very flat here. The distance between high and low tide, which the pier was here to bridge, was a good 300 yards, and Beth's limp seemed to be getting worse by the minute. The two of them had no chance to get the jelly-like bundle of Veronica's inert flesh and bone onto a distant shipboard without causing damage to it, or to themselves, and Teeple looked around for solutions — or, rather, straws to grasp at.

But even there the choice was limited. Leaving Veronica behind was not an option, and all he could see that looked somewhat workable was the pier itself. It was barely wide enough for a small car, but there was no railing on either side. Nothing to knock off side mirrors or hang up door handles on, and Teeple told Beth to leave Veronica be and get back in the car.

He took a shortcut out of the parking lot, across a lawn and several flower beds, and onto a gravel footpath along the waterfront. At the beginning of the pier, he aimed the center of the car's hood at the center of the pier's threshold and gave gas to scale the step up. The bottom of the car scraped hard against wood, but nothing vital seemed to have fallen off, and the weathered wooden floor planks felt sturdy enough under the wheels. The tires had no more than a couple of inches clearance on either side, so, clutching the steering wheel with both hands, Teeple drove on slowly with bated breath.

The rattling of the floor planks made the crawling, flimsy little car sound like a tank charging at full speed, and at the far end of the pier, a man in a black turtleneck was waving a hand to make them stop. The pier looked even narrower at the end than at the beginning, and Teeple realized his mistake too late. He and Beth were going to be barely able to squeeze out of the car themselves, and the only way to get Veronica out of the backseat would be by pushing her into the water.

He had no choice.

The man at the end of the pier seemed to have realized that, too, and was becoming more frantic the closer they came. He was holding the boat's bow rope wrapped around a cast-iron pylon, but with the stern rope loose, he could not let go of his end to throw himself on the charging car's hood.

The gangway onto the boat was heaving and sliding back and forth, and Teeple turned on the headlights. The white-crested waves on both sides of the boat looked evenly spaced in the light beam, fit for a travel poster of a serene seaside resort, which meant that the seemingly wild rise and fall of the boat was predictable.

"Put on the seat belt," he told Beth, but would not put on his. With the car's tires barely skirting the edge of disaster, he could not split his attention between common good and personal safety. Nor could he waste time on speculations that the small boat had shallow draft and the water most likely was not deep here. He had to concentrate on driving, not drowning.

The trick was to hit the front edge of the jittery gangway just right, slow and square, when the far end was at the peak, just as it began to go down. Once the front wheels were on, he had to slam the gas pedal into the floor, uncouple the clutch the moment the rear wheels cleared the gangway, hit the brakes, and ram in the reverse while flying. He needed the absolute braking power on landing; because there was going to be no second chance to hit the deck square and with blocked wheels. The boat was barely wider than the car's length.

"Hang on, Beth."

Then the car was airborne, and he hit the brakes and the clutch to ram in the reverse while in the air. They landed on the deck with a thud and screeching tires, skidding into what looked like a solid rail post. The front of the hood crumpled, but the railing held.

"Ugh," Teeple heard Veronica gasp in the back.

The hard landing had knocked the air out of her, and he understood how she felt as his own chest slammed into the steering wheel. On second thought, though, it was not his chest that hurt. The pain was where Beth's fingernails were digging into his biceps, and it went away when she turned to check on the moaning and groaning in the backseat.

Gasping for air, Veronica was rattling a door handle to get the hell out of this nutty place, and Beth took a deep breath of relief to speak for all of them.

"Still alive, I guess."

The car engine had stalled on landing, and Teeple sat back to stare at his hands on the wheel. They were trembling. The front of the car was hanging over pitch-black water, and he closed his eyes to let the memory of the old river back home pass. *The cows on the banks used to be impressed to see him prod Primo head on into the swift winter current. There were holes under the swirling surface, and the cows appreciated his bravery, risking it all for just a fickle chance of meeting Roni on the other side. Roni, the runner-up for Miss California 1969 . . .* the same old girl who was now cursing him from the backseat.

"Are you nuts, driver?"

Out on the ship's deck, men in black turtlenecks were coming out of hiding now that the car had landed, and reasons why Teeple should not have done what he had came at him in a torrent. What the bloody hell was he thinking? They all talked at the same time, but none of them seem to have the authority to dress him down. They all showed equal restraint in their choice of words to chastise him for almost killing them or capsizing the boat or both, and Teeple assumed that someone else was on board to do the cursing later.

He got out of the car to have another go at getting Veronica out of the backseat. There was plenty room on both sides of the car now; but she would not cooperate, and the black turtlenecks stopped grumbling about the bloody stunt and stepped forward to help.

The old girl's bombed, they concluded. Teeple better leave her to them. He and Beth were to go straight to the cabin. They were expected there.

The boat engine came on, throbbing at full throttle, and as the bow turned away from land to point into an offshore fog bank, the wind stirred up a fishy smell. There were fishing nets rolled up under the bridge. The railing had been scuffed by ropes and fishing hooks, revealing multicolored layers of paint stacked up like miniature geological formations, and Teeple expected the inside of the cabin below the bridge to be equally scored and dented.

38

Inside the boat's cabin, Verhagen was sitting at a cluttered chart table, clearly not in charge of navigation.

He looked sick.

His red-rimmed, watery eyes were oblivious of the charts before him, his old three-piece suit looked more ill fitting than ever, and Teeple's first reaction was to ignore his misery. On second thought, though, the old man must have come out here knowing what boats and boating did to him, and Teeple groped for a less grudging intonation.

"What are you doing here?" he said, his voice deliberately void of emotion. He was sure that whatever Verhagen had in mind was purely utilitarian and functional and could not help frowning when the old man went into a sort of pleasantries.

"I know how you feel, Hank."

"Do you?"

"It was the only way to get things done. You know it, I know it." Verhagen shrugged a deliberately dismissive shoulder. His aim was to accentuate confidence in the future, but with the sea getting worse the further away they were from land, rising stomach gases made him sound unconvincing. "So, in the end, what do we have? We all must admit it worked."

Through the porthole behind Verhagen's back, Teeple could see they were in the offshore fog bank now. There was no way to tell where they were headed, but the old man did not look concerned. He seemed preoccupied with avoiding Beth's eyes, just like Heather had on the train, and Teeple put an arm around her shoulders.

"You two haven't met, I suppose," he said, beginning to feel very tired of the falsely flippant routine. "Or have you?"

Verhagen made no answer, and Beth watched him silently from the safety of Teeple's protective embrace. The old man looked pathetic, grinding his teeth to keep his stomach from popping out while trying to sound cool.

"Blewitt's offering you a deal, Hank." Verhagen paused to let his stomach settle. "He'll let you off the hook, no thanks expected. You can wash your hands of wrongdoing and walk away from it all, free as a bird. No marital vows required to keep Miss Beth safe."

The boat took another hairy pitch and roll, and the old man held his breath a moment longer before he dared to go on. "I give you my word, Hank. Miss Beth will be tucked away in style."

"You gave me your word about her before."

"Did I?" This was neither the time nor place to split hairs, and Verhagen, sick as he was, made sure Teeple understood that. "You got to remember one thing, Hank. I had nothing to do with the pick of a hiding place. It was Blewitt's idea: a cute little cottage on a distant shore — distant from Washington, that's to say, but close at hand out here."

"What the hell are you talking about?"

"It's a done deal, Hank. A thatch roof, white picket fence, a rose garden, the works, plus a bonus: a live-in maid and an assistant gardener."

"Both of them armed and on Blewitt's payroll?"

"They will be instructed to do Miss Beth's bidding for as

long as she sticks to her end of the bargain and stays in seclusion for the duration of Richard Fitch's term in the White House."

"Might be eight years."

"Let's hope not."

"Ever wondered what her hopes are?" Teeple glanced at Beth. She had been listening to the old, sick-like-a-dog man with a puzzled frown. He sounded rattled and shaky, which at his age could have easily been interpreted as senile, and for a moment she seemed to be leaning toward that possibility.

Verhagen noticed it, too, but kept on talking to Teeple without the least effort to dispel Beth's unfavorable impression of him.

"Long story short, Hank—Miss Beth is a liability. Given her street-marching past, it's crystal clear that we have no jurisdiction over her discretion, and, like I said, the cottage's got a hell of a rose garden. She won't be biting her nails in exile. Plenty flora to tend to: tea roses, floribundas, ramblers, grandifloras, you name it."

The exacting list of rose varieties seemed to finally convince Beth to take the old man seriously, and Teeple felt her finger nails digging into his biceps again.

"How do you know she likes gardening?" he said, but Verhagen knew better.

"Most women do."

"She's not most women."

"Hmm." The old man turned to the porthole to check on the progress of Veronica's extraction out of the wrecked car on deck. "Actually, that is where the rose-garden idea came from."

"Roni?" Teeple groaned. Was she still jerking him around like she used to? Even when she was whacked out of her skull?

"Blewitt told me the thatch-roof cottage idea dawned on him when he saw a picture on the cover of a book on Miss Veronica's bedside table back in Beverly Hills," Verhagen said, continuing to gaze out of the porthole to put romance in a more realistic perspective by observing things the way they were. The black turtlenecks out there used a crowbar to rip off the car door, threw it overboard and began getting Veronica's limbs out of the wreck by hand, one by one. It seemed like a good time to explain the rest of the thinking behind the thatch-roof cottage. "In his macho mind, Blewitt figured that if one woman was into daydreams, Miss Beth would be also . . ."

The old man's stomach was on the move again, but Teeple did not care.

"No," he said, firming up his grip on Beth's shoulders.

"No what?"

"No daydreams. No roses. No cottages."

"Are you jumping to her conclusions?" Verhagen looked hurt. "Off the top of my head, I could name you a hundred people, including myself, who would kill for that kind of a deal. Roses, picket fences, the sun, the sea, with all expenses taken care of. Some kind of a retirement, no?"

"She's not retirement age," Teeple said, quietly.

"Call it a vacation then. An English seaside holiday. We'll be there at first light, as the Brits say." Verhagen paused as the cabin door opened and two black turtlenecks edged inside the confined space, trying to hold Veronica Pitt upright between them.

They seemed to have managed to pry her out of the car wreck without bleeding wounds. The only thing that had come off in the process were her blue high heels. The red jacket was in reasonably good shape, with both sleeves on, and the white skirt had only one tear and a few stains that were not blood. The hem was riding high up her shapely Miss-California-runner-up thighs, and her bare feet and buckling knees made her look flat-footed.

One of the men carried the blue heels in his hand and dropped them on the floor to help the other one fold the body into a sort of sitting position at the chart table. She would not open her eyes, and the men stepped back to stand by the door.

With their necks bent sideways under the low ceiling, the men looked larger than life, but neither of them would move a finger as the rolling and pitching of the boat made Veronica slide back and forth on the bench. Even semiconscious, she looked miserable and cold, and Beth went down on her knees to put the blue shoes back on to keep at least the feet warm. Then she got up and went to sit at the open end of the bench to prevent the inert ex-beauty queen from falling out.

They made strange bench fellows.

A glamorous woman in blazing red and skintight white with boldly exposed miles of shapely legs seeking comfort on the shoulder of a run-of-the-mill girl in dull brown whose limbs were hidden in baggy pants and clumsy hiking shoes.

As usual, Verhagen's thoughts were running away with him as he watched the odd couple in pensive silence. Something about the similarity in the difference had caught his attention, and he heaved a sigh when Veronica began to snore.

"A penny for her thoughts," he said.

"Roses and picket fences," Teeple shrugged. "Haven't you just told me that?"

"Did I?" The old man shook his head sadly. Over the years, he had seen a lot of things that made no sense, yet could be easily explained by a simple argument. "Fooled with hope, men favor deceit. Who said that, do you know?"

There was a twinkle in the old man's eyes as he came to think of that now, and Teeple knew better than to interrupt his train of thought, wicked or not.

"By the way, my wife just called . . ." Verhagen went on with another sigh, wishing she were here with her special teas and digestive biscuits. "She told me someone organized a dead body in my bedroom to send me a message."

"Saying what?"

"What would happen if I ever tried to get around Blewitt." Verhagen smiled a little, not particularly distraught by the antics of a stressed-out man. "Because, between a rock and a hard place, Blewitt has to trust me to carry out all his wishes to the letter. He has no choice. It wouldn't be merely inappropriate but outright stupid of him to come anywhere near that cute little cottage himself for as long as his master's son is on display in the White House—if you know what I mean."

Verhagen let the end of the sentence dangle, then turned his eyes to the two hulks by the door to translate his rambling thoughts about the fate of the two women on the bench into a simple, terse command. It had to be done his way, or else.

"At sunup, the brown one goes on land," he decreed, stressing the usage of colors in lieu of names. "The colorful one stays on board."

There was no hesitation in the old man's voice as his watery, red-rimmed eyes moved away from Beth's baggy brown pants to rest on Veronica's boldly exposed thighs. Magnificent, were they not? No other pair like that under the sun. Or was there?

Who was the judge of that, his smile seemed to be asking, and when Teeple looked at Roni's—sorry, Veronica's—legs, too, he thought he saw what the devious old man meant.

39

The sunrise flared up in the boat's wake, making the proverbial white cliffs of Dover ahead look pink. But the pink grew fainter the higher the sun rose, and by the time the boat dropped anchor off a picturesque sandy beach, the cliffs looked as white as on postcards—complete with one lone, cute cottage with a thatch roof and a white picket fence perched on the edge of a mighty white rock face. A sight to behold.

And, as Verhagen had decreed the night before, the brown one was getting off here, no ifs or buts.

Two black turtlenecks took her on land in a row boat. There was no room for the hiking boots in the little boat, and her legs in baggy brown trousers were hanging over the side from the knees down.

The wind was coming off shore now, bringing the smell of morning dew and roses, and the men in the row boat were pulling hard at the oars.

She was going to be fine; Teeple had no doubt about that as he watched the disembarkation from the boat's railing. Past the shimmering turquoise water of the bay, the lone white cottage on the edge of the white cliff was half submerged in picket fences and pink roses—leaving him mercifully free of pangs of conscience.

The sun was stroking the back of his neck with warm approval, and remorse could not have been further from his mind when he dropped his eyes to the shapely pair of bare legs standing next to him by the boat railing.

"After all this time, who'd have thought," he told her, wrapping an arm around her shoulders to pull her closer. "You look great."

"I do?"

"Trust me."

"The heels help, I guess." She drew a hand through his arm to cuddle. The sleeve of her red jacket looked a touch too long, and she could not help smiling as she looked down to the daring miniskirt and on to her feet. She was not at all sure about the shoes. "Don't know about the blue, though."

"Looks fine on you."

"Not my size, really." Looking back up, she sent a wary sidelong glance to the boat's cabin, where Verhagen had been nursing his sea sickness in strict seclusion. "The old man's got to suspect something."

"Why should he?" Since sunrise, Verhagen had not as much as glanced out of his porthole, and Teeple grinned at the red sleeve in the crook of his arm. "In these threads, you made it a breeze for him to see his orders carried out to the letter."

"Me? I made it a breeze?" she cried. "It was your idea. You took the chance."

"Nah."

"You've never seen me in anything but baggy pants and flat shoes before. How could you've known?"

"A hunch."

"Oh."

"I never thought a bunch of screws in a shin could ruin your looks."

The boat engine came on. The bow turned away from the

cute little cottage on the cliff where the "brown one" was being settled in, and Teeple patted the red sleeve on his arm. The truth was, he had lied a little about his cool under fire the night before. He had had his doubts back then, considering it a reckless gamble to have Beth put on Veronica's finery, just hoping that her legs would pass Verhagen's visual. He remembered he had felt like a man putting his life savings on a roulette table until he actually saw Beth wiggling into the skin-tight miniskirt.

"Well, look at you," he told her now and left it at that.

"Well," she laughed, drawing still closer. "I told you the heels help."

She wanted him to know she could not care less about the color and size of designer shoes, because she could not care less about fashion when he was with her. She wanted to tell him all that and more, but before she could get a word out, a gust of wind took her breath away, and she changed her mind. They'd have plenty of time to get serious about life later — if ever. As for right now, the sun was in her eyes, the wind was in her hair, and she had to laugh when she looked down at Veronica Pitt's shoes on her feet.

She did fill them.

* * *

And she made sure to wear the blue heels as a good-luck charm under her white wedding gown when she and Hank stood before a preacher on the terrace of her spectacular New York penthouse.

The sun was shining, a helicopter overhead was taking pictures for the family album, the preacher was a solemn woman in floor-length garb, and the lawyers present at the ceremony all wore white ties and tails. Beth's father had had them set up an ironclad trust fund effective for as long as the kids stayed together, and he personally arranged for his private jet to stand by to fly the newlyweds to some fun honeymoon place — like Paris, for instance. Why not, huh?

"Gee, thanks dad," they told him. "But . . ."

"Ow, come on. A week at the Ritz is what we used to do for fun in the old days," he grinned and patted Hank on the back. They were about the same age, and he loved the thought of his daughter marrying a man just like himself—someone he could trust to take a good care of her.

He had, of course, no idea that his mature son-in-law had already taken his little girl for a wild ride in the City of Light. Yet he did not seem disappointed when they told him they preferred California to Paris.

"OK, just tell the pilot to fly the other way," he grinned, patting his son-in-law's back again. It seemed he had not been getting enough of that. "How about teaching me to ride a bronco one of these days?"

"When do we start, dad?"

"Sooner than you think, son." Between the two of them, a couple of tough old birds of a feather, the father-in-law made no bones about counting on frequent visits.

And both Hank and Beth could tell he meant it when they saw him standing out there on the tarmac, watching the private little jet take off. He had been braving cold wind and rain with a grin because he was thinking of visiting the kids out there in warm and sunny California real soon.

CALIFORNIA
SPRING 2000

The first winter of the new millennium had been short and benign. The Santa Ynez River caused no damage to speak of on the old Teeple land, and by the time the water was back to normal, the grazing ranges began to turn yellow. Red poppies and blue bells were withering fast in the spring sunshine, and the ranchers down the coast were grumbling about a darn sunny summer comin' up.

By the end of April, there had not been a cloud in the skies for weeks in a row, and Hank and Beth wore summer hats and shirts with the sleeves rolled up. Beth had never been out west before, but she had taken riding lessons as a child and had no problem getting used to Western saddle and to handling horses with a loose rein. She bought a good supply of cowgirl shirts, blue jeans and work boots in Los Olivos, at the same store with the weathered sales counter and creaking oak-wood floor where Hank had once been dumb enough to buy an engagement ring for a beauty queen—a memory that gave him a lump in his throat as he watched Beth put the cowgirl gear on.

No beauty queen since Christopher Columbus could hold a candle to Beth Teeple. She looked out of this world in tight work jeans and brawny boots, making life feel as good as it could ever get.

Because, once the law suits about the complicated ownership of the heavily mortgaged property were settled, they planned to do a lot of work on the old house themselves—like the barn door, for instance. Nothing had been done about the sagging old hinges for much more than thirty years. The rock musician who had bought the ranch for a song from Hank's father had broken his neck in a fall from a stage during a reenactment of Woodstock in the yard, and an environmental regulatory group took over the property to regulate the endangered species of aquatic salamandridae up in the lake.

In view of the deceased musician's fame, a subcommittee of a senate committee headed by Richard Fitch had also put the same regulatory group in charge of the marijuana field the rock musician had planted behind the farm house to promote organic farming. No fertilizers, no machinery. The dead musician's soul mates worked the marijuana field with just hoes and water buckets, and scientists from all kinds of universities would come over to compile statistics on the organically grown plant's effects on the retardation of global warming.

So when the local sheriff, a simple guy acting under pressure from simple uneducated local voters, had the marijuana field burnt, the pot growers accused the establishment of crime against humanity. They demanded an amendment to the Constitution, but Beth's millions did wonders in settling irreconcilable differences about making the world a better place to live in. She and Hank bought the ranch back at an outrageously inflated price, and for a few million more they even got the environmentalists off the newts' backs too.

Because what was money to hearing the old stories about Primo, the river, the cows and the lake up on the hill right on the spot and, as their neighbors would say, straight from the horse's mouth. It made Beth see the true meaning in the old folk wisdom about getting the boy out of the country but not the country out of the boy.

They got a new herd, 500 head to start with, and the day they let them out on the range, they got a long letter from Veronica

Pitt. She was not happy in the little seaside cottage on a distant shore, she wrote. Nor was she crazy about the clothes she had to wear day in and day out. Brown made her look oh-so-drab. All in all, though, she still got one hell of a kick out of swapping places with Beth after Hank told her, when she sobered up that night on the boat, what had really happened back in Paris. It made her feel ever so much better about everything, like for instance watching Richard 'Slick Dick' Fitch's recent inauguration speech on television. Listening to the new American president's drivel about the principles of decency and integrity gave her a brand new lease on life—a purpose that had made kicking the habit child's play. It felt ever so great to know that Slick Dick had no clue she finally had him by the balls. The enlightened leader of the free world hadn't the faintest what she knew about his sinister self, and she was in no hurry to figure out how to knock that low-life bastard off his lofty perch. Not a bad thing for a girl to mull over while clipping roses, was it? Worth staying sober for sure, she wrote, and Hank and Beth were happy to hear that.

But they really did not care what kind of surprise she had in mind for the magnanimous man himself. Washington was far away, and, as the old saying went, where the mountains were high, the emperor was far.

With their new cows beginning to migrate towards the foothills, where the rattlers were coming back to life at this time of year, Hank and Beth were in the saddle every day. She could not get enough of the open range, the big blue sky and the lake up on the hill. The two of them would often stop up there to rest her bum leg after a day in the saddle—just before sunset, when the ocean down below began to reflect the mauve sky and the ground felt warm and cozy in the cool evening air.

Way out there, far beyond the glowing horizon before them, thousands of miles and millions of years away were the Malacca Straits, pirates, contrabands, letters of credit, insurance claims and tons of crisp dollar bills swirling in the fly-infested hot dust that Danny Craig had died in.

In a way, Danny would be there with them on a summer evening at the lake. They often talked about him, how he had brought the two of them together. Then, sometimes, Hank would think of his father and mother, how relieved they would be if they could see him and Beth, not the crazy Pitt girl, tie their horses to the trunk of the old, fallen mesquite tree up there by the lake.

He was sure they would get a kick out of that kind of family picture: their son and his darn-pretty wife, with a couple of fine horses behind them, watching a majestic sunset from a muddy water's edge.

Because every now and then, the majestic silence would be interrupted by the clank of tackle when a horse shook its head or stamped a foot, making the newts in the lake shoals look up and worry. The green little critters in the mud did not trust the world outside their pond. They were frightened of people — but when they saw Hank and Beth sitting at the water's edge holding hands, their bulging little eyes and big wide mouths were clearly smiling.

THE END

More about the author and his work:
www.pourbooks.com